ALSO BY VICTORIA HOLMES

Rider in the Dark
The Horse from the Sea

VICTORIA HOLMES

Heart of Fire

HARPERCOLLINSPUBLISHERS

Heart of Fire

Library of Congress Cataloging-in-Publication Data
Holmes, Victoria.
    Heart of fire / Victoria Holmes.— 1st ed.
        p.   cm.
Summary: In 1923, Maddie's family is reunited when her brother
finally comes home to England after fighting in the Great War, but
when she discovers that he is an impostor, Maddie faces the loss of
both her new brother and his horse, which she has grown to love.
    ISBN-10: 0-06-052037-X (trade bdg.)
    ISBN-13: 978-0-06-052037-3 (trade bdg.)
    ISBN-10: 0-06-052031-0 (lib. bdg.)
    ISBN-13: 978-0-06-052031-1 (lib. bdg.)
    [1. Impersonation—Fiction. 2. Mistaken identity—Fiction.
3. Horses—Fiction. 4. Horsemanship—Fiction. 5. Brothers—
Fiction. 6. England—Social life and customs—20th century—
Fiction.] I. Title.
PZ7.H7377He 2006   2006000366
[Fic]—dc22   CIP
                                                   AC

Typography by Karin Paprocki

1 2 3 4 5 6 7 8 9 10
❖
First Edition

FOR JANET—STILL DANCING,

WHEREVER YOU ARE

ACKNOWLEDGMENTS

I WAS HELPED IN my research by the following people, who have been infinitely generous with their time and knowledge. Any historical inaccuracies are entirely my own.

Roger Philpott and Houghtons Ruby (Harry) of Pittern Hill Stables, Warwickshire, who taught me everything I know about riding sidesaddle; Ann Marshall, who let me wear her beautiful vintage riding habit; Trevor Batley of Stansted Park, Hampshire; the staff at Polesden Lacey, Surrey; Gary Marston of Gaydon Heritage Motor Centre, Warwickshire; the British Show-Jumping Association; Nick Greenall, for knowing about World War One aeroplanes; and Rhidian Williams, for translating the Welsh words.

The villages of Hamstead Marshall and Hundred House and the Grand Hall at Olympia are all real places. The layout of Sefton Park is based on Stansted Park, Hampshire, and the Craven Estate, Berkshire, but all characters are fictitious and any similarity to any persons alive or dead is entirely coincidental.

1

BERKSHIRE, ENGLAND 1923

THE BAY GELDING'S EARS twitched back and forth as he cantered toward the jump, and Maddie felt his stride falter. *It's not
too high, it's not too high,* she told herself—and it really wasn't, it was
only a wooden pole laid across two straw bales. If Maddie had
stood beside it, the rail would have barely come up to her knees.

Starling propped on his forelegs, throwing up his head and
making the reins flap against his neck. Just when Maddie was
convinced he was going to slither to a stop, he took a huge leap
over the rail. Maddie lurched backward, the top pommel jab-
bing painfully into the back of her right knee, and only managed to save herself from toppling off altogether by grabbing a
handful of mane.

Starling landed with a thud, stumbling as Maddie caught up
with him a few moments too late. Her right leg had slid so far
up the gelding's shoulder that her boot was tangled in his
mane, and her bowler hat had slipped over one eye so that she

couldn't see anything except a narrow strip of grass under Starling's front hooves.

"That was useless!" she exclaimed, hauling herself straight as Starling jogged to a standstill and took advantage of his trailing reins to snatch a mouthful of grass. "I just can't do it!"

"How many times do I 'ave to tell you, Miss Maddie? You need to fold to the right." A slight, wiry-limbed figure was limping across the paddock toward her, his face creased with a frown. Toby Chalk, the head groom at Sefton Park, was clearly as frustrated by Maddie's lack of riding talent as she was herself.

"Fold to the right?" Maddie echoed crossly. "I'm not a piece of paper, Toby! How can I fold to the right?" She yanked off the brown leather gloves and rubbed at the angry red marks around her wrists. No matter how many times she told her grandmother that she didn't have hands the size of a doll's, Lady Ella insisted that Maddie wore them whenever she rode.

Toby took hold of Starling's bridle and lifted the gelding's head. "Try again, Miss Maddie," he said. "This time, remember to kick 'im on when you come into the jump. Just because you don't 'ave a leg on his right-hand side, doesn't mean you can't give 'im a tap with the whip."

Maddie stared mutinously at the groom, drawing herself up to her full height. On the ground, she was barely an inch over five feet tall, but sitting on Starling, even though the gelding was less than fourteen hands, she could look down at the top of Toby's flat tweed cap. "I don't wish to ride any more today," she told him. "Please can we go in now?"

She pressed her knuckles against Starling's mane, letting the warmth of his neck comfort her. Poor old Starling; it wasn't his fault she couldn't get the hang of jumping. Behind them, the clock in the stable yard chimed eleven, and Maddie shut her eyes, letting herself imagine what she would be doing if she was back in London, in her parents' Kensington townhouse. On a gray, rainy day like this, her mother would have ordered the fire to be lit in the sitting room, and morning tea would be served in warm cups, with toast and bramble jam. The postman would have brought yet another square of thick, creamy paper (Maddie's favorites were the ones that had scalloped edges), inviting the Harmans to a musical evening or a birthday party or a poetry reading, and Mrs. Harman would be frowning as she tried to remember if they were free on that date.

There would be rapid footsteps in the hallway and the door would swing open to reveal a young man with a narrow, high-cheekboned face and gray eyes. Sitting on Starling in the windswept field, Maddie felt her cold cheeks stretch in a smile. Theo! She missed her brother so much.

Was it a real memory? Maddie wasn't sure. It was four years since she had lived in Kensington with her parents; the sitting room, the invitations, the fire, the people—most of all, the people—everything was gone now.

Her eyes flew open and her fingers clenched around the reins, making Starling sidestep restlessly. She reached down to soothe the pony while inside she recoiled with the familiar stab of grief. All the days, weeks, months she had spent at her grandparents' home hadn't made the pain any less sharp. Maddie was fifteen now, and sometimes she was afraid she would forget everything that had happened before she came to live on her grandfather's country estate. There was no point in wishing for her old life in London; her parents were dead, and she hadn't seen Theo since he left to fight in the Great War seven years ago, when Maddie was eight years old.

Invalided out of the army after a mustard gas attack, Theo had gone to seek his fortune in Namibia, swapping the trenches in France for an African diamond mine. He hadn't been home since, not even for their parents' funeral. Maddie wondered if he even remembered he had a family back in England. Had he stayed away because their mother and father had been so upset by his decision to fight in the war? Their father had never mentioned Theo's name after that day, and Maddie remembered thinking that he was behaving as if her brother had died.

And now Father and Mother were dead, from the influenza epidemic in 1919 that had killed more people in Europe than the war itself. Theo was still alive, he had always been alive somewhere, and they had let him just disappear. It wasn't fair, and it was all the fault of the stupid war!

Maddie gathered up the reins; now that the lesson was over, it didn't matter if she held them like a bunch of radishes. She glanced down to see Toby looking up at her with a strange expression in his pale blue eyes, and she wondered why he hadn't gone over to open the gate.

"I wouldn't have thought you'd be the type to give up so quick, Miss Maddie," Toby said.

She stared at him, puzzled.

"Your father wouldn't 'ave," he went on.

Maddie bristled; she was partly indignant that her grand-father's groom was speaking to her like this, and partly desperate to hear about her father from someone who had known him as a child, when he was growing up at Sefton Park. Curiosity won, and she stayed quiet.

"He didn't much like 'orse riding, that's for sure"—Toby took her silence as an invitation to go on—"but I can remember 'im falling off half a dozen times before 'e finally made it over that hedge." He nodded toward the dense row of brambles at the bottom of the field. Maddie felt a jolt of sympathy for the sturdy, chestnut-haired boy she had stared at a hundred times in the gilt-framed painting that hung in her grandmother's salon. She had been told often enough that she had inherited her father's stubborn streak, along with his fox-colored hair and hazel eyes.

Well, if her father could learn how to jump, so could she!

She thrust her hands back into the gloves, not bothering with the fiddly little buttons at the wrists. She wasn't ready to be defeated by two straw bales and a pole. "I'll try the fence again, please, Toby," she said, as if she hadn't just told him she was giving up.

Toby didn't say anything, just nodded and stepped away to let her turn Starling toward the rail again. Maddie tried to swallow the anxious lump that had formed in her chest. It was only a little jump. *Fold to the right,* she reminded herself. *How hard could it be?*

Starling broke into a canter before Maddie was ready and she nearly dropped the curb rein. "Slow down, please," she begged under her breath as she made a grab for the trailing rein. She could feel herself bouncing around in the saddle; Toby said she would sit much more firmly if she could keep her right leg tucked tightly around the top pommel. Maddie wanted to tell him to try riding in a sidesaddle, with his right toes pointing down and his left toes pointing up, and see how easy he found it to keep still.

She tugged on the right rein and Starling swerved toward the fence. If she could just remember to fold to the right, left shoulder over right knee. But Starling was cantering faster now, his hooves slipping on the damp grass. Maddie felt herself slipping backward, and even Starling's mane seemed out of reach as he took off far too early, grunting with the effort of clearing the rail. Maddie's right leg shot up and she felt herself tipping slowly sideways, with the grass rushing up to meet her.

Everything slowed down for one endless heartbeat before she hit the ground with a thud, hip then shoulder then head then legs, like a rag doll.

CHAPTER

2

⌘

THE FALL KNOCKED THE BREATH out of her and for a moment Maddie lay still, listening to Starling's hoofbeats canter away. *I can't do it,* she thought bleakly. *I don't care how many times my father fell off learning to jump.*

She opened her eyes to see Toby staring anxiously down at her. "Are you all right, Miss Maddie? Let me help you up." He reached out his hand.

"Thank you, I can manage," Maddie said, feeling her cheeks flush with embarrassment.

She pushed herself up so that she was sitting by Toby's feet. Her jacket was twisted uncomfortably around her ribs and one button had popped off, leaving a tuft of white shirt sticking out. The apron had flipped up to reveal her legs, thankfully clad in navy breeches although a slice of cold air on her left knee made Maddie suspect there was a nasty tear in them. Her stirrup lay beside her on the grass where it had slipped out of the safety clasp, and Toby hid his own awkwardness by bending down to snatch it up.

Looking around, she saw Starling slither to a halt beside the gate, his reins trailing and the saddle skewed on his back. "Is he all right?"

"Aye, he's fine." Toby put his hand under Maddie's elbow. "Come on, miss."

"Honestly, I can manage," Maddie insisted, scrambling to her feet. She wound the heavy apron around her waist, buttoning it into place, and started to walk as fast as she could toward the paddock gate. Her right hip ached where it had hit the ground, but she was determined not to limp.

Starling sniffed curiously at her sleeve when she reached the fence, but Maddie ignored him and wrenched open the gate so hard it banged against her knuckles. As she stumbled across the cobbled yard, keeping her head down so no one could see her scarlet face, she felt the pony's patient brown gaze follow her.

Behind her, she heard Starling's metal shoes ring against the cobbles as Toby led him out of the paddock. It wasn't Starling's fault she had fallen off. He was a sweet pony—sturdy and short-legged, with a coat the color of beechnuts, and a wiry black mane that Ollie the stable boy had to damp down with water before it would lie flat.

Maddie walked faster, making it clear that she was going straight indoors—not that Toby would expect her to help unsaddle her pony. She headed around the edge of the house, crunching over the gravel that swept up to the steps. To her relief, Sidney the boot boy was polishing the brass bellpull, and the front door stood open. With any luck, she would be able to slip across the hall and up the stairs before her grandmother realized she had come inside.

An imperious voice stopped her dead when she was halfway across the hall. "Madeline? Is that you? I saw you fall! Come in here, please."

Feeling her heart sink, Maddie walked through the double doors that led into her grandmother's salon. The elegant room looked out through ceiling-high windows onto the back lawn, then the riding paddock, and beyond that the wood known as Knight's Copse. Sir Wilfred's estate stretched between the villages of Hamstead Marshall and Enborne, nearly a thousand acres of bright green Berkshire countryside.

Maddie's grandmother was in her favorite chair, a high-backed, sparsely padded seat that looked big enough for two people when it was empty, but seemed full to overflowing with Lady Ella's rustling old-fashioned skirts whenever she sat down.

"Come here, Madeline, and stand where I can see you," she ordered, tapping her lorgnettes against the arm of her chair.

Maddie shuffled across the carpet, conscious that her skirt was smeared with mud and bits of grass, and she was almost certainly leaving damp footprints on the priceless Persian rug.

Lady Ella arched her thin eyebrows as she surveyed her granddaughter. "Madeline, horse riding really isn't as difficult as you think it is. Toby's being very patient with you, but I'm afraid that you're not trying as hard as you could."

Maddie felt a bubble of frustration swell inside her. "I am trying!" she insisted. "But I don't see why it matters so much if I can ride or not. It never mattered when Mother and Father were alive."

Lady Ella's face darkened. Maddie waited for a stern reply, but her grandmother just looked down at her lap. "I know how much you want to go back to London, believe me, Maddie. But you live here now, and riding is one of the things that you do in the country. Try not to hate it so much, my dear."

Maddie wanted to argue that she didn't hate riding; she was just fed up with being so dismally bad at it. She was about to ask if she could go to her room when Lady Ella went on, "Now, we'll say no more about today, but next time you fall off, I want you to get straight back on and try again. Do you think I didn't take a tumble or two when I was learning to ride? And take that miserable look off your face, Madeline. Anyone would think it was the end of the world!"

Maddie turned away, biting her lip. It wasn't falling off Starling that felt like the end of the world! Why couldn't her grandmother understand that there were more important things than jumping one stupid fence? Tears coursed hotly down her cheeks, and she was thankful that the hall was empty as she made for the stairs. She just wanted to go home! Really home, to Kensington; if Theo came back from Namibia it wouldn't matter that her parents were dead, because she could live with him. Her breath came in ragged gasps, and she found herself hating her grandfather's collection of bird paintings even more than usual, crowding the wood-paneled staircase with their beady-eyed stares and lurid feathers. Why did her mother and father have to die? She didn't want to live at Sefton Park, she wanted to live in London, far away from endless empty fields and rainy skies, and horses, horses everywhere. She hated her grandparents, she hated the countryside, and she wanted her brother back so she could go home. . . .

Blinded by tears of fury and self-pity, Maddie burst into her bedroom and flung herself down on her bed, giving in to her sobs as if she was five years old again.

———— ⟨⟨⟨⟩⟩⟩ ————

"MADDIE? ARE YOU IN THERE?"

There was a soft tap at the door, before it opened just enough for Maddie to see an anxious, heart-shaped face framed with short dark brown hair. She rolled onto her back, wincing as a hairpin jabbed behind her ear. She'd got as far as taking off her riding jacket and skirt, but she hadn't unpinned her hair and she was still wearing her grubby, torn breeches.

"It's all right, Louisa, you can come in."

The door opened farther and Maddie's sister slipped into the room. She was taller than Maddie, and reed-thin like their mother, with glossy brown hair and pale gray eyes. Before their parents died, Louisa's hair had swung below her waist, but last year she had gone to London with her friend Rosie and come back with it cut in a startling bob that curved around her head, the same length as her chin.

Louisa went over to the closet and took out a clean dove-gray blouse. "Come on, Mouse," she said, using the nickname their father had given Maddie when she was very small.

"I don't want to get up," Maddie muttered, turning her face

away. Just because Louisa was twenty-two years old, it didn't give her the right to act like she was Maddie's mother.

Louisa laid the blouse on the bed and went back to the closet. "Dinner will be ready in half an hour," she said briskly, as if Maddie hadn't spoken. At the foot of the stairs, the grandfather clock chimed six, sounding muffled and tinny through the pillow against Maddie's ear. She sighed and heaved herself up to a sitting position. It was raining again, the drops pattering against the window like someone tapping the glass with a very small stick. Louisa was standing at the foot of the bed with a skirt in each hand. "Blue or dark green?"

Maddie shrugged. Louisa narrowed her eyes, then put the blue skirt next to the blouse and placed the other one in the closet. Shutting the door, she came over and sat on the end of the bed.

"Ella told me about your fall," she began. Louisa never called their grandmother "Grandmama" like Maddie did. "Did you hurt yourself?" she asked, her eyes concerned.

Maddie shook her head. "Only my pride," she admitted, unbuttoning her riding shirt. "And it was my fault. I think poor old Starling got quite a shock—and Toby," she added.

Louisa grinned. "Shocked by the way you ride? I doubt it."

"It's not funny!" Maddie protested, threading her arms into the blouse. She slithered off the bed and bent down to tug off her breeches. "I just don't see why I have to learn to ride.

You've never had to." Her voice came out muffled and squeaky with her head upside down.

"I guess Ella decided you couldn't teach an old dog new tricks," Louisa replied lightly.

Maddie stepped into the skirt and buttoned it up, wincing as the fabric pressed against her bruised hip.

"I know it's not easy," Louisa went on sympathetically. "Ella is trying her best, but it must be hard for her too. She hardly expected to be surrounded by young people again at her age. As soon as I have a house of my own, you know you can come and live with me."

"In London?" Maddie asked hopefully.

Louisa looked down at her hands. "Well, I don't know. Who's to say what will happen in the future?"

Maddie went over to her dressing table. "George Edwards might have something to say about your future," she said impishly to her sister's reflection, and was rewarded by a flush of pink spreading across Louisa's cheeks. "Although I suppose you could run away from him quite easily if you didn't want to listen."

Louisa lifted her head. "Don't tease," she scolded. "George would give anything to be able to walk without a stick. I doubt you'd cope as well if you lost a leg."

"Half a leg," Maddie corrected her. The first time she had met the Right Honorable George Edwards, he had interpreted her stare at his wooden leg as pity; to reassure her, he had jabbed his forefinger into his thigh to show that it was flesh and blood, then given his shin a hefty thwack with his stick, the hollow thud making Maddie jump right out of her chair. Louisa had told her that George lost it in a motorcycle accident in 1915, two weeks before he was due to be sent to France to fight in the trenches.

"Just think, Lou," Maddie went on, "if you marry George, you might get to see what his leg looks like without the false bit!"

Louisa's voice was very dry. "No doubt I would, though that's hardly what goes through my mind every time he proposes."

"Tell me again, how many times is it now?"

"Only twice, as you well know. Now come on, or we'll be late for dinner. And for your information, my most recent answer was still no, but I'd rather Ella and Grandpapa didn't find out. You know how they feel about George."

"Oh yes," Maddie agreed, slipping her feet into her house shoes. "Grandmama would be dreadfully disappointed to know that you'd turned down the chance of becoming Lady Edwards for a second time!"

Louisa shooed Maddie toward the door. "Get along with you, you minx! George is a very kind man, and he's been a good friend to us both since we came here."

Maddie's glance fell on the small silver frame next to her bed. The photograph inside had faded, blurring the faces of the people at the center of the picture, and making the steam train in the background look like a strange, ghostly caterpillar. But the taller of the two figures was recognizably in a khaki soldier's uniform, his cap tipped to one side as he bent down to put one arm around the little girl standing beside him.

Before getting into the carriage, Theo had leaned close to Maddie, his face red and shining inside his hot uniform, and already unfamiliar under the peaked cap. "I'll be all right, Mouse," he whispered. "I've got nothing to be scared of, as long as I've got your penknife with me." She reached up to feel the shape of the folded knife in his breast pocket, long and thin, a bit like Father's cigars but flatter. She had chosen it because the handle was exactly long enough to have her brother's name engraved in swirly writing: *Theodore Wilfred Harman.*

"Do you think Theo would like George?" she wondered out loud.

Louisa looked surprised. "I . . . I don't know. I mean, we don't know what Theo is like now, do we? He might think George had an easy war, not seeing what was happening in the trenches."

Maddie was suddenly desperate to hear more about her brother. Apart from giving him the knife, she had few clear memories of him. She felt that she should have paid more attention before he went away, as if she should have somehow known he wouldn't come back. She was scared that her happiest memories, of Theo making their parents laugh, or reading to her when everyone else thought she was asleep, were fading away like mist. It was easier to remember the shouting and the slamming doors when Theo announced that he had signed up to fight. Maddie's parents had insisted there were other ways to settle disagreements, without sacrificing innocent lives; Theo argued that every Englishman had a duty to serve his country.

Before Maddie could ask her sister to share some of her own memories, the gong rang at the foot of the stairs.

"Come on, Mouse, it's dinnertime," said Louisa, getting up from the bed and shaking the creases out of her skirt. They ran downstairs, past the bird paintings, and slowed to a walk just before entering the breakfast room, where they ate when they didn't have guests.

Lady Ella was already seated at one end of the table. She glanced up and smiled as Maddie and Louisa came in. Sir Wilfred was carving a shoulder of lamb at the opposite end of the table, forking the slices onto a serving plate held by the scullery maid, Faye. Maddie knew her grandmother hated having to use the scullery maid to serve meals—George Edwards's parents had a pair of scarlet-liveried footmen to wait at table, even when they weren't entertaining—but since the war it was much harder to find domestic servants.

For a while, Maddie concentrated on chopping green beans into pieces that were short enough to fit into her mouth without stabbing her cheeks. But she put down her knife and fork when Louisa announced that she was going to London the next day, to stay with her friend Rosie Williams.

"Who will you and Rosie be seeing in London, my dear?" Lady Ella asked, not quite hiding the anxious note in her voice. Maddie knew why she was worried. Lou's friends may have been from the right sort of background—most of them had been raised on huge country estates like Sefton Park and all of them were wealthy—but Rosie Williams and her other best friend Lily belonged to the new breed of women who didn't think political reform had gone far enough and were campaigning to extend the vote to all women over the age of twenty-one, just as it was for men. Lady Ella Harman couldn't understand why any woman would want to do something as vulgar and manly as voting.

"I'm not sure yet," Lou replied, helping herself to a bread roll. "I think Clarissa de Montfort is in town with her fiancé, Algernon—you know the Ponsonbys, don't you, Grandpapa? And Bertie Farnsworth has asked us to play golf on Saturday."

Maddie hid a smile. Her sister had just listed the people their grandmother would approve of most among her friends: Clarissa de Montfort would only campaign for the vote if it was going to give her instant access to the latest fashions from Coco Chanel, and Algernon and Bertie had impressive private fortunes as well as respectable jobs in the city.

Sure enough, Lady Ella looked pleased. "Well, that sounds like a charming weekend. If Rosie can't drive you back on Monday, your grandfather can always have Henry meet you at the station."

"Thank you, Ella, but I'm sure Rosie won't mind. She loves any excuse to drive her new motorcar."

Sir Wilfred glanced up from his lamb. "It's a Baby Austin, isn't it?"

"Yes, that's right," said Louisa. "It's so much fun! It has a top speed of fifty miles per hour, you know—not that Rosie would ever go that fast," she added hastily when Lady Ella gasped.

"Quite right too," said Sir Wilfred, skewering a boiled potato on his fork. "I'm not sure women should drive at all, I must say."

"Oh, you'd be surprised, Grandpapa." Louisa smiled. "Rosie says it's not that different from operating a sewing machine."

"Then you'll have to remind me not to let Miss Williams mend my shirts!" Sir Wilfred replied, his eyes twinkling.

Maddie stabbed her fork into her last green bean and sat back in her chair. Maybe Louisa was right, and Sir Wilfred and Lady Ella were trying as hard as they could to raise their grand-daughters in the way they thought best. But she was going to have to figure out how to tell them that she would never be able to ride, that however hard she tried and however patient Toby and Starling were with her, she just wasn't any good at it.

The next morning, Maddie escaped another jumping lesson by saying she needed to practice a tricky piece of Chopin. She wasn't much better at playing the piano than riding, but at least no one had ever hurt themselves falling off a piano stool. After half an hour of Maddie muttering crossly under her breath when her fingers couldn't find the right notes anywhere among the keys, Lady Ella waved from her chair to indicate that she'd heard enough for one day.

"Madeline, dear, I'm suffering one of my headaches. Do you think you could ask Kate to bring me a glass of lemonade?"

Maddie carefully shut the lid of the piano and jumped up from the stool. She let herself out of the salon as quietly as she could and went to the breakfast room to ring the bell for her grandmother's maid. When Kate had vanished to the kitchen in search of lemonade, Maddie sat down on one of the cushioned window seats in the hall. The house was very quiet; her grandfather was reading the newspaper in the library and Louisa was upstairs, packing for her weekend away. Maddie rested her chin on her hands and stared out at the columns that framed the front door. Beyond them, the fountain in the driveway sent tiny rainbows sparkling into the air. After yesterday's rain, the sky had cleared and the sun felt warm through the windowpane.

A damp muzzle pushed against Maddie's leg. As she reached down to ruffle the silky ears of Charlie, her grandfather's Irish setter, a movement outside caught her eye, and she turned to see a pony and trap bowling along the drive. A thin chestnut horse trotted behind the trap, tethered to the cart by a short rope.

Maddie frowned. Her grandparents hadn't said they were expecting any visitors. Two people sat in the trap: the driver, wearing a flat tweed cap and a waistcoat over his shirtsleeves, and a smaller figure next to him swaddled in a greatcoat, with his hat pulled well down as if he found the mild February day as cold as midwinter.

The trap rolled to a halt and the smaller man climbed down, lifting out a khaki-colored bundle before fishing in his pockets for a coin to pay the driver. Maddie studied him curiously. He was thin and deeply suntanned as if he had spent a long time outdoors. The left side of his face was dragged down by a long scar, as wide as a finger by his forehead, thinning to a pinkish thread by the time it reached his chin. When he had been paid, the driver twisted around to untie the chestnut horse and handed the end of the rope to the man. The trap wheeled around and set off back down the drive, leaving the man and the horse standing in the center of the spotless gravel. The visitor took off his hat and the wind lifted his light brown hair as he raised his scarred face to look up at the house.

And suddenly it wasn't the face of a stranger after all. He was older than Maddie remembered, of course, and his skin was brown and creased as if he had spent a long time in the sun, but the high cheekbones and the wide-set eyes were exactly as she had always pictured them.

Maddie felt a hundred emotions leap inside her: joy and astonishment and fear and disbelief all mixed together. She swung her legs off the window seat, pushing Charlie away, and ran to the front door.

"Lou!" she shouted. "Come quickly! Grandmama! Grandpapa! Theo's come home!"

4

⁕

MADDIE WRENCHED OPEN the door and flung herself out onto the top step. She hesitated for a moment, looking down at the man and the horse standing in the middle of the drive. "Theo," she whispered.

The man looked at her without saying anything, his gray eyes narrowed against the sun.

"Theo!" Maddie said a little more loudly, but before she could move, Louisa burst out of the door and jumped down the steps to fling herself into the arms of the visitor.

"Oh my goodness, I can't believe it! Theo!"

The man stepped back as if he wanted to study her at arm's length. Then he looked over Lou's shoulder at Maddie and nodded. "Yes," he said. "It's . . . it's me."

Lady Ella appeared in the doorway. She stared at the khaki-clad figure in the driveway and reached out with one hand to lean against the door frame. Her other hand went to her mouth and she swayed.

Sir Wilfred came up in time to steady her. "Are you all right, my dear?"

"Theodore," murmured Lady Ella, lowering her hand.

Maddie started to feel impatient. Was everyone going to stand around saying Theo's name all day? Another figure appeared behind Sir Wilfred. It was Matthew the butler, wearing a spotless linen apron over his dark gray trousers and white shirt. He must have come straight upstairs from polishing the silver when Maddie had started shouting.

"Shall we invite the gentleman inside, Sir Wilfred?" he suggested quietly.

"Oh yes, good idea," said Sir Wilfred. "Show him to the library, please, while I take Lady Ella to the salon."

Maddie's grandmother straightened up. "No, no, I'm perfectly all right. Don't fuss, Wilfred." She moved to the top of the steps and held out her hands. "Theodore! Welcome home!"

Theo smiled awkwardly and held up the horse's rein to show that he couldn't come up the steps. "Hello, Grandmother," he said, and when he spoke, his teeth looked very white against his brown skin. "I wonder, could I leave the mare in the stables?"

"Of course," Louisa answered, looking around for someone to take care of the four-legged visitor. The driveway was deserted, so she waved at Maddie. "Maddie, take the horse, will you? We can't leave Theo standing out here all day!"

Maddie trudged down the steps. It looked as if she was going to get left with the horse while everyone else went inside with Theo. He was her brother too! But as she drew near, she suddenly felt shy, and she couldn't meet his eyes as he held out the rope to her.

"Thanks, Maddie," he said, and his voice sounded different from how she remembered, with a lilting, singsong accent that suggested he had been speaking another language for the last seven years. She fumbled clumsily with the rope, her fingers brushing against Theo's as she nearly dropped it.

They both flinched and snatched their hands away. "Sorry," Maddie muttered. "I'm not very good with horses."

Theo's mouth twisted in a half smile. "Don't worry, you'll be fine with this little lady. She's tired enough to be quiet as anything."

Maddie lifted her eyes to meet his, gray and almond-shaped just like their father's. How could she feel shy around her own brother? She stood next to the horse and watched as Louisa led Theo triumphantly up the steps to the front door.

Lady Ella stared at him as if she couldn't quite believe what she was seeing, then put her arms around him and pulled him toward her. Maddie felt a bit stunned—her grandmother had never hugged her like that. Theo allowed himself to be pressed against Lady Ella before he drew away and held out his hand for Sir Wilfred to shake. His grandfather took it for a moment, then dropped it and clapped Theo on the back, ushering him inside. The front door swung closed behind them.

Maddie stood on the gravel in her house shoes feeling rather foolish. The mare tugged at the rope, and Maddie turned to frown at her. "Don't start playing up," she warned. "I don't even know your name, and I'd much rather be inside with Theo than stuck out here with you."

"Talking to yourself, Miss Maddie?" called a cheery voice, and Maddie felt her cheeks go crimson. Fred the under-gardener was pushing a wheelbarrow around the side of the house.

"Theo's come back!" she blurted out. "He brought this mare with him." She held up the end of the rope to explain why she was standing out here and everyone else was inside.

Fred put down the handles of the wheelbarrow and crunched across the gravel toward her. "Shall I take 'er to the stables, miss?"

"Thank you, Fred," Maddie said warmly. She thrust the rope into Fred's hand and hurried toward the front door.

She ran all the way to the library, where the door stood open. Matthew was putting a tray with five glasses and a jug of lemonade onto a side table. Sir Wilfred stood with one hand on the back of the sofa, quietly watching his family; Maddie couldn't have guessed what he was thinking at that exact moment, not for a thousand pounds. Lady Ella and Louisa were sitting on the sofa on either side of Theo, who was looking rather red in the face as if he wasn't comfortable with being the center of attention. Maddie hoped that he wouldn't turn tail and go straight back to Namibia. Surely he'd understand they were just pleased to see him?

Matthew handed her a glass of lemonade, and Louisa patted the cushion next to her. "Come and sit down, Maddie," she urged. "Theo's been telling us why he left Namibia. There was an accident in the mine!" Her eyes opened very wide and her sleek brown hair swung about her face like a spaniel's ears.

"An accident?" Maddie echoed. "Is that . . . is that how you got hurt?" Lou glared at her, but Theo nodded, his fingers straying to the scar on his face.

"A roof beam fell on me," he explained. "I was lucky to get out alive. The tunnel I was in collapsed after an explosion and I had to be dug out."

"Thank the Lord you weren't more seriously hurt," Lady Ella gasped.

Theo looked down at his hands. "Like I said, I was one of the lucky ones. My best friend wasn't. He . . . he didn't make it out."

"I'm so sorry," Louisa said, and Maddie nodded. But it was hard to feel sad for long about an unknown stranger when she had her brother safe and well in front of her, and she had to put down her glass and clasp her hands in her lap to stop them twitching about with excitement.

"You should have known about the accident," Theo went on, sounding puzzled. "The doctor at the hospital said he wrote to you to say I would be coming home. Didn't you get the letter?"

Sir Wilfred shook his head. "No, we've heard nothing. But that doesn't matter now. All that's important is that you're home, and we can start thinking about your future."

Theo stiffened. "Well, I'm not sure what I'm going to do," he began. "I mean, I might not stay in England—"

"But surely if the mine has collapsed, there's nothing for you back there?" Lady Ella protested. "Theo, you can't possibly think of leaving us again when you've only just arrived!"

Theo blinked. "No, no, of course not. Sorry, I'm just tired, you know, the journey, being here . . ."

Sir Wilfred reached down and patted his shoulder. "I understand, old chap. Don't worry, there'll be plenty of time to talk. I'll ask Matthew to show you to your room, shall I?"

Maddie jumped up. "I'll take him, Grandpapa."

Louisa stood up as well. "I'll come too. I'll ask Matthew to send a telegram to Rosie, letting her know I won't be coming to London. You told Mrs. Kirby to make the Blue Bedroom ready, didn't you, Ella?"

Her grandmother nodded. "Yes, that's right. Theo"—she looked up, one hand resting on his arm—"please take as much time as you wish to rest. I'll send Mrs. Kirby up with a light luncheon, but Wilfred and I would be delighted if you could join us for supper."

Theo looked awkward. "That's very kind of you. Of course I'll have dinner with you, but I'm not sure how hungry I'll be. . . ."

"I can ask Patrice to prepare whatever you like," Lady Ella went on. "He trained at the Georges Cinque Hotel in Paris, you know. Although I'm not sure if he is familiar with African dishes."

Theo's mouth twisted in a brief smile. "In that case, I won't ask for curried goat. Really, anything will be fine. We ate whatever got put in front of us. Jonathan always said I'd have eaten the tin plates if I was hungry enough!" His face clouded, and his scar flushed pink as it stretched with his frown.

Maddie reached out her hand to him. "Come on, Theo," she said. "I'll show you upstairs."

He nodded, then looked past her out of the window. "Is the mare all right?"

"Yes, she's fine. One of the gardeners took her to the stables." Curious, she added, "Did you bring her all the way from Namibia?"

"Not exactly. At least, she came from Namibia, but I didn't see her until I'd been on the ship for a couple of days. Her owners were bringing her to England to sell and I liked the look of her, so I made them an offer." He glanced at Sir Wilfred. "I . . . I'm afraid it took the last of my cash. We put all our savings into a new set of mine shafts that didn't turn up anything like the quality of diamonds we had been promised. When I got out of hospital, the mine's doctor gave me what I was owed, and that was enough for the ticket home and the mare."

Sir Wilfred patted the back of the sofa. "There's no need to worry about that now. We can talk over dinner."

Theo followed Maddie out of the library.

"It's this way," said Maddie, pointing toward the door leading to the stairs. Then she stopped, flustered. "I'm sorry, I keep forgetting you must know your way around."

There was a pause, then Theo smiled. "Don't worry, Mouse. It's a long time since I was here, so maybe it's just as well if you tell me which way to go. At least that way I won't end up in a linen cupboard!"

"It's a deal," laughed Maddie. Something struck her and she stared at him. "You called me Mouse!"

Theo looked uncertain. "Well, that's what we used to call you, isn't it? Although I suppose you're too old for a silly nickname like that now."

Maddie went over and touched his arm—part of her wanted to hug him, but there was a reserve about her brother that made her keep her distance. "I wouldn't mind if you called me that until I was a hundred! In fact, I want you to promise that you'll never stop calling me Mouse, ever. Promise?"

Theo held up his hands. "Very well, I promise."

Maddie turned and started up the stairs. "Do you remember Grandpapa's bird paintings?" she said. The one nearest to her showed a peacock fiercely arching its neck, catlike, at a small brown peahen.

"The bird paintings, yes," said Theo. "You were always terrified of them, weren't you?"

"I still don't like them very much," Maddie admitted. She hoped Theo wouldn't think she was being childish.

To her relief, Theo just said, "I can't say I blame you. There are a lot of beady eyes, aren't there? Ella said she'd put me in the Blue Bedroom, didn't she?" He had reached the top of the stairs. To his right was the door to Maddie's bedroom, and opposite that was Sir Wilfred's dressing room. Louisa's bedroom was directly behind them, and straight ahead was a long corridor with doors to the other bedrooms.

Theo looked at each of the doors, then walked down the corridor to the very end. "If I remember right," he said, putting his hand on the doorknob directly in front of him, "it's this one here. And the bathroom is just next door?"

"That's right," said Maddie. She watched him open the door to the Blue Bedroom, suddenly terrified of letting him out of her sight. "Theo, wait!" she gasped, and he paused to look back at her.

"Yes?"

Maddie twisted her hands together. "You . . . you won't leave straightaway, will you? Please?"

Theo let the door close and walked over to her. "It's all right, I won't be going anywhere in a hurry. I don't have anywhere to go, for a start."

"But this is your home now!" To her dismay, her voice shook. "It's been so awful, with Mother and Father dying, and having to live here when I don't know anybody. Now it looks like Lou is going to marry George Edwards and I don't want to stay here on my own, I want to live with you and Lou. . . ."

Theo put his hand on her shoulder. "It's all right, I'm here now," he said quietly.

CHAPTER

5

‧‧‧‧‧‧‧‧‧‧

"Help! Get me out! I can't see! Help!"

Maddie sat bolt upright. Who was shouting?

"Get me out of here!"

The shouts were coming from the other end of the house.
Maddie pushed back the counterpane and swung her legs out
of bed. What was going on? She grabbed her dressing gown
from the chair in the corner of the room and opened the door.
Luckily there was enough moonlight spilling through the window above the stairs to see all the way to the end of the corridor.

"Theo?" she whispered.

The house was silent. Maddie started to creep down the
corridor toward the Blue Bedroom. Theo had stayed in his
room all afternoon, emerging half an hour before dinner to go
down to the stables to see the mare. Louisa had gone with him;
Maddie had wanted to go too but when she had seen them
heading off arm in arm with their heads close together, matching dark brown hair exactly like their mother's, she had suddenly felt shy and had stayed in the hall, playing with Charlie,
instead.

Dinner hadn't been quite the celebration that Lady Ella had hoped for, either. Theo had praised all of the food—tomato soup to start, followed by chicken in a creamy mushroom sauce—but he hadn't eaten much, and looked positively gray with tiredness. Maddie had felt oddly disappointed, as if her brother should have entertained them on his first night back in England with tales of lions and giraffes, and diamonds as big as hens' eggs; then she told herself that Theo had only just got out of hospital and could hardly be expected to leap straight into the role of court jester.

"Theo? Are you awake?" she whispered as she padded closer to his bedroom door, her bare feet making no sound on the carpet.

Suddenly the door flew open and her brother stood there, outlined in the silvery moonlight with a pair of Sir Wilfred's blue-and-white pajamas hanging off his thin body. The good side of his face was in shadow, so the only part Maddie could see was stretched and misshapen by the jagged scar.

"Is everything all right?" she asked, her voice coming out as a strangled croak.

Theo stared at her for a moment. "Yes, I . . ."—he looked down at his pajamas and flinched as if he was surprised to see them—"I thought I'd go and see how the mare was. She might be unsettled, being in a strange stable."

"But it's the middle of the night! You really don't need to go down to the stables. Toby sleeps there, and he'll see to the mare if she needs anything."

Theo rested one hand on the door frame. "I guess I'd forgotten about that," he said. "We had staff at the mine to do cooking and washing, things like that, but we always looked after the horses ourselves."

"You had horses?" Maddie said in surprise. "You didn't ride before . . . before you went away."

Theo shrugged. "That just meant I had to learn fast when we got out there. You can't use motorcars in the African bush, the sand gets into the engines." He scraped at a speck in the paint on the door frame. "J—Jonathan taught me to ride. He'd grown up around horses, you see."

"Jonathan Price was your friend, the one who didn't make it out of the mine?" Maddie said softly. The name was familiar from the letters Theo had sent home every Christmas. "Were you with him when the accident happened?"

"No. He was farther along in the tunnel. After the roof collapsed, they managed to dig me out, but they couldn't reach him."

Maddie studied her brother closely; the shadows on his face made it impossible to tell what he was thinking. "Is that what you were dreaming about?"

Theo turned his face toward her, and she swallowed as his scar glistened in the moonlight. "I'm sorry. I didn't mean to wake you. I thought the dreams would stop when I came back to England."

Her heart twisted with pity. "It's all right, honestly. You won't have woken Grandmama or Grandpapa, they sleep through anything. And Lou's room is too far away for her to hear. Why don't you go back to bed now, see if you can sleep until morning?"

"I'd still like to check the mare."

"I promise there's no need," Maddie insisted. "Toby will see to everything. She's only a horse, after all."

He looked at her, his eyes wide. "What do you mean, only a horse? She's had the same journey I have, all the way from Namibia, but it's worse for her because she doesn't understand what's happening or where she is."

Maddie flushed. "I'm sorry. But really, Toby will look after her, and you need to rest. Come on, get into bed." She shooed him back into the room as if he was a child. Theo sat on the bed and rubbed his hands through his hair.

"Can I ask you something?" Maddie stood in the doorway and fiddled with the belt of her dressing gown.

Her brother lowered his hands to look at her. "What?"

"Your accent sounds different. I mean, I don't think you sounded like that when you went away. Did you speak a different language in Namibia?"

Theo pushed himself off the bed and went over to stand by

the window. The heavy velvet curtains hadn't been drawn, leaving shafts of pewter light sloping across the floor. He knelt on the window seat and stared down at the lawn.

Maddie wondered if she had offended him. Then, without turning around, he said, "The Europeans in Namibia speak Afrikaans, which is a bit like Dutch. Jonathan and I had to pick up a few words so we could talk to people in other mining companies. But I think the main reason I sound different is because Jonathan came from Wales. He dreamed in Welsh when I first met him. He used to wake us up all along the trench, singing some daft song or other. Anyway, I was around him so much that I must have picked up some of his accent. Sometimes he was the only person I spoke to for days, especially when we first went to Africa."

"Did he teach you to speak Welsh as well?"

"Only a few words."

"You must miss him a lot," Maddie said.

Theo's eyes clouded. "More than I can say," he murmured. "I owe him everything." He took a long, shuddering breath. "It's harder than I thought, being here."

Maddie didn't know what to say. "You need to sleep," she said. "I'll see you at breakfast. Good night, Theo."

"Good night." He didn't move from the window seat, but turned his head to stare out of the window again.

Maddie wondered if he was seeing scorched orange sand instead of damp, moonlit English grass. She padded back to her room with her head whirling. She remembered her mother telling her over and over to be careful what she wished for, because it might come true. She had wished and wished for Theo to come back—but not sad and broken and scarred like this. Deep down, she had always known that he would be haunted by what he had seen in France, just like Toby and the other men in the village who had made it home again; but she had assumed that once he was back, he would leave all his bad memories on the other side of the English Channel, and everything would be as it was before.

Maddie gave herself a shake as she climbed back into bed. She couldn't possibly expect Theo to feel instantly at home. After all, they hadn't even been living at Sefton Park when he went away! Tomorrow she'd take him on a grand tour, around the fields and down the lane to the chapel where their parents were buried.

At least they had him here, safe and well. Poor Jonathan's family would never get their son back; how awful for them to know that he made it through all those worrying months when he was fighting in France, only to die in a place even farther away.

Maddie swallowed. She was letting her imagination run away with her! She folded the pillow more comfortably under her cheek. She had to concentrate on Theo, and make him understand that he'd done the best possible thing by coming home.

6

AFTER HER DISTURBED NIGHT, Maddie slept later than she had intended and by the time she came into the breakfast room the grandfather clock at the foot of the stairs was chiming half past nine. The room was empty, and there was a half-filled rack of cold toast in the center of the table.

Pippa the kitchen maid came in to clear away the used dishes. "Good morning, Miss Maddie," she said. "Shall I fetch you some fresh toast? There's scrambled eggs as well if you'd like."

Maddie poured herself a glass of orange juice. "No, thanks, Pippa. I'm not very hungry. Has Theo eaten?"

"Yes, he and your grandfather were down a good hour ago. Sir Wilfred is in the library now and Master Theodore said he was going out to the stables." Pippa's brown eyes sparkled. "Oh, Miss Maddie, we're all so pleased your brother's come home!"

Maddie grinned. "I'm pleased too, Pippa! I think I'll go out and find him. Has my sister been down yet?"

"Yes, miss. Henry has driven her to Newbury to do some shopping for your grandmother."

Finishing her juice, Maddie put the empty glass on the table and went to fetch a coat from the lobby. She whistled for Charlie. Her grandmother's maid, Kate, was passing on her way to the kitchen and she tutted under her breath because Maddie would *never* whistle in Lady Ella's hearing. Then Maddie opened the side door with the dog at her heels like a burgundy-colored shadow.

"Let's go and find Theo," she said as they crunched along the gravel path that led to the stable yard. Ahead of them, there was an excited yap. Charlie lifted her head, recognizing Toby's brown-and-white spaniel, Jinx. She darted around the corner, her plumy tail waving.

Maddie broke into a run and stopped dead at the edge of the stable yard. Charlie and Jinx were in the middle of the cobbles, rolling ecstatically on their backs to let Theo rub their tummies. Maddie's brother was bent over them, his cap in one hand as he fussed their velvety ears. His face was flushed and his hair stood on end, and for the first time Maddie thought he looked truly happy.

A door banged as Toby came out of a stable. Behind him, a big black horse thrust his head over the door, his lip peeled back to reveal huge yellow teeth. Thor was Sir Wilfred's favorite hunter, although at eighteen he was getting close to retirement. Every time Maddie saw his heavy, Roman-nosed head, she thanked her stars that she'd never be expected to ride the bad-tempered thoroughbred. He was nearly seventeen hands high, and just looking at him gave her a crick in her neck; the thought of being hoisted onto his back made her feel positively dizzy.

"Good morning, Miss Maddie." Toby nodded to her across the yard.

Theo glanced up from the dogs. "Hello there," he said.

Maddie felt shy as she remembered their strange conversation in the night. "Hello," she said. To hide her confusion, she went over and crouched down to smooth Jinx's ears. "I see you've met the most important people around here."

"I'm not sure that fellow would agree with you," Theo replied with a half smile, nodding toward Thor, who was watching them with his ears pricked.

"Thor just thinks he's important," Maddie said. "I wouldn't waste any time trying to make friends with him."

Theo stood up and brushed down the knees of his breeches. They looked rather baggy, and Maddie wondered if he had had to borrow some of Sir Wilfred's clothes. He certainly hadn't arrived with much luggage, if that rucksack was all he had brought. "Well, I'd like to meet everyone before I choose who my friends are going to be," and his unusual, lilting accent took away any sting in his words.

"Perhaps you'd like to go for a ride this morning, sir?" Toby offered. "Sir Wilfred suggested you could take Wayfarer."

Theo's eyes lit up. "Thanks, Toby. Will you be coming too, Maddie?"

Maddie was starting to wish Jonathan Price had never taught her brother to ride. "I was going to show you around the estate today, but it might be easier if we went by bicycle," she said. "I could show you more things," she added lamely.

Theo frowned. "We can always get off the horses and tie them up if there's something particular to see."

Maddie drew her brother to one side and said quietly, "Theo, don't you remember me saying that I don't like riding? I'm no good at it. The last time I rode Starling, I fell off!"

Theo grinned. "Well, maybe you just need some more practice. We don't need to go fast." He glanced hopefully at the stable door with Wayfarer written above on a brass plaque, and Maddie knew she was beaten.

"I'll need to go indoors and change," she warned.

"Of course," he said. "I can help Toby tack up." He turned and started to walk across the yard.

"Where are you going?" Maddie asked.

Theo stopped and looked at her, uncertainty in his eyes. "To the tack room?" he said. "It is this way, isn't it?"

Toby emerged from a doorway on the other side of the yard carrying a saddle, a bridle slung over his shoulder. "Actually, sir, it's over here now. Sir Wilfred had the old feed room converted a couple of years back, when the new feed store was built." He slung the saddle over Wayfarer's stable door and took off his cap to scratch his light brown hair. "I'm surprised you knew where it was at all, sir. I shouldn't think you visited the stables more'n half a dozen times when you came here with your parents."

Theo stared at him, then shrugged. "It's strange, the things you remember." He went over to Wayfarer's stable and rubbed the cob's dark chestnut nose as he stuck his head over the door. "Shall we get you ready, old fellow?"

Toby put his hand possessively on the saddle. "Thank you, sir, but there's no need for you to do anything."

Theo stepped away from the door. "Oh, right," he said. "I didn't mean to interfere."

"I'll just go and change," said Maddie, feeling like the odd man out. She didn't think she'd ever picked up a grooming brush in her life, and she couldn't have saddled Starling if her life depended on it. She knew Theo would be different after being away for so long, but she was beginning to wonder if she had anything in common with her brother at all. She would ask him lots of questions about his life in Africa while they were riding, and hopefully that would make them feel a bit less like strangers.

Maddie returned to the yard just as Toby was leading Wayfarer out of his stable. He halted the cob and tightened the girth, then clicked at him to make him walk over to the mounting block.

Theo put out one hand to stop him. "I can get on here, thanks," he said. Toby said nothing, just ducked under the reins and held the right stirrup as Theo swung himself into the saddle. He sat lightly, his feet finding the stirrups without needing to look down.

Maddie could hear Ollie the stable boy leading Starling across the yard. She hoped Theo would keep his promise of not going too fast. She couldn't bear the humiliation of falling off in front of him. To distract herself from the butterflies that were swooping around in her stomach, she said to Theo, "Have you seen your mare this morning?" She thought it would be polite to ask, since she had only just stopped him from paying the horse a visit in the middle of the night.

"Yes, she's looking grand. Toby said she finished her haynet last night, and nearly knocked him over this morning trying to get at her feed."

"Oh," said Maddie, wondering why Theo sounded as if that was a good thing.

"Ready, Miss Maddie?" said Ollie, leading Starling up beside her.

Maddie took a deep breath and let Ollie give her a boost into the saddle. Starling always stood like a rock, but it felt dreadfully undignified to have someone gripping her left leg like a pincer while she flailed for the pommel and heaved herself into the saddle.

If Theo thought she looked less than elegant, he didn't say so. He waited until Ollie had tucked the ankle strap over Maddie's right boot, covering her legs with the heavy apron, then gathered up Wayfarer's reins. "Ready when you are," he said, and Maddie scooped up her own reins, nearly stabbing Ollie in the eye with the end of her whip.

They rode along the track past the cottage where Stan the head gardener lived.

"We can go to Hamstead Marshall this afternoon if you like," Maddie suggested. "It's not far to walk to the village."

Theo nodded. Maddie looked down at Starling's mane. Perhaps he was still tired from the journey; he certainly wasn't being much more talkative than he had been at dinner. She fished around for something that might interest him.

"Toby was in the war too, you know."

Theo's face went dark. "A lot of men were. I'd rather not talk about it, if you don't mind."

Maddie picked at a loose thread on the handle of her whip and tried not to feel cross. She was just trying to make conversation! "Come on, let's go to the church first," she said, kicking Starling forward.

They walked side by side along the track, Theo dropping behind when the hedgerows on either side became more overgrown and wet branches stretched out to soak their legs. He craned his neck to look over the hedges, standing in the stirrups to look down the hill at the canal.

"Does it look the same as you remembered?" Maddie asked curiously. "It must be very different from Africa."

"Yes," Theo replied. "I haven't seen this much green since . . . well, not for a good few years."

If Maddie had hoped her question would prompt Theo to tell her more about the things he had seen, it didn't work. He stared around as if he wanted to study every blade of grass, and hardly seemed aware that Maddie was there at all.

The path narrowed still further and a small copse of pine trees appeared in front of them. A gray stone building crouched among the trees, looking more like a farmyard barn than a church. Strictly speaking, this was the private chapel for Sefton Park, but Hamstead Marshall was a small enough village for all the local people to use it.

Maddie reined Starling in by the little wooden gate leading into the churchyard. "We could get off here if you like," she suggested, suddenly feeling self-conscious. Had Theo understood the significance of her bringing him here?

"This is where our parents are buried, isn't it?"

Maddie fiddled with the button on her glove. "I thought you might like to see their grave. Seeing as you didn't come back for the funeral." She bit her lip, not wanting to sound like she was angry with him. She had been angry enough back then; she and Lou had sent a telegram to Theo, and even delayed the funeral to give him time to get home, but he hadn't replied for over a month, by which time it was too late. Louisa and Maddie had buried their mother and father without him.

"You should have come back!" she burst out, the words escaping her before she could stop them.

Theo's face was unreadable as he kicked his legs out of the stirrups and swung himself onto the ground. "I wasn't there when the telegram arrived. I wrote to you explaining, didn't I? Jonathan and I had gone to look at a new site in the north. We didn't see the telegram until three weeks after the funeral."

Maddie didn't trust herself to say anything. She let Theo lift her out of the saddle and waited while he tethered the horses to the gatepost. Wayfarer flattened his ears at Starling, but the pony ignored him and turned away to snatch a mouthful of hawthorn leaves.

Theo unlatched the gate and held it open for Maddie, who kept her head lowered as she wound the apron around her and buttoned it onto her hip. The sting from her fall had faded, but the riding habit felt heavy and uncomfortable. Still without speaking, she walked along the path to the dove-colored grave-stone that bore her parents' names. She knelt down to clear away some weeds that were pushing their way through the white gravel covering the grave.

She felt Theo stand behind her. She could tell by the shape of his shadow that he had taken off his cap and was looking at the inscription on the gravestone. *Philip and Amelia Harman,* it read. *Beloved father and mother of Theodore, Louisa, and Madeline. You will be missed forever.* Two sets of dates were engraved underneath, showing the beginning and end of the lives of Maddie's parents.

"That's . . . nice," Theo said.

Maddie stood up and turned to face him. "Nice?" she echoed in disbelief. "Is that all you can say?"

Theo's eyes filled with alarm and sadness and something else that Maddie couldn't recognize. "I'm sorry," he said. "It's just hard . . ."

"I know," Maddie finished for him. "It's hard being back here. You said, last night." She pulled up a weed and fiddled with the leaves. "So, did you and Jonathan find any diamonds in the new site?" she asked, changing the subject.

"Not that time, no."

"What about the other mine? Were there lots of diamonds there? What do they look like before you dig them out?" In her head, Maddie imagined a sparkling cave lined with chips of glittering ice.

Theo shrugged. "They just look like rocks." He turned and started to walk back along the path.

Maddie stood up, hitching her habit straight on her hip, and followed him. "In your letters, you said that you were scared of being underground at first, but Jonathan wasn't. Did you get used to it in the end? Did Jonathan help you?"

Theo stopped and turned to face her. "Look, I don't want to talk about what happened in Africa. I'm back, so what does it matter?"

"But I'm interested," Maddie faltered. "You talked about it so much in your letters, and I always tried to picture what everything was like."

"It's not important now," said Theo, spinning on his heel and crunching away.

Maddie wondered if he was angry because she had mentioned Jonathan. She knew what grief felt like, and she could see the same pain carved into Theo's face whenever he spoke about his dead friend. She slipped through the gate in the hedge as her brother was untying the horses.

"Is it Jonathan?" she asked quietly.

Theo whipped around and stared at her. "What do you mean?"

Maddie pinched a fold of her riding habit between her fingers. "I know how it feels to lose someone. I . . . I just want to say that I understand how much you miss Jonathan."

Theo led Starling over and looked down at Maddie, his face twisted with anger and grief. "You're wrong, Maddie," he said, sounding bone-weary. "You don't understand at all."

MADDIE FLINCHED. "I'M SORRY," she began, but Theo had turned away to check Starling's girth.

"Come on, let's go back," he said, lowering the saddle flap.

Maddie wished they were back already. She couldn't work out what she'd said to make her brother so angry.

She would have preferred to ride back on her own, but she had to wait beside Starling for Theo to lift her back into the saddle. She didn't meet his eyes as he hoisted her up, not holding her leg like Ollie did but putting both hands around her waist as if she were five years old. As soon as he had put her left foot into the stirrup, she gathered up the reins and pulled Starling's head away from the hawthorn bush.

"Steady on, he's not done anything wrong," Theo protested, but Maddie ignored him and nudged her pony into a rapid walk down the lane. Behind her, she heard Theo swing himself onto Wayfarer's back and follow, the cob's hooves crunching heavily over the loose stones. To her relief, Theo didn't try to talk to her as they rode back along the track to the stable yard.

Ollie came out of the tack room when he heard Starling's

hooves on the cobbles and came over to help her dismount. Maddie shook out some damp leaves from the folds of her habit and bent over to button the apron around her waist.

"How was Wayfarer for you, sir?" Ollie addressed Theo as he led Starling across the yard.

"Fine, thank you," Theo replied. "Sir Wilfred must have a good eye for a horse."

"Aye, that he does. We're going to turn that mare o' yours into the top paddock. Would you like to see?"

"Yes, I would." Theo sounded as if he was recovering from the quarrel in the churchyard.

Maddie lifted her head. She'd hardly looked twice at the mare yesterday with all the excitement of Theo coming home, but now she was curious to see the horse that had come all the way from Africa with her brother. She didn't even know the mare's name, she realized.

Theo had led Wayfarer into his stable, and Ollie was coming out of Starling's stable with the saddle over his arm.

"Where is the chestnut horse?" she asked.

Ollie nodded at the stable next to Thor's. Maddie went over to the door and peered inside. The stable was shadowy after the bright sunshine, but she could make out the mare on the far side, her head hanging low and her eyes half closed as if she was dozing. Her head shot up when Maddie appeared, and she turned toward her with her small ears pricked and her nostrils flaring rapidly in and out.

"Hello there," Maddie said. She started to stretch her hand over the door, then stopped with her hand dangling in thin air, feeling foolish. The horse was much too far away to stroke.

The mare shifted toward her. She halted in the middle of the straw, still too far away to touch, and looked at her with huge, curious eyes. Maddie stared in fascination at the mare's eyelashes, which were the same shade of brown as the horse's eyes, and the longest she'd ever seen. A broad strip of white ran down her nose, slipping at the bottom to include her right nostril but not her left. Her tail was so long that the bottom few inches lay tangled on the straw, and her mane hung lower than her neck. It was a shade darker than her coat, which was the exact color of firelight, even in the gloomy stable.

Feeling very daring, Maddie unbolted the door and slipped inside. The mare watched her, unblinking; the only way Maddie could tell she wasn't a statue was by the way her sides heaved gently with each breath. Maddie realized with a jolt of surprise that she had never been inside a stable before. Starling was always brought out to her in the yard. She looked around. A haynet hung from a steel ring in the wall beside her, half filled with hay. A triangular manger was fixed in the corner on the other side of the door, about the height of Maddie's waist. She couldn't tell if there was any feed left inside. She guessed there probably wasn't, remembering Theo telling her how enthusiastic the mare had been about her breakfast.

Maddie took a step closer to the mare and reached out to touch her mane, imagining what the tangled hair would feel like under her fingers. The straw dragged at her skirt, and she rested her other hand on the haynet to steady herself. Suddenly the mare's head snaked around, quick as lightning, and nipped Maddie smartly on her forearm.

She clutched her arm and stared at the horse in dismay. The sleeve of her riding habit was thick enough that the mare's teeth hadn't pierced the cloth, but it had hurt all the same, like a sharp pinch. The mare flattened her ears and curled back her top lip. Maddie wasn't going to wait around and get bitten again. Still holding her arm, she turned and forced her way through the straw toward the door. Luckily she hadn't bolted it and it swung open easily, letting her burst out into the yard.

Her cheeks burned when she saw Theo standing in the middle of the cobbles. "She bit me!" Maddie exclaimed.

Her brother came over. "Are you all right?"

Maddie took her hand away from her arm and they both peered at the sleeve. There was a faint row of damp tooth marks in the cloth just below Maddie's elbow. "It's not too bad," she admitted.

"Still a shock, though," Theo said. He walked past her and leaned over the mare's door. "You were inside the stable, right?"

Maddie nodded.

"I expect you got between her and the manger," Theo guessed. "Horses don't like thinking they can't get to their food."

Maddie stared at her brother. "Are you saying that it was my fault I was bitten?"

Theo was watching the mare pull at her hay. "Horses aren't malicious creatures," he said. "She wasn't doing it for fun."

"No!" Maddie agreed. Embarrassment was making her angry. "She was doing it because she was greedy!" She wheeled around and started to walk across the yard. She couldn't even talk to a horse without getting something wrong! When she reached the path that led to the side door of the house, she kept going, heading for the back lawn. She didn't want anyone to see her looking so flustered and red-faced.

Rapid footsteps sounded behind her and a hand touched her shoulder.

"Maddie, wait."

It was Theo. He let his hand fall back to his side and looked down at the ground. "I'm sorry," he said. "Sorry that you were bitten, and sorry about . . . about not coming back for our parents' funeral." He shrugged. "I don't know what else to say."

Maddie turned away to walk across the lawn. "I don't know, either," she said miserably. "Everything I say seems to come out wrong. Even Lou gets disappointed because I won't tell her I like living here, and that I don't mind her going off to London all the time. But I do mind, and I wish she'd understand that. I thought everything would be all right if you came back, but it isn't." She broke off, hoping she hadn't offended him.

But her brother was walking with long strides to keep up with her, and when he looked at her, his gray eyes were kind. "It's all right. I know this hasn't been the sort of homecoming you read about in books." He forced a wry smile, which only reached the unscarred side of his mouth.

"And maybe I shouldn't expect you to act like you've been here forever on your first day back," Maddie admitted. She looked around at the smooth green paddocks, then back at the big square house, whose windows seemed to watch them unblinkingly. "I don't think it feels like home to me, either."

"I'm sorry to hear that," Theo said. He seemed about to say something else when they were disturbed by the sound of hoofbeats on grass. Theo's face lit up. "Look!" he said. "They're putting the mare out."

Maddie wasn't sure why he was so excited about putting a horse in a field, but she gazed obediently across the paddock. The chestnut mare jumped around like a fiery fish at the end of the rope that Toby was holding, while Ollie shut the gate behind them.

"She seems a bit frisky," Maddie commented.

"She's a beauty, don't you think?" said Theo, as though being frisky was a good thing.

Maddie glanced sideways at him. He looked more alive and filled with feeling than she had seen him yet.

"Come on," he urged. "You can't dislike horses that much."

"I don't dislike them at all," Maddie told him. "I . . . I'm just not very used to being around them, I suppose."

She watched Toby unbuckle the mare's headcollar. The horse sprang away like a trout freed from a line. She cantered a few strides, then stopped and tossed her head so that her mane rippled in a dark orange wave. With a snort, she started to trot along the line of the fence, flicking out each hoof with her front legs perfectly straight. Her tail was kinked high over her back, spilling over her quarters like a waterfall. Suddenly she stuck her nose between her knees, bunched her hind legs under her, and bucked once, twice, three times, before setting off at a fast canter with her head in the air.

"I'm not sure I like all that leaping about," Maddie confessed.

"That's not leaping about!" Theo protested. "That's dancing! Look at the way she moves, like she's floating over the grass."

"I suppose so," Maddie said. The mare certainly looked very different from the way Wayfarer pounded over the ground, or even Starling, whose strides were short and choppy.

"I'd guess she's got some Arabian in her," Theo went on, not taking his eyes off the mare. "That's a type of desert horse, smaller than English thoroughbreds but bred to run long distances without getting tired. In Namibia, we always tried to buy horses with Arabian breeding. See her dished face?"

Maddie guessed he was referring to the way the mare's nose was slightly concave, so that it looked wider around her nostrils than just below her eyes.

"That's a real Arabian face," Theo explained. Suddenly he turned to Maddie. "Would you like to name her?"

Maddie stared at him in surprise. "Doesn't she have a name already?"

Theo shrugged. "She must have done once, but I never asked the people that I bought her from on the ship." He paused, then added, "Don't hold it against her, that she nipped you in the stable. I can show you how to handle her so that she doesn't do it again. She needs a name if she's going to stay here."

And if the mare stayed, Theo would stay too. . . .

Maddie nodded. "All right. But I haven't named a horse before," she warned him. Something inside her fluttered with excitement.

"Doesn't matter. Just think of something that'd suit her, and is easy to remember."

Maddie rested her hands on the wooden rail and watched the mare approach them. She had slowed to a trot once more, her hooves swishing over the grass. Theo was right, she did look as if she were dancing. A memory flashed into Maddie's mind of a hot, crowded theater, and a spotlit stage far below where a slender girl clad in an orange-and-scarlet dress was swept into the air by a man wearing a dark green coat.

"Firebird," she said out loud, and Theo looked at her with his eyebrows raised.

"Perhaps we could call her Firebird?" she went on. "It's the name of a ballet that Mother took me to see in London, not long after you went away." She swallowed the sharp stab of grief for the life she had lost along with her parents. "Because the mare looks like she's dancing, like you said, and because she's the color of flame."

Theo smiled. "I think Firebird is a perfect name."

The mare stood in the center of the paddock, sniffing the air.

"Welcome to England, Firebird," Maddie whispered. "Welcome to your new home."

CHAPTER

8

⟨≈≈≈⟩

A CLOUD COVERED THE SUN, making Maddie shiver, so she left Theo watching Firebird and went back into the house. She couldn't believe she'd named the mare!

She felt her face stretch in a smile, and a voice said, "Penny for your thoughts?"

Louisa was standing in the lobby, taking off her heavy car coat.

"Theo let me name the chestnut mare!"

"Didn't she have a name already?"

Maddie shook her head. "No, or at least Theo didn't know what it was. Don't you think Firebird is the perfect name for her?"

Lou looked puzzled. "Well, she's the right color, I suppose."

"And he's going to teach me how to handle her so I don't get bitten again," Maddie went on.

"She bit you?"

"It wasn't her fault," Maddie said hurriedly. "Theo says I must have stood between her and her manger."

"I didn't have you down as such a keen horsewoman,

Mouse," Louisa teased.

Maddie felt herself go red and bent down to undo her boots. "Did you get everything you needed in Newbury?" she asked.

"Yes. Ella wants to have a lunch party next Saturday, to welcome Theo home." Louisa paused. "I'm not sure how Theo will feel about that."

"Me neither," Maddie agreed, thinking of Theo's reaction to her questions about the mine. She suspected that was the last thing Theo would want, to be paraded around like an exotic vegetable. "But he can't be surprised that Grandmama wants everyone to know he's come home," she said out loud. "It's not like it's a big secret!"

"No, of course not." Lou's voice faded as she walked back into the hall, and Maddie heard her taking the post from Matthew. "Hey, Maddie! There's a letter from Namibia!"

She ran into the hall to find Louisa holding a rather dog-eared white envelope. The address, in faded blue ink, was hardly legible but the postmark clearly said Windhoek, Namibia.

"Do you think it's the letter about the accident?"

"Could be," said Lou, slitting the envelope open with the letter knife. She took out a single sheet of thin paper and held it out so Maddie could read it as well.

Dear Sirs,

We regret to inform you that Major Theodore Wilfred

*Harman has been injured in an accident in mineshaft B7 on the
day of 7th December 1922. He has been discharged from hospital
and will be returning to England on the next available boat.
Should you have any inquiries, I would be glad to help if it is
within my power.*

     Yours faithfully,

       Dr. Christopher van der Valk, M.D.

The letter was dated 18th January, nearly six weeks ago.

"It must have been delayed because the address is hard to read," Lou decided, studying the envelope again. "Not that it matters now."

"No," Maddie agreed. "We should tell Theo it's here. He might want to write to say he got home safely."

"Good idea," said Louisa. "And then he can start to make plans for his future back here. Perhaps I should take him to London with me this week, see if he wants to look up any old friends."

Maddie felt herself go cold at the thought of Theo leaving Sefton Park so soon. She wanted the chance to get to know him before he went away again, even if it meant spending time with him in the stable yard, where he seemed more comfortable than anywhere else. She realized that part of her was looking forward to learning more about horses, especially Firebird.

To her relief, Theo didn't seem to view the letter as a reason to start sorting out a new life for himself in London. It didn't make him talk about the mine any more, either. Instead, he fitted quietly into the weekend routine at Sefton Park, joining Lady Ella for afternoon tea and walking in the garden with Sir Wilfred before supper. Maddie found herself waiting rather anxiously for him to suggest they go to the stables for her first lesson in horsemanship. She was too shy to remind Theo in case he hadn't meant her to take his offer seriously. Perhaps he would mention it the following day.

But Sunday morning was taken up by the family's visit to the church, where Lady Ella seemed determined to introduce everyone to "my grandson, Major Harman, newly returned from Africa." During the sermon, Maddie asked Lou in a whisper why Theo was still called Major Harman; Lou explained that once you reached the rank of major or higher, you were allowed to keep your title even if you stopped being a solder.

From Theo's expression, Maddie didn't think he wanted to be reminded about the war every time someone said his name.

On Monday, she came downstairs to find Theo and Louisa having breakfast together. "Morning, Mouse," said Lou, putting down her empty teacup. She turned to Theo. "I need to write some letters this morning, but we could go to Newbury this afternoon if you wanted."

Theo nodded as he carefully sliced the top off a boiled egg. "Thanks, Louisa." His face looked worse this morning, his scar crimson as if he had been rubbing it in the night. But his eyes were cheerful when he looked up at Maddie. "Hello there," he said. "Would you like to come with me to see Firebird this morning?"

Maddie slid into her chair and unfolded a napkin on her lap. "Yes, please." The governess who taught her lessons wasn't due to come until tomorrow, and she usually rode on a Monday morning anyway. But her stomach flipped over with nerves when she remembered the way the mare had bitten her, and then she thought of her undignified plummet off Starling and began to wonder if this was such a good idea after all.

Her brother was waiting for her in the stable yard by the time she had finished her breakfast; she had drained the last sip of tea and even eaten the corners of her toast, which she normally left at the edge of her plate. It was another warm morning, even though it was only February, and Theo was in shirtsleeves, the oversized shirt billowing out on his back like a sail. Maddie wondered if Louisa was going to take him to buy some new clothes that afternoon so he didn't have to keep wearing Grandpapa's.

Theo beckoned her over to Firebird's stable. A saddle was resting on top of the door, with a bridle draped across it. "I thought we'd start by tacking her up."

"Toby usually does that," Maddie said without thinking.

An expression that she couldn't read flickered across Theo's face. "You can't always rely on other people to do things for you. Don't you want to be able to do things for yourself?"

Maddie shrugged. Driving her own car like Rosie Williams, wearing dresses from the fashion plates in Lou's magazines, or going to house parties in London—those were things that she wanted to do but couldn't. Putting a saddle on a horse didn't seem nearly as much of a challenge.

Theo seemed to read the hesitation in her eyes. "Perhaps it would be best if I tacked up and you watched?"

Maddie nodded. "Yes . . . please," she added, in case she sounded ungracious. She followed Theo into the stable, telling herself there was no need to be nervous while he was there. She made sure she was standing well away from Firebird's manger, but not too close to the haynet either. Did horses feel possessive about their water buckets as well? Maddie inched away, just in case.

The mare watched them from the back of the stable, her coat glowing like embers. Maddie felt a tingle of excitement as she let the mare's name echo in her head. *Firebird.* It seemed to suit her even more this morning.

Theo held the bridle in one hand and draped the reins over Firebird's head with the other. "The thing about being around horses," he explained, "is that you have to be confident and calm around them all the time. They can tell if you're scared, see, and that will make them scared too. They're not predators, so if they think there's something to be frightened of, they'll either run away or try to fight back. Be gentle and quiet, and always let them come to you. There's no point chasing them, because you'll never catch them."

Maddie watched as he stood close to Firebird's shoulder and lifted the bridle so that he could ease the bit into her mouth.

"There's a good girl," he murmured. Maddie winced as the metal clanged against the mare's strong yellow teeth.

"Don't be afraid to praise her," Theo said over his shoulder. "Horses always want to please us, which makes it too easy to take advantage of them."

"Did Jonathan tell you all this?" Maddie asked curiously.

He blinked. "Sorry?"

"You said Jonathan taught you to ride. Is this what he said to you?" Maddie winced as she remembered the expression on her brother's face when she had tried to talk to him about Jonathan before. She held her breath, hoping she hadn't made him angry again.

To her relief, Theo just shrugged. "I guess. I mean, yes. He really loved horses. It wasn't hard to learn from him." He turned away to fasten the leather straps that went around Firebird's nose and under her chin.

"Would you like me to pass you the saddle?" Maddie offered, steering away from dangerous topics.

"Thanks," said Theo.

She heaved the saddle off the door, staggering a little—she hadn't realized how heavy these things were, and this was a man's saddle, smaller and lighter than a sidesaddle. Theo took it from her and showed her how to place it high up on Firebird's withers before sliding it into place on her back.

"So the hair lies flat underneath, see?" he said, glancing at her to check she understood. "I thought I'd ride Firebird today," he went on, "but you could ride her tomorrow, if you like."

Maddie's nerve failed her as she pictured Firebird leaping across the paddock with her heels in the air. "I think I'll keep to Starling for now," she stammered.

"You do know Starling's too small for you, don't you?" Theo said with a frown. "If you get any taller, you won't be able to ride him at all. That might be why you find it so hard to jump. It can be easier on a horse with longer legs."

"But I don't want to ride a different horse," Maddie said stubbornly. "I like Starling."

Theo ducked his head under the saddle flap to buckle the girth. "Well, let's see how you feel after you've seen me ride Firebird." He ran his hand under the girth, making the hair lie flat, and took hold of the rein. "Come on, old girl," he said. Firebird turned to him and blew softly down her nostrils. Theo bent down and put his nose against hers, blowing back. Maddie stared at him in astonishment.

"It's how horses greet each other," Theo explained.

"Like blowing a kiss?"

"Kind of," he agreed, smiling. Behind him, Firebird nudged him, leaving a smear of foam on his shirt. The mare didn't look the least bit likely to bite him—in fact, she seemed to be treating Theo like her best friend. Maddie realized she was feeling jealous of a horse and told herself to stop being ridiculous.

Ollie had tacked up Starling for her and was holding him in the middle of the yard. He lifted Maddie into the saddle while Theo mounted Firebird. The mare danced sideways, her hooves clattering against the cobbles.

"Steady, lass," Theo murmured.

Maddie looked away, hoping Theo couldn't tell how nervous she was. What if Firebird made Starling misbehave as well?

But Theo was already riding out of the yard. "I thought you could show me some more of the estate," he said, twisting around to look at Maddie.

Trying to untangle her reins and kick Starling forward all at the same time, Maddie just nodded. When her hands were more or less in the right place and Starling had jogged to catch up with Firebird, she said breathlessly, "If we turn right at the bottom of the drive, we can go down the hill to the canal and join the track that leads to Home Farm."

They rode in silence along the lane that sloped steeply down to the canal, past the church. Theo sat lightly in the saddle, letting Firebird arch her neck and snort curiously at the ground. On the canal below, a man shouted on a barge and the mare's head shot up, her nostrils flaring in alarm.

Theo leaned forward and laid one hand against Firebird's neck. "Steady, girl, you're all right."

"She looks as if she's scared of everything," Maddie commented.

"Everything must seem strange if she's used to Africa," Theo pointed out. "I think she's doing fine. She's been well-schooled, wherever she was before."

Maddie studied the mare as she walked down the hill, trying to see how Theo could tell what Firebird had been taught in the past. Her strides were smooth and she flicked her toes up daintily with each step, as if she wanted to dance but couldn't with a rider on her back. Maybe that was what Theo meant.

Suddenly Starling stumbled and started to limp. Maddie gasped and clung on to the top pommel.

Theo slid off Firebird and led her over. "Ease up, old fellow," he said, placing a hand on Starling's chest to bring him to a halt. "I think he's got a stone in his hoof."

"I thought I was going to fall off again," Maddie confessed.

"No danger of that," said Theo. "You'd stagger about too if you had a stone stuck to the bottom of your foot." He took a small silver penknife from the pocket of his breeches. "Let's see if we can get it out."

Maddie's heart flipped over. "My knife! You've still got my knife!"

Theo paused and looked down at the knife. The engraving, *Theodore Wilfred Harman,* was clearly visible on the handle. "Yes," he said quietly. "I still have the knife. It saved my life. There's no way I'd lose it now."

"It saved your life?" Maddie echoed. "How?"

Theo didn't reply because he was busy running his hand down Starling's front leg, encouraging the pony to lift his hoof and rest it in Theo's hand. Maddie watched him use the tip of the knife to prise a large stone out from beside the fleshy triangular lump in the center of Starling's foot.

"How did the knife save you?" she repeated.

Theo lowered Starling's hoof to the ground and patted the pony's neck. "It doesn't matter."

"Yes, it does!" Maddie protested. "I gave you that knife, and now you tell me it saved your life? How can I not want to know?" She scooped up the reins and turned Starling so she could look at her brother, who had swung himself onto Firebird again.

Theo's expression darkened, his face almost unrecognizable behind the scar. "I don't want to talk about it."

Maddie clenched her hands around the reins, feeling her temper flare. "It's another secret, I suppose. Like just about every single thing you've done for the last seven years. For goodness' sake, Theo, what are you trying to hide?"

9

TOO FURIOUS TO WAIT FOR her brother's reply, Maddie dug her left heel into Starling's side and grabbed his mane as he set off at a trot back along the lane.

Behind her, she heard Theo call out, "Maddie! Come back!" but she kicked Starling again until he broke into a canter. He wasn't limping now, but she steered him onto the grass beside the road in case his hoof was still sore from the stone. A small part of her was astonished that she had spoken like that to her brother, but another, louder voice told her it was Theo's fault. Why did he have to be so secretive? What had he done that he couldn't tell his own family about?

As she neared the gate that led onto the driveway, Maddie glanced over her shoulder. To her relief, Theo wasn't coming after her. She hoped he would stay out for hours and hours. With any luck, he'd get lost and not come back for days. Maddie knew she was being absurd: Grandpapa's estate was big, but not big enough for a horse and rider to disappear. Even if Theo didn't know where he was, he would soon find a farm-worker to tell him how to get back to the house.

If Ollie was surprised to see Maddie return alone, he didn't say so. Instead, he helped her down and led Starling into the stable, leaving Maddie to trail into the house wondering why she had ever wished for her brother to come back. Louisa was writing letters in the drawing room and her grandmother was in her salon, so Maddie read in her bedroom until the gong rang for luncheon. She heard Theo return about half an hour before, passing Grandpapa on the stairs and telling him that he'd had a good ride, that the mare was obviously well-schooled if a little fresh. Grandpapa had grunted sagely and remarked it was no surprise if there was a tickle in her toes, with all the spring grass she was having.

Maddie clamped her hands over her ears and stared at her book. *Horses, horses, horses!* That's all anyone thought about around here. She considered missing luncheon altogether but knew it would only make her grandmother ask awkward questions. But she didn't have much appetite, and pushed her Dover sole listlessly around her plate after a couple of mouthfuls.

"Madeline, stop playing with your food!" Grandmama scolded from the end of the table.

Maddie looked up guiltily and dropped her fork with a clatter.

"Is everything all right?" asked Louisa. "You look awfully strange."

Maddie could feel Theo's eyes burning into her. What did he think she was going to say? *Theo's knife saved his life and I want to know why?* "I'm fine. I'm just not very hungry."

"So it would seem," Grandmama said. "Perhaps you'd like to leave the table, since it would be a shame to waste your dessert as well."

Feeling like a naughty child, Maddie slipped off her chair and went out of the breakfast room—now that Theo had been back for a few days, they had stopped using the formal dining room for family meals. But they would be eating there on Saturday, when Grandmama had invited "just a dozen of our closest friends" for a luncheon party.

Maddie didn't want to go upstairs again, not when the sun was slanting temptingly through the windows of the hall. Instead she went to the lobby and pulled on her garden shoes, then took a shallow basket and a pair of pruning shears and slipped outside. The lawn sank invitingly under her feet and a handful of starlings swooped over her head, looking for soft fluffy things to line their nests. Charlie bounded over from the hedge where she had been investigating the tiny paths used by rabbits and voles.

"Come on, girl," Maddie called to the Irish setter. There wouldn't be many flowers out yet, but she could cut some early daffodils and take them to her grandmother as an apology for her behavior at lunchtime.

Leaving the flower beds closest to the house untouched, Maddie headed for the bottom of the garden. For a while she thought about nothing except laying each flower carefully in the basket so the petals weren't crushed. Charlie wandered off to sniff around the fence posts at the edge of the paddock. A fresh molehill attracted her attention, and Maddie watched the dog probe it with one paw, as if she knew there was a mole somewhere under there but couldn't figure out how to reach it.

There was a snort from the other side of the fence, and Maddie looked up, startled. Firebird was stretching her head over the top rail toward her. Her top lip twitched as she snuffled at the daffodils in Maddie's basket.

She was about to snatch the basket away when she remembered what Theo had said about horses being easily frightened. She didn't want to scare Firebird. Very slowly, she lowered the basket to the ground, putting it out of reach from the nibbling lips. When she straightened up again, Firebird's head was still close, the liquid brown eyes studying her curiously.

"Hello, girl," Maddie said. Firebird's nostrils flared in and out, and Maddie felt hot, damp breath against her hand. Almost without thinking, she bent down and put her face close to the horse's muzzle. It seemed perfectly natural to puff down her nose, and the thrill that she felt when Firebird blew back made her blink in surprise. She was talking to a horse, in horse language! She blew again, shorter and quicker this time, and Firebird did the same.

Maddie stood up with a shout of laughter, and the mare wheeled away in alarm. Maddie instantly felt cross with herself. But Firebird only cantered away for a single stride, then stopped and took a pace back toward the fence. Maddie reached her hand slowly over the rail.

"Come on, little one," she whispered. "It's all right. I won't hurt you."

The mare arched her neck and snorted—and Maddie somehow knew it meant *I'm not quite certain about this.* She shut her eyes and kept completely still, even though her heart was hammering. She felt a warm velvet muzzle push against her fingers, and long whiskers tickled her wrist. She opened her eyes to see Firebird standing right in front of her. The mare's tiny golden ears—which Maddie suddenly noticed arched inward at the tip, like beech leaves—pricked forward, then relaxed, and her muzzle rested heavily in Maddie's hand.

Maddie took a long, shaky breath. She had done it! She had made friends with Firebird, all by herself. Very slowly, she reached up with her other hand and rested it at the top of Firebird's neck, just under her long mane. It was softer than she had imagined, more like spun silk than Starling's wiry hair. She rubbed her fingers gently against Firebird's neck and watched the mare's eyes close.

For the first time she could remember, Maddie wasn't thinking about London, or her parents, or about Theo being difficult to talk to. All that mattered was being here with this horse, not scaring her, not asking her to do anything apart from trust her and be her friend.

CHAPTER

10

⟨∾∾∾⟩

FOR ALL HER EXCITEMENT about making friends with
Firebird, Maddie felt shy about telling Theo after their argu-
ment, and she wasn't too disappointed when they didn't have
any time on their own for the rest of the week. She was kept
busy with lessons with her tutor, Miss Finnigan, who clearly
didn't think a long-lost brother reappearing was sufficient
excuse for forgetting the causes of the English Civil War.

Louisa took Theo to Newbury to be measured for shirts and
suits at their grandfather's tailor; Sir Wilfred advised Theo to
wait until he was in London to be measured for a dinner suit,
but from the look on Theo's face, which Maddie glimpsed
from the corner of the library where she was looking for a
volume of poetry, he was in no hurry to start going to formal
dinners. She suspected that he wasn't hugely enthusiastic about
Grandmama's luncheon party, either, because he shook his
head when Lady Ella asked him if there was anyone he wanted
to invite, and politely said he'd prefer to leave all the arrangements to her. He didn't even seem pleased when Louisa told
him that she'd invited all of her London friends, who used to

be his friends—then she stopped awkwardly and said that they were still his friends, of course, only . . . Theo had looked at her with sympathy in his eyes and said he knew what she meant.

Trapped indoors by the rain one afternoon, Maddie stared out of the drawing room windows at Firebird, who didn't seem to mind the wet at all. Theo was in the library with Sir Wilfred, reading the newspaper. Maddie had heard him remark to Grandpapa how unusual it was for a thin-skinned desert horse to be content to stay out in the rain, but Maddie thought it was one more example of how perfectly Firebird was settling into Sefton Park. She couldn't forget the way the mare's breath had felt against her hand, and how she had let Maddie smooth the hair on her neck in tiny circles. Maddie watched her dance through the raindrops with her neck arched and her mane clinging to her rain-slicked coat. However awkward things were with her brother—they had barely exchanged two words since their quarrel on Monday—she would wish Theo home a thousand times over if it meant Firebird came with him.

On Saturday, the day of Lady Ella's luncheon party, the first guests arrived shortly before eleven. Maddie was practicing the piano in her grandmother's salon, prodding the keys half-heartedly while she craned her neck to watch Firebird cantering around the paddock, chasing rooks off the grass. Even though it had stopped raining, Maddie hadn't been able to go out to see the mare because she was dressed in her luncheon outfit. Louisa had helped her choose a dark green pinafore dress with a pale green chiffon sash, over a pristine white blouse. She had matching dark green velvet house shoes, and Lou had tied her hair back with a green ribbon. Lady Ella had proclaimed she looked "most suitable"; Maddie thought she looked as if she was about to run away and join Robin Hood and his Merrie Men.

She heard the butler open the front door. "Good morning, Miss Williams, Mr. Farnsworth. I trust you had a pleasant journey down?"

"Oh yes, Matthew," replied a warm, enthusiastic voice. "Though I'm not sure Bertie was too pleased when I got forty miles per hour out of the Baby Austin. Were you, Bertie?"

There was a low reply that Maddie couldn't hear. She swung her legs off the piano stool and went out to the hallway. Her sister's best friend, Rosie Williams, was taking off her driving coat and handing it to Matthew. Rosie had a pretty, heart-shaped face, pale green eyes that slanted upward like a cat's, and blond hair that was bobbed even shorter than Louisa's. Today she was wearing knee-length culottes and a short-sleeved blouse, and when she came over to hug Maddie, a waft of spicy, exotic scent floated around her.

"Maddie! How lovely to see you! Where's this mysterious brother of yours? I can't believe he's been here for days and days, and Lou hasn't once brought him up to London to see us!"

The tall young man behind her handed his hat and gloves to Matthew and grinned at Maddie. "Don't mind Rosie, she's been wittering all the way from London about seeing Theo again. I did try to tell her the poor chap probably wanted some peace and quiet before we descended on him!"

Before Maddie could reply, her grandfather appeared at the library door. "Good to have you here, Farnsworth," he declared, shaking Bertram's hand.

Another couple followed Rosie and Bertram through the front door, their clothes looking rather crumpled from being squashed in the back of Rosie's tiny car.

Louisa came running down the stairs to greet her friends, kissing cheeks and exclaiming at Clarissa's latest outfit, a straight-waisted dress in layers of peach chiffon, with matching high-heeled shoes. "But where's Theo?" everyone wanted to know, and Maddie saw Sir Wilfred look around as if his grandson might be hiding behind one of the tall Chinese vases that stood at the edge the hall.

Lady Ella swept into the hall and raised her eyebrows when she realized the guest of honor was missing. "Is he in the stable yard?" she asked Maddie.

"I don't know, Grandmama," she confessed. "Shall I go and look for him?"

"Yes, please do," said Lady Ella. She gestured toward the door of her salon. "Shall we go through, everyone? Matthew, could you bring refreshments?"

The butler nodded and headed for the lobby, where a staircase led down to the kitchen. Maddie was just pulling on her tweed jacket, ready to look for Theo in the stable yard, when the back door opened behind her and her brother came in. His gray eyes looked almost black in the wood-paneled lobby, and Maddie couldn't tell what he was thinking.

"The guests have arrived," she said, feeling awkward. She didn't want Theo to think she was chasing him around like Charlie after a rabbit.

Theo didn't say anything, just took off his coat and bent down to untie the laces on his boots. Maddie felt as if she was leading him to the gallows, from the way his shoulders were hunched and his eyes didn't meet hers. Through the window, she saw Firebird in the paddock at the bottom of the lawn. The mare was cantering along with her head lowered to make another rook flap noisily into the air.

"Don't you want to see your old friends?" Maddie blurted out. "You're not the only one who fought in the war. Bertie was in the King's Hussars, and Clarissa's brother was killed at Passchendaele."

Theo didn't say anything, and Maddie went on, "What did you expect? Did you think you might be able to come back and not see anyone you used to know?"

Theo just shook his head, and pushed his feet into his indoor shoes before heading past her into the hall. Sighing, Maddie followed him. She hoped her brother would have enough manners to be polite to their guests however much he would rather be somewhere else.

The other guests had arrived and were already in the formal dining room. George Edwards was looking pink and pleased as he sat next to Lou, and his parents were seated on either side of Sir Wilfred. The final members of the party were Mr. and Mrs. Granville, old friends of Maddie's grandfather.

Everyone stopped talking when Theo entered the room. There was a stunned pause, and Maddie guessed her grandmother hadn't warned them about the scar on his face.

Before anyone could say anything, there was a deafening clap from outside. Sir Wilfred looked at the window and scowled. "Blasted fellow across the lane must be shooting pigeons again," he muttered.

The sound of the gunshot seemed to break the ice that Theo had brought into the room. Bertram Farnsworth stood up and came over to shake his hand, clapping him on the back at the same time. "Good to see you, old fellow. You're looking very fit, I must say! Must be all that African sun."

Clarissa lifted one hand to her cheek. "It wouldn't agree with me at all. I'd be scorched!"

While everyone made suitably admiring noises about

Clarissa's complexion, Theo slid into his seat and bent his head to unfold his napkin on his lap. He looked like a little boy who didn't want to be made a fuss of, and Maddie felt a pang of sympathy for him as she walked around the table to her chair.

While the servants brought in bowls of watercress soup, Terence Granville turned to Theo. "So, Theodore, tell us about these mines of yours. Good prospects in diamonds down there?"

"Not if the tunnels collapse," Theo said bleakly, and Lady Ella gasped.

"Well, no, of course not," blustered Mr. Granville.

"We heard about the accident, and we're so sorry about your friend," Rosie put in.

Theo shrugged and crumbled the bread roll on his side plate. Louisa met Maddie's eyes, looking as desperate as she felt.

Algernon tried next. "Do you have any plans for what to do next, old boy?"

"I'm waiting until I feel a bit more settled," Theo replied.

"Yes, of course," Algernon agreed heartily. "Plenty of time for that. But if you want me to put in a word at the bank, just let me know."

When Theo didn't say anything, Clarissa said, in the tone of someone who isn't at all fazed about making polite conversation, "The Rothschilds are having a boating party next month. It will be so much fun, especially if Teddy FitzHammond makes it back from Balmoral. Are you coming, Louisa?"

Suddenly Theo pushed back his chair and stood up. "Excuse me," he muttered. "I have a dreadful headache. Please, enjoy your lunch." He turned and pushed his way out of the dining room, almost cannoning into Faye who was bringing in a dish of butter.

There was a stunned silence.

Lady Ella opened her mouth with an effort. She had gone deathly pale, with two spots of bright red on her cheeks. "I'm so sorry," she stammered, and Maddie felt quite sorry for her.

She put her napkin on the table and stood up. "I'll go after Theo, Grandmama," she offered.

Lady Ella nodded. "Yes, dear. And perhaps you could ask Mrs. Kirby to take him a tonic for his headache?" She was already recovering her composure, behaving as if her grandson was nothing more than a little unwell and hadn't just wrecked her carefully planned luncheon.

Maddie hurried out of the room. She was about to head upstairs, guessing that if Theo really had a headache he would have gone straight to his bedroom, when she felt a draft around her feet. He must have gone out to the stables and not closed the door behind him. Shoving her feet into her galoshes, Maddie followed.

As she walked along the gravel path, more rooks landed in the paddock, fluttering to the ground like a handful of sooty handkerchiefs. Maddie waited for the thud of hooves that meant Firebird was chasing the birds away. But the only thing she heard was the cawing of the rooks, and Jinx barking in the stable yard.

Maddie stopped. Why hadn't Firebird chased the rooks? She walked across the lawn, craning her neck to see both sides of the paddock. It was a large, square field lined with rails on two sides and a thick, bristly hedge on the other two. There were three tall oak trees in the far corner, but Firebird wasn't standing underneath them. Apart from the rooks, the paddock was completely empty.

Maddie spun on her heel and rushed to the stable yard. She skidded to a halt on the cobbles, panting.

"Toby!" she cried. "Come quick! Firebird has gone!"

CHAPTER

11

⬦⬦⬦

THE GROOM APPEARED AT the doorway of the tack room.

"Has anyone taken Firebird out of her field?" Maddie demanded.

"No, miss." Toby looked puzzled. "We only put her out a while ago."

"But she's not there now!"

"Is there something wrong?" Theo appeared at the end of the stable block.

"Firebird's not in her field!"

Theo's face darkened. "Have you checked if the gates are open?"

He led the way across the yard at a run, heading for the archway in the back row of stables that led to the paddocks. Maddie followed, holding her skirt with both hands to keep it from tripping her up.

"I'll bring a headcollar," Toby called after them.

Maddie reached the gate a few paces behind Theo and stopped, gasping for breath. It was firmly shut, even though Theo rattled the latch.

"Come on," he said. "We need to check the other gate as well." He swung himself over, then paused and opened it to let Maddie walk through before setting off at a run.

She stumbled behind him, hoping Grandmama and her guests weren't watching from the dining room windows and wondering why she hadn't brought Theo back indoors. Right now, his dramatic departure from the luncheon didn't seem important compared with finding Firebird. Could she have been stolen?

Theo had reached the other gate and was shaking his head at Maddie. This one was safely shut, too. She searched the ground for hoofprints, but this gateway had been so boggy that Toby had put down a layer of gravel so it was impossible to see if a horse had passed through recently.

A loud whining noise made them both look up. Toby was riding into the field on a motorcycle, a headcollar lying across his lap. He bounced across the grass and came to a halt beside them. "Here, take this," he panted, stepping off and pushing the motorcycle over to Theo. "I'd head that way first." He nodded across the neighboring field, which sloped down to the largest of Sir Wilfred's fishing lakes. "I doubt the mare left by t'other gate," he went on. "She couldn't have come through the stable yard without me noticing. But there's a footpath across this field, an' it's possible ramblers could have let her slip through this way."

Theo took the handlebars and swung his leg over the seat of the motorcycle. Toby handed him the headcollar, which he slung over his shoulder.

"Wait, I'll come with you," Maddie burst out. She'd never ridden on a motorcycle before, and she was hardly dressed for it now, but Theo didn't know his way around the estate like she did. There was no point sending him out to get lost, not when Firebird could have gone anywhere—as far as the marshy, leg-twisting ground beside the canal, or worse, the railway line on the other side.

Theo looked at her in surprise. "Are you sure?"

But she was already bunching up her skirt and climbing on behind him, resting her feet on tiny stalks of metal that jutted out from the center of the back wheel. She tucked her skirt under her and wrapped both arms around Theo's waist.

Theo pressed the accelerator, and the motorcycle's engine buzzed, making Maddie's teeth rattle. She braced herself as Toby opened the gate and the motorcycle lurched through, its wheels spinning on the gravel.

"Hang on!" Theo shouted over his shoulder, and then they were away, skimming over the grass and following the field down into the dip where a house that had been destroyed by fire had once stood.

Maddie felt the wind whip her hair free from its ribbon to lash against her cheek like tiny stinging brambles. She could hardly breathe and the fumes from the exhaust made her eyes stream, but she had never done anything so exciting in her life. If she hadn't been so worried about where Firebird could have gone, she would have loved every second.

As they neared the far side of the field, Theo took his thumb off the throttle and the motorcycle slowed down. "Can you see her anywhere?" he yelled.

Maddie leaned away from him to look from side to side. There was no sign of a chestnut mare in the field, but in the far corner the gate stood open. She risked letting go of Theo for a moment to point. "She might have gone that way!" she shouted.

He nodded and steered the motorcycle along the fence. The ground was lumpier here, and Maddie felt her teeth rattle as they jolted over the ruts. This gateway was still bare earth, and among the old cattle tracks she clearly saw a trail of equine hoofprints, neat shallow crescents in the mud. She pointed and Theo sped up, bouncing through the open gate and following the trail down a grassy slope to the track that led through the estate.

Maddie started to feel more worried. If Firebird had made it this far, she could have gone in several different directions— farther into the estate, past the fishing lake, or left toward the canal and the railway line. "Firebird, where are you?" she muttered under her breath.

Theo turned the motorcycle right, heading away from the lane. Beside them, the land dipped down sharply to Sir Wilfred's fishing lake. A flicker of movement under some willow trees on the far side caught Maddie's eye. She tapped Theo on the shoulder.

"Over there!" she said.

Theo stopped the motorcycle at the edge of the lane. Maddie slithered off and shook her head to make her ears stop ringing. Theo propped the motorcycle on its stand, then shaded his eyes with one hand to peer across the lake. A distinctive chestnut shape was standing in the dappled shadows under the trees.

"That looks like our girl," he murmured.

Maddie started to run across the grass, but Theo caught her arm. "Steady on," he said. "We don't want her to think we're chasing her, do we? She'll wait for us, don't worry."

Maddie nodded and slowed to a walk. As they drew near, Firebird lifted her head and pricked her ears, watching them. A few blades of grass were sticking out of her mouth, and she started to chew calmly again. Maddie guessed this was a sign she knew exactly who they were and didn't mind them coming over to say hello.

Theo unhooked the headcollar from his shoulder and hid it behind his back, shooting a grin at Maddie as he did. "No point letting her know we want to take her back, is there?" he whispered.

Maddie grinned back. She didn't care if they lassoed Firebird like cowboys, as long as they could take her safely home. *It's only a horse,* whispered a tiny voice inside her head; but something else replied, *Firebird's much, much more than that.*

When they were a dozen yards from the mare, Theo held out one hand, indicating to Maddie that she should wait here. She stood still and watched as he walked up to Firebird and let her sniff him before gently placing one hand flat on her nose. With his other hand, he brought the headcollar out from behind his back and slipped it over her head, all the time talking to her in a low, soothing voice. When he had buckled it into place, he turned to Maddie and beckoned.

She waded through the knee-high grass as fast as she could without startling the mare. Theo stood back, holding the rope attached to the headcollar, to let Maddie press her face against Firebird's warm, damp neck.

"Oh, Birdy," she murmured. "I was so worried about you! You're a good, good girl for letting us find you, do you know that?"

She looked up to see Theo watching her with his eyebrows raised. "Birdy?" he echoed, looking amused. "I thought she was a horse, not a bird? Last time I looked, she didn't have feathers."

Maddie felt herself go red. "Firebird's a bit formal, don't you think? Anyway, you call me Mouse, and I don't have whiskers and a tail!"

Theo grinned. "Sounds fair enough. It's good to see you're getting on with her now."

Maddie ran her hand down Firebird's shoulder. "I breathed down her nose like you showed me, and it really seemed to make us friends." She looked up at Theo, an idea forming in her mind that she knew she had to say out loud before it vanished again like a burst bubble. "Do you think I could try riding her?"

Theo's grin stretched wider, and Maddie didn't notice his scar at all now, just the warmth in his eyes and the way his face lit up. "I think that's a grand idea," he said. "Don't worry, Firebird—Birdy—will look after you. And I won't let you try anything too ambitious—not straight off, at least! Come on, let's get her back to the yard."

He handed the lead rope to Maddie as if she led horses around every day. She clicked her tongue at the mare, just as she had seen Toby and Ollie do dozens of times, and the horse moved off with a toss of her head. She seemed quite happy to walk beside Maddie along the edge of the lake and back onto the gravel track.

Maddie watched her in delight. She was going to ride Firebird! She felt a rush of love for the beautiful little mare. She had come a long, long way to Sefton Park, almost halfway around the globe, and there was no doubt in Maddie's mind that this was where she belonged now.

CHAPTER

12

⸘⸘⸘

BY THE TIME MADDIE AND Theo had returned to the yard, Lady Ella's luncheon guests had left. Maddie braced herself for an uproar when they went back into the house, but Lady Ella and Sir Wilfred seemed too embarrassed to mention Theo's departure. Beyond a rather strained inquiry about his headache, nothing more was said.

Maddie was kept busy all week with lessons, church, and driving to Hungerford to see friends of Grandmama, but she found time to visit Firebird every day. She was sure the mare recognized her now—why else would she lift her head and whinny when Maddie called to her, and trot over to blow gently on her hands with her neck arched and her nostrils flared like tulip petals?

Patient and familiar though Starling was, Maddie had never felt like this about a horse before. Firebird was like a friend, and even when Maddie was drinking tea in a stuffy house in Hungerford, answering endless questions about her lessons and what Louisa was up to, she found herself wondering what the chestnut mare was doing. Toby and Theo had decided her escape must have been the fault of ramblers, letting her slip through when they were opening the gate, so Toby had fixed a sign to the top rail that read *Please keep firmly shut.*

But when she was finally sitting on Firebird, Maddie decided she would give quite a lot to be looking down at Starling's sturdy neck right now. The mare's neck looked as narrow as a rail, and her shoulders were almost hidden beneath the heavy sidesaddle. She snatched at the bit, and Maddie nearly dropped the reins.

"That's it," Theo said encouragingly. "Sit nice and tall, just like you would on Starling."

"But Birdy's so much taller!" Maddie protested. The cobbled stable yard looked a long way down.

"Don't be ridiculous. She's only a couple of hands taller than Starling. What's he, thirteen hands and three inches? Well, Firebird's probably not much more than fifteen two."

Maddie pursed her lips. Even if it was only a matter of inches, sitting on Firebird still felt very, very different from being on Starling.

Theo finished checking the girth and looked up at Maddie, his eyes gleaming like sun on water. "Ready?"

She nodded, trying to sort out the reins again. The leather gloves seemed tighter than ever today, and the sun felt hot on her back. *Please don't let me fall off,* she begged silently.

With a toss of her head, Firebird followed Theo under the

archway. The schooling paddock was next to the field where Firebird grazed, separated by a hawthorn hedge. A sparrow swooped out with a startled *chack,* and the chestnut mare shied. Maddie grabbed the top pommel and glared at Theo. He shouldn't have let her ride Firebird! She was just going to make a fool of herself again.

If Theo guessed she was having doubts, he didn't show it. He glanced back to make sure Maddie was still on board, then unlatched the gate. "In you go," he said, swinging it open.

With her heart pounding, Maddie steered Firebird into the paddock. The mare pricked her ears when she saw the open stretch of grass, lengthening her stride and arching her neck so that Maddie could only just feel the bit at the end of the reins.

"Trot when you're ready," Theo called, coming to stand in the center of the paddock.

Maddie opened her mouth to protest that she hadn't got used to walking yet, but Firebird must have been trained to obey voice commands because she sprang forward, her hooves thudding lightly on the grass. Flustered, Maddie scooped up the reins and tried to sit up like Toby had taught her. The mare's trot was certainly much smoother than Starling's, who bounced along like a jack-in-the-box, but Maddie could already feel herself toppling backward. Her right leg slid forward, the tip of her boot emerging from under the apron to nudge Firebird's silky golden mane. As Maddie's weight tipped back even farther, the mare's stride faltered and she stumbled.

Maddie yanked the mare crossly to a halt. "I told you I can't ride!" she burst out. "It's no use! I'm just going to fall off again."

"Steady on there—both of you," said Theo, coming over and resting one hand on Firebird's nose. He narrowed his eyes. "You know, I think we can do something about your position."

"But this is how Toby told me to sit!" Maddie argued.

Theo shrugged. "Let's have a look anyway." He started to unhook the strap around Maddie's right ankle that held the apron in place, and she drew up her foot with a gasp.

"What are you doing?"

He frowned, making his scar twist like a crimson snake that was trying to devour his face. "I need to see what your legs are doing. You're wearing breeches, aren't you?"

"Well, yes," Maddie faltered. She lowered her leg, and Theo unhooked the strap and folded back the heavy skirt, handing it to Maddie to drape over her left arm.

Theo took hold of her right ankle. "What you want to do is keep this tight against the saddle flap, down here." He pushed her leg against the thin piece of leather that covered Firebird's shoulder.

"Ouch," said Maddie.

He glanced up at her. "Don't be such a baby," he scolded, but his eyes were warm. "This leg is what's going to hold you in place," he went on. "Can you feel it gripping the top pommel?"

Maddie nodded.

"Right, now lean forward a bit so your weight isn't on the back of the saddle. But use your right leg to keep yourself there. You don't want to put any extra weight on the stirrup."

Maddie tilted forward until the top pommel was digging into the back of her right thigh, and her left leg swung lightly in the stirrup.

"That's better," Theo said approvingly, unfurling the apron back over her legs and hooking the strap around her ankle.

"But my leg hurts," Maddie protested.

"You'll get used to it. Now, let's see you ride like that."

Feeling the muscles in her back already beginning to protest, Maddie gathered up the reins. She wouldn't have admitted it in a thousand years, but sitting like this did make it easier to hold her hands above Firebird's neck, without banging them against the top pommel. A thought struck her, and she looked down at Theo again.

"How do you know so much about riding sidesaddle?"

He shook his head. "I don't. I mean, I've never tried. But I could see you were losing your balance before, and this seems the logical way to keep you in the right place. Jonathan always used to say riding was one part skill and nine parts having the sense to figure out how to stay on board!"

"He must have been a very good teacher," Maddie said.

"I suppose he was. He was always more comfortable around horses than people, that's for sure." Theo smiled as if he was seeing something far away. "I used to say he'd be quite happy if we all woke up with hooves and tails."

"Shall I try riding around the paddock again?"

Theo nodded as if he was trying to jolt himself back from his memories. "Just remember to keep that right leg tight against Firebird's shoulder, and hold yourself steady with the top pommel."

Maddie nudged Firebird with her left heel and touched the whip to her flank on the other side. The mare leaped straight into a trot, tucking her nose into her chest so that Maddie had to shorten the reins and wedge her thigh even more firmly against the top pommel. But it worked! Now Firebird's strides felt smooth and even, and she could tell when the mare started to lean inward when they reached the top of the field. Instinctively, Maddie touched her whip against her inside flank to keep her from cutting the corner.

"Well done!" Theo shouted from the middle. "Keep her going, nice and steady!"

Maddie stuffed the reins into her right hand and leaned forward to pat Firebird with her left. "Good girl!" she whispered.

But when she sat up again, her grip on the top pommel had loosened and she felt herself tipping backward again. She tried to sit up, but her right leg slid forward and she started to bounce in the saddle. Firebird's stride became choppy, and Maddie slowed her to a walk.

"It's no good," she told Theo, steering Birdy into the center of the paddock. "It feels like there's a big hole behind me, sucking me backward."

Theo took off his cap and folded it in half. "That saddle's a bit too big for you," he said. "That's why you feel as if you're slipping back. Here, put this underneath you."

Maddie pushed herself off the saddle and stuffed the folded cap underneath her. It felt a bit lumpy, but once she had wriggled around, it propped her forward, making it easier to hook her right leg around the pommel.

Theo pushed her ankle against Firebird's shoulder. "And keep your foot tight in, to hold you steady. With your toes pointed down. If your foot doesn't stay hidden under that skirt, I'll know it's not in the right place!"

Maddie grinned at him and gathered up the reins again. This time she was ready for Firebird to respond to the lightest touch on her sides, and she felt herself relaxing into the gliding, springy trot. Theo's cap kept her tipped forward just enough, and even though her back still ached and her right ankle was being rubbed raw, Maddie could tell she was sitting properly at last.

"Now try cantering!" Theo called, and she shortened the reins, sat up straight, and kicked her left heel against Birdy's flank.

With a snort, the mare struck off on her right leg and cantered along the edge of the paddock. Maddie laughed out loud.

She felt as if they were floating! Firebird's mane flew up with every stride, flicking against Maddie's gloves, and when she glanced down she could see her front hooves striking the grass, one-two, one-two, one-two.

They rounded the corner by the stables and Maddie squeezed with her left heel, urging the mare to go faster. As they set off along the long side of the field, she heard a buzzing sound and looked around, expecting to see a horsefly. Firebird flattened her ears, and Maddie felt the mare's hindquarters slip sideways as she tried to dodge away from the noise. She pulled on the reins to slow Birdy to a trot. The buzzing got louder, and out of the corner of her eye she saw Theo looking at the sky and pointing. Maddie glanced up.

There was an aeroplane flying straight for her!

It was a biplane, with two oatmeal-colored wings held together by wooden struts. Firebird threw up her head in alarm, and Maddie was nearly jolted out of the saddle. She grabbed for the reins, pressing her right ankle against the saddle flap to keep herself from falling off. The mare sidled and swung right around, trying to look up at the plane.

"Hush, Birdy, it's all right," Maddie tried to soothe her. Couldn't that fool of a pilot see there was a horse down here?

Just when she thought the plane was going to land right on top of them, it swooped up again, circling over the church and nearly clipping the flagpole where the red-and-white St.

George's flag was stretched taut by the breeze. Maddie caught a glimpse of some black letters painted on the side, G-A ANG, and a tiny, helmet-clad head halfway along the fuselage before it vanished behind the pine trees.

Firebird's ears flicked as the buzzing faded away, and Maddie leaned forward to pat her. The mare's neck felt damp and warm through Maddie's gloves, and there were specks of white foam in her mane.

"Good girl, good girl," Maddie praised her. She looked around for Theo. He shrugged as if he didn't know what the plane had been doing, either, and made a circle with his hand to show he wanted Maddie to circle in the other direction.

But before she could gather up the reins, the buzzing sound returned, roaring up from behind the church like a swarm of angry wasps. Firebird leaped sideways, her hooves slipping on the grass.

"Steady, girl," Maddie gasped, trying to keep her right leg clamped against Firebird's shoulder. The biplane was heading straight for them again, its wings dipping from side to side like a giant, clumsy bird. The engine sputtered once, twice, and for a dreadful moment Maddie thought it was about to crash. Then the low, deafening hum started up once more, and the plane swooped toward the field on the far side of the house, so low Maddie could see the stitching on the canvas stretched over the fuselage.

With a startled whinny, Firebird bolted. Maddie felt the folded cap shoot out from underneath her. Her legs were sliding all over the place and she clamped her hand on the top pommel to stop herself from rolling off backward. But her lack of balance didn't make any difference to Firebird's stride. Faster and faster the mare galloped, heading straight for the hedge that divided the schooling paddock from the field where she grazed.

"No, Birdy! Stop!" Maddie cried, trying to pull on the reins. But Firebird kept going as if she had been fired out of a cannon.

The hedge loomed in front of them, at least a foot higher than the mare's ears and woven from a thousand needle-sharp brambles. They were going to crash straight into it! Maddie shut her eyes and wrapped her hands in Firebird's mane.

She felt the mare's strides slow down, and for a moment she thought Firebird was going to stop in time, then the noise of hoofbeats vanished and Maddie felt herself being pushed up, up into the air. She opened her eyes and saw the hedge underneath her, with Firebird's forelegs stretched out in front. Then the ground on the other side was racing up to meet them and they landed with a thud, Firebird's legs crumpling as Maddie's weight caught up a second later. The horse pitched forward and Maddie flew out of the saddle, turning a somersault in the air before landing heavily on the grass.

13

STUNNED, MADDIE LISTENED TO the mare's hoofbeats thundering across the paddock and waited for her chest to stop hurting so she could breathe again. As Firebird's hooves faded away, they were replaced by running footsteps, and Theo's face appeared above her.

"Maddie, are you all right?"

Maddie sat up carefully, rubbing her bruised ribs. "I think so," she said. She didn't feel as shaken as she had when she fell off Starling. She was more worried about what had happened to Firebird. She had bolted out of sheer panic, thanks to the fool in that plane! Maddie hoped her grandfather had seen what had happened, and would come out to order the pilot off his land immediately.

"Where's Firebird?" she asked, looking around.

"She's fine. Toby caught her at the gate," said Theo. He helped Maddie to her feet. "Are you sure you're all right? That was a mighty leap Birdy took over the hedge! She cleared it by a good yard."

Maddie nodded. "It felt as if we were going to take off after the plane," she said, remembering the way she had looked down at the hedge as they flew over.

Theo was looking at her with an odd expression in his eyes. "You know, I've never seen a horse jump like that before," he said. "Especially not an Arabian. They're more famous for their speed than their spring," he added.

Maddie smiled a little shakily. "I knew she was special."

They started to walk over to the gate, where Toby was holding Firebird by her reins. The mare's head was held high, her small curved ears pricked as she strained to see where the plane had gone.

Halfway across the field, Theo suddenly said, "Do you know something, Maddie? Seeing Birdy clear the hedge like that, I don't think it was ramblers who let her out of the paddock the other day. I think she was scared by that gunshot we heard from the dining room, and jumped the hedge!"

Maddie stared at him in alarm. "Really? Is that a bad thing? I mean, how will we make sure she stays in her field from now on?"

Theo pursed his lips. "I'm not sure," he admitted. "Maybe we should put her out with another horse for company."

Maddie nodded. Much as she hated the idea that Firebird might be able to escape from her field at any time, part of her tingled with excitement that they had found this out about the flame-colored mare.

"What happened?" Toby asked as they drew near. "Did that plane scare her?"

"Yes," Theo replied. "Maddie fell off when Firebird jumped the hedge. She cleared it by a yard! Did you see?"

Toby shook his head. "I was watching the plane land. Look!"

Maddie turned to see several figures running across the lawn toward the field on the other side of the schooling paddock. The biplane stood in the middle of the grass, looking like a large clumsy insect. The pilot was climbing out of the cockpit. He paused before jumping down to unhook a stick strapped to the side of the fuselage, and Maddie realized it was George Edwards. What on earth was he doing with a biplane?

"It's a good job I hadn't put the rest of the horses out," Toby remarked. His eyes gleamed. "I hope Mr. Edwards won't mind me taking a look. That plane's a beauty!"

Maddie frowned. It wasn't a beauty, it was dangerous! Firebird snorted and tossed her head, flicking specks of white foam over Maddie's jacket. Maddie ran her hand down the mare's slippery neck.

"I'll take her in and wash her down, Master Theo," Toby offered.

"We'll come with you," said Theo, before adding, "unless you want to go inside, Maddie. That was quite a nasty fall."

She shook her head. "I'm fine, honestly. The ground's pretty soft after all that rain." She rubbed her side, wondering what the housekeeper would say when her riding habit was covered in mud for the second time in as many weeks. She followed Theo under the archway and across the cobbles to where Toby was unbuckling Firebird's bridle, a headcollar looped ready over his arm.

Even with her head hanging low and her coat streaked with mud and sweat, Maddie thought Firebird was the most beautiful creature she had ever seen. Beside her, Theo took off his jacket and rolled up his shirtsleeves. Maddie waited for Toby to point out that he could manage on his own, but to her surprise the groom just nodded to a bucket that stood beside the door to the tack room.

"You can start washing her down," he said.

Theo took the bucket over to the water pump and started to fill it, heaving energetically at the handle. Suddenly rapid footsteps sounded on the path that led to the house, and Fred the under-gardener appeared around the edge of the stable block.

"Master Theo, Miss Maddie, Miss Louisa sent me to tell you to come and see Mr. Edwards's plane. He's landed it in the far field!"

He nearly landed it on my head! Maddie was tempted to reply. Instead she looked at Theo, who was carrying the bucket back from the tap. "We ought to go," she began hesitantly. However strangely he had arrived, George Edwards was still a guest.

To her relief, Theo handed the cloth to Toby. "I'll come back and see the mare later," he promised. "Could you bandage her legs, please, in case they swell up after that jump? We should probably keep her in the stable until the plane has gone."

Toby nodded. "Right you are."

Maddie only had a moment to feel puzzled about how comfortable her brother seemed to be around the stable yard before she and Theo were hurrying out of the yard and across the back lawn toward the plane.

Louisa was standing in the field beside George, with Lady Ella and Sir Wilfred watching over the fence. They turned when Theo and Maddie approached, and she saw that her grandmother's cheeks were pink with excitement.

"Well!" gasped Lady Ella. "George has bought a plane!"

Louisa called from the field, waving. "Come and see!"

Theo opened the little gate and they walked across the grass to the plane. It was silent now, its tail resting on the ground and the propeller on its nose completely still.

George grinned at them, leaning on his stick. "What do you think, eh? It's an Avro 504K, good as new and hardly flown since 1917. She was used as a training plane during the war," he explained. "You can see there's room for an extra person up there, just in front of the pilot. Come on, Maddie, help me persuade Lou to come up for a spin!"

"Not if you're going to scare any more horses!" Maddie retorted. Theo put his hand warningly on her sleeve.

"The plane frightened Birdy," Maddie told Louisa, who was looking at her in surprise. "She bolted and jumped the hedge. I fell off!"

George went bright red. "I say, I'm sorry about that. It's a bit tricky to see what's going on underneath, you know, especially when you're thinking about where to land. I was just glad there was a flag on the church to tell me which way the wind was blowing."

Theo asked him a question about the plane, and Maddie guessed he was trying to steer the conversation to safer waters.

Lou turned to Maddie as George and Theo walked toward the plane, talking about rotary engines and ground speed. "I didn't realize you fell off," she said. "Did you hurt yourself?"

Maddie shook her head. "Not really, it was a soft landing. But Lou, it was amazing! Firebird felt as if she had wings!"

"What's this about someone else having wings? It's an epidemic!" called a voice behind them, and Maddie turned to see Rosie Williams waving to them from the gate.

"Come over here, Rosie!" Lou called. "I was hoping you'd get here in time to see George's new toy."

Rosie ran across the grass, looking sensibly dressed for scooting about in fields in long trousers, neat little boots, and with a jumper slung over her shoulders. "It's more impressive than my Baby Austin," she agreed, eyeing the plane. "Are you going to have a turn in it?"

"I haven't decided yet," Louisa admitted.

"What about you, Maddie?"

She shook her head. "No, thank you! Not after it scared Firebird."

Rosie frowned. "Who's Firebird?"

"The mare Theo brought back with him from Africa," Lou explained.

"Yes, and we've just found out she's a brilliant jumper!" Maddie added. "When the plane scared her, she cleared that hedge by miles!" She pointed to the other paddock.

Rosie raised her eyebrows. "In that case, you should read an article in a magazine I have in the car. It's about a horse that won one of these new show-jumping competitions, the King George the Fifth Gold Cup, I think. Doesn't that sound like the sort of thing you should enter Firebird in?"

"What a brilliant idea!" Maddie was already picturing a huge golden cup. "Theo!" she called. Her brother looked up from where George was showing him something on the propeller.

Maddie ran across the grass. "Rosie just told me about a jumping competition for horses called the King George the Fifth Gold Cup. She thinks we should enter Birdy!"

"Steady on," said Theo. "Just because she's jumped one hedge doesn't mean she can be entered in competitions."

"But you said you'd never seen a horse jump like she does!" Maddie reminded him.

George gave a low whistle. "I know some fellows who've jumped at Olympia—where the Gold Cup is held," he added, seeing Maddie look confused. "You'd be jumping against the best in the world, you can be sure of that. Not that you'd be able to ride yourself, Maddie. It's only open to chaps." His blue eyes twinkled kindly at her.

"But that's all right!" she said. "Theo can ride her, can't you, Theo?"

To her dismay, her brother shook his head. "No, Maddie. Don't get carried away. Firebird's much smaller than the thoroughbreds who'll be in that competition, and she's not professionally trained like them, either. She wouldn't stand a chance, and it wouldn't be fair to make her try." He turned back to George. "What did you say the horsepower was in this engine?"

"Er, one hundred and ten," said George.

Maddie felt her shoulders slump with disappointment. Maybe she had let herself get carried away by Rosie's suggestion, but Theo didn't have to be so miserable about it. She walked back to the gate, scuffing her shoes against the grass.

"Is everything all right?" asked Lou.

Maddie shrugged. "Theo doesn't think I can enter Firebird in the jumping competition."

"Well, it does seem a bit sudden, since she's only jumped one hedge so far," Lou pointed out.

"Two, actually," Maddie told her. "She jumped out of her

field last Saturday, when that gun went off."

Rosie leaned forward and gave Louisa a quick hug. "Sorry, Lou, I have to dash off. I only dropped in to say hello. It's taken me ages to get here from Swindon, and I'm beginning to feel as if I'll never get home. I'll see you on Tuesday for the rally in Hyde Park, yes?"

Lou nodded. "Definitely. Shall I come up on Monday to organize the leaflets?"

"That would be great, thanks. For a moment there, I was afraid George would turn your head with this plane of his, and you wouldn't want to come to the rally anymore."

"Not in a thousand years!" Louisa declared. "What's one plane compared with the chance to get votes for all women? It's a disgrace that we can't vote until we're thirty!"

Maddie glanced around, hoping her grandparents hadn't heard. To her relief, the garden was empty. When she turned back, Rosie was already running across the lawn, back to her motorcar.

Lou grinned. "I don't know where that girl gets her energy from! She makes me feel quite tired just watching her. Come on, Mouse. Let's leave the men to talk about wings and engines until they're blue in the face."

The next day, Maddie woke up feeling as if there was a cold, heavy stone in her stomach. She wondered if it was because she was still disappointed about Theo's reaction to the idea of entering Firebird in the Gold Cup. Rosie had left the magazine behind for her, and she'd stayed awake late into the night reading about Nightwatchman, the horse that had won the Cup last year. But then she remembered what day it was, and the stone sank even farther. It was March 12, her mother's birthday.

Downstairs, the house was deserted, with only the sound of Patrice thumping away at a batch of dough in the kitchen to show there was anyone else awake. Maddie put on her galoshes and opened the side door. The sky was hazy and tinged with pink like the inside of a seashell. Pausing only to gather what she needed from the garden, she walked to the shed where the bicycles were kept. She carefully laid her armful of daffodils in the basket and swung her leg over the saddle, tucking her skirt underneath her to keep it out of the way of the wheels. Then she rode down the narrow lane that led to the church.

Leaving the bicycle propped against the yew hedge, she lifted out the flowers and let herself into the graveyard.

To her surprise, she wasn't alone. There was someone already at her parents' grave, kneeling on the grass with his cap in his hands.

"Theo!" Maddie exclaimed.

Theo looked up, startled.

"Did you remember what day it was?" Maddie whispered, going over and kneeling down beside him. She started to put the flowers one by one into the vase wedged in the stones on the grave. It was already full of rainwater, so she didn't need to fill it from the water butt by the church.

Theo nodded. "Do you do this every year?" he asked, watching Maddie put the last daffodil into the vase.

"The flowers? Yes. At least, I bring some in the morning, and Lou brings some at night."

Theo picked up a piece of shingle and rolled it between his hands. "I didn't want them to think I'd forgotten," he said, without looking at Maddie.

"They'd never think that! They knew you hadn't forgotten about us, even when you were in Africa. They were so proud of you."

Theo turned to stare at her. "Really? I . . . I didn't know. I mean, they always said the right sort of things in their letters, without asking when I was coming home. But it didn't seem to make much difference to them if I was in France, Namibia, or in a London bank, like everyone else."

"Of course it mattered!" Maddie protested. "They worried about you all the time, and they would have been thrilled if you'd come home, even just for Christmas. They were proud of you for doing what you wanted to do, however dangerous it was, and not what other people might have thought you should do—like working in a bank!" She smiled, even though she could feel tears running down her cheeks.

She was relieved when Theo smiled as well. But then his face went dark again. "I tried to do the right thing," he said quietly, and Maddie wasn't sure if he was speaking to her or to their parents, "but I feel like I've let everyone down by coming back like this, with nothing to show, nothing to make people really proud of me. I only wanted to be part of a family again. . . ." His voice cracked and he put his hand over his face.

Maddie's heart ached for him. "Don't cry, Theo. Mother and Father would be so pleased to have you home. That's the only thing that matters now, I promise. You don't have anything to prove. We love you because you are Theo, that's all."

He lowered his hand and looked at her, his eyes searching hers as if he wanted to say something but couldn't find the words. "I'm really grateful to you, Maddie, do you know that? To all of you. You've given me so much, made me feel so welcome, in spite of everything."

Maddie frowned. "But what did you think we would do, Theo? We're your family!"

Her brother stared at her, his eyes hooded and the scar on his face standing out more sharply than ever. Then he took a deep breath and echoed faintly, "Of course, you're my family."

They walked back along the lane together, Maddie wheeling her bicycle beside Theo in a rather awkward silence. She couldn't help thinking there was something she'd missed in their conversation by the grave, but it was too late to go back and ask Theo what it was. As soon as they reached the yard, she propped her bicycle against the wall and ran over to Firebird's door.

"How are you today, my beautiful girl?" she murmured, peering into the shadowy stable.

She jumped back, startled, as a head appeared above Firebird's back. "Toby! I didn't see you there!"

The head groom walked around the mare's quarters and let himself out of the door. There was a bucket slung over his arm containing strips of fluffy white cotton and two rolled-up bandages. "Good morning, Miss Maddie," he said. "Morning, Master Theo," he added as Theo walked across the yard.

"Is Firebird all right?" Maddie asked, eyeing the bucket of bandages with alarm.

"There's some heat in her legs this morning." Toby addressed Theo, and Maddie listened in dismay. "We'll keep her in for today, and see how she is tomorrow. I doubt it's anything serious, but I don't think she should be ridden for a couple of days."

"That's not surprising, given the way she jumped that hedge yesterday," said Theo. "We could try hosing her legs, too."

"Aye, that's a good idea. I'll get Ollie to do it—unless you'd like to do it yourself, sir?" Toby looked expectantly at Theo, who nodded.

Maddie let herself into Firebird's stable and buried her face in the long flame-colored mane. "Hurry up and get better!" she whispered. Jumping the hedge hadn't frightened her at all—on the contrary, all Maddie could think about was the feeling of flying through the air, and cantering around the paddock as if Birdy had been dancing, and she just wanted to do it all over again.

On Monday, Louisa took the train to London, pink-cheeked with excitement about the suffragist rally. Nancy Astor, the Conservative politician and the first female Member of Parliament, was going to be making a speech. The whole family went to see Louisa off from the station because Lady Ella wanted to do some shopping in Newbury, and Theo's new suits were ready to be picked up. Maddie saw her grandmother's face fall after she had waved good-bye to Louisa on the platform. For all the excitement about George's plane, Louisa had never seemed less likely to accept his proposal of marriage.

They weren't expecting Lou back until Wednesday, when Rosie was going to drive them both from London, but on Tuesday evening a telegram arrived for Sir Wilfred. Matthew brought it to the breakfast room where they were having dinner, apologizing for interrupting their meal but saying the delivery boy insisted it be read at once.

Maddie watched her grandfather's face drain, then flush

with color as he silently read the telegram. She put down her knife and fork. When he had finished reading, Sir Wilfred folded the telegram and laid it carefully beside his plate before looking up.

"It would seem that Louisa has been arrested," he announced.

CHAPTER
14

——— ⊗⊗⊗ ———

MADDIE'S GRANDMOTHER GASPED and put her hand to her throat.

"The telegram is from Bertram Farnsworth. Apparently he has arranged for Louisa and Rosie to be released on bail, and they are staying at his parents' house. He will bring Louisa home tomorrow, and until then there's nothing we can do, or need to worry about." Sir Wilfred pushed back his chair and started to leave the room, but Lady Ella stopped him.

"What on earth was she arrested for?"

He turned and looked at her, his eyes somber. "Affray," he said, before walking heavily out of the room.

Affray? Maddie tried to remember what Louisa had told her about past rallies. That could mean anything from refusing to leave a public area to hitting a policeman! She didn't think Lou would have attacked anyone, however much she was provoked, but she couldn't help feeling a tiny thrill of excitement. Her sister was like one of the suffragettes before the war, risking the harshest punishment for the sake of getting votes for women! She looked at Theo, expecting to see the same mix of concern and admiration in his face, but he was studying his plate, his expression unreadable.

Maddie tried to nudge him under the table with her foot, but she missed. He must have felt the swish of air, though, because he looked up.

"Do you think Lou's all right?" she whispered.

He nodded. "She'll be fine. We can find out what happened when she comes home tomorrow." He put his napkin on the table and stood up. "Grandmother, would you like me to send Kate to you?"

"Yes, please, Theo. Tell her I shall be in my salon." Lady Ella went out of the room, walking more slowly than usual as if she had aged ten years since the telegram arrived. Even the rustling of her skirt seemed muted. Theo held the door for her, then went to ring the bell for Kate.

Beginning to feel alarmed for the first time since the telegram arrived, Maddie went to find her grandfather's Irish setter, Charlie, hoping for a pair of sympathetic ears while she wondered what Lou could have been up to at the rally.

The next day, Maddie was in Firebird's stable, running her hands down the mare's legs to see if the swelling had gone down, when she heard a motorcar rolling up the drive. She ran from the stable yard to see George getting out and walking around to open the door for Lou.

He smiled and raised his stick in greeting, looking remarkably cheerful considering the trouble Lou was in.

Louisa stepped out of the car and looked briefly at Maddie but didn't say anything. Holding George's arm, she walked up the steps beside him and vanished through the front door. Maddie ran around to the side door and kicked off her galoshes, pulled on her house shoes, and went into the hallway. To her disappointment, it was empty. There were people talking in the library, but the door was shut and she couldn't hear what they were saying. Feeling left out, she sat on the window seat and watched as Charlie padded over to push her nose into Maddie's lap.

"I wonder what's going to happen to Lou now?" she murmured into the dog's velvet-soft ears. Charlie blinked solemnly up at her.

There was the sound of the side door opening, and a moment later, Theo appeared. "Is Louisa back?" he asked.

Maddie nodded. "George Edwards brought her in his motorcar. They're in the library with Grandpapa and Grandmama."

As she spoke, the paneled door opened, and Lady Ella stood in the doorway with her hands clasped together. Maddie didn't think she looked like someone whose elder granddaughter was on the verge of going to prison.

"Wonderful news, Madeline, Theodore!" she exclaimed, and

Maddie stared at her in confusion.

"George has done Louisa the very great honor of asking her to be his wife, and Louisa has said yes!" Maddie's grandmother beamed as if all her Christmases had come at once.

Louisa followed her out of the library, looking rather flushed. "That's right," she said. "George has been so kind and understanding. I know we're going to be very happy."

Maddie went over to hug her sister. "Congratulations!" she said. "I'm really pleased for you." She meant it—now that Theo was home, the thought of Louisa leaving Sefton Park to be Lady Edwards wasn't nearly so daunting.

George and Sir Wilfred had emerged from the library by now, and were doing the sort of things with Theo that men always did to celebrate good news, shaking hands and slapping backs and muttering about brandy and cigars, even though it wasn't yet lunchtime.

The butler coughed politely behind Sir Wilfred. "Shall I bring refreshments to the drawing room, sir?"

"Yes, please, Matthew. Make sure you bring a decanter of brandy, as well—or champagne?" Maddie's grandfather looked questioningly at George. "Would you like champagne, George?"

"Brandy will be fine, Sir Wilfred." George smiled, placing one hand on Lou's waist.

"So is everything sorted out now? From yesterday, I mean?"

Maddie didn't want to dampen everyone's excitement but she was desperate to find out if her sister was going to prison or not.

"Oh, that was nothing more than a misunderstanding," George said generously, but Lou pulled away from him and frowned.

"A little more than a misunderstanding, I think," she said. "After all, I can't deny that I tore the policeman's coat."

Maddie gasped.

Lou smiled. "Don't worry, Mouse. I didn't wrestle him to the ground! It's just that policemen are so terrified of what a group of angry women might do, they didn't need any excuses to arrest us. Rosie and I were lucky—we only spent an hour in the cells before Bertram arrived, breathing fire like our very own dragon, and whisked us out."

"Will you have to go to prison?" The words were out before Maddie could stop them, but to her relief Lou laughed and shook her head.

"Goodness me, no! We were let off with a caution, which is nothing more than a warning not to do something like that again. Not that I will, of course," she added, catching a look of alarm in George's eyes. "I think Rosie was rather disappointed that we weren't going to be made martyrs to the cause, but they couldn't have put us all in prison. They took so many of us from the rally that they wouldn't have had one big enough!"

"Are you coming, Louisa, dear?" Lady Ella called from the drawing room.

Maddie followed Louisa and George as they trooped in and sat down on a sofa opposite Lady Ella. Sir Wilfred was in his favorite leather armchair by the fire, and Theo was standing by the window, watching Thor and Wayfarer graze in the field where George had landed his biplane a few days before. Maddie sat on a padded footstool and glared at her grandmother's fat little Peke, who wheezed out from behind the coal scuttle and curled his lip bad-temperedly at her.

"Now," Lady Ella began, looking expectantly at Louisa and George. "Sir Wilfred and I would like to host a small celebration to announce your engagement. I thought"—she glanced at her husband, and went on—"I thought we could have a summer party, like we used to. Before the war and before . . . well, before everything."

Maddie felt a tingle of excitement.

"Let's make it a masked ball, not just an ordinary party. After all, we have two reasons to celebrate this year," Lady Ella went on, smiling at Theo. "Everyone deserves to share in our good fortune, and masked balls are such fun! And we could arrange some fireworks, just like the Granvilles did last year. What do you think?"

"That would be very generous of you, Ella," said Louisa. "But there's no need to go to such trouble. We can just as easily put an announcement in the *Times*."

"Nonsense!" Lady Ella exclaimed. Her eyes softened, and she added, "It has been too long since we had a proper party here, and even though Sir Wilfred and I may be a little long in the tooth to dance until dawn, it would give me an enormous amount of pleasure to be able to do this for you."

Louisa smiled. "In that case, how can I say no?"

Sir Wilfred reached down and rested his hand on Lady Ella's shoulder. "Excellent idea, my dear," he said. "It's high time this place came to life again, and what better reason to celebrate than our granddaughter's engagement, and the return of our grandson?"

At the window, Theo was pleating the edge of the heavy velvet drape between his fingers. He didn't look up.

Lady Ella picked up a notebook bound in dark brown leather. "Let's start making some plans right away," she said, slipping a pencil out from the spine of the notebook and holding it poised above a blank page.

Maddie noticed Theo slip out of the room, and she followed him, knowing there was nothing she could add to her grandmother's planning spree. She caught up with her brother in the hallway, where he was rubbing Charlie's tummy as the Irish setter lay sprawled on the rug, her feathery tail thudding against Theo's foot.

"Are you all right?" Maddie asked, crouching beside him.

"I just don't like parties and that sort of thing," said Theo without looking up.

"Come on, Theo, it will be fun! Especially if we have fireworks. Don't you remember Papa telling us about Grandmama's famous summer parties? I was always so cross he wouldn't let me go to one! Grandpapa is right—it's time Sefton Park came to life again."

Theo's face was hidden in shadow as he continued to make a fuss of Charlie. "But things were different then," he said quietly. "I'll be like some sort of fairground sideshow, with everyone wanting to look at me and ask me about Africa and the war. . . ."

Well, it's not like you'd tell them, is it? Maddie thought. She dug her fingernails into her palms to stop herself from saying something too sharp. "I know you don't like this sort of thing, Theo," she said, "but Grandpapa and Grandmama would be very disappointed if you didn't put in an appearance."

Theo said nothing. He was still looking down at Charlie, and she could see only the scarred side of his face so it was impossible to tell what he was thinking.

Maddie stood up, brushing auburn dog hairs off her skirt. She'd been so excited by the thought of the party, and Theo was making everything far too complicated. "Look, Theo, this ball is going to happen whether you like it or not, so you'd better get used to the idea. Lou and George will be the center of everyone's attention, not you. Anyway, you'll be wearing a mask, if you're scared of what people might think about your scar." She swallowed, knowing that she'd never mentioned his damaged face before. But it was too late now. She turned and walked across the hall, planning to go outside and let the fresh air cool her burning cheeks. Before she reached the door, she stopped.

"And with your mask on, it doesn't matter who or what you are underneath. You can even pretend to be someone else if you want!"

Maddie wheeled around and slammed the door satisfyingly behind her.

15

THE NEXT FEW WEEKS PASSED quickly, and even though Maddie was looking forward to the masked ball, the stable yard soon became a haven from Grandmama's endless appointments with dressmakers, firework specialists, and the long-suffering Patrice, who became more short-tempered with every addition or alteration to the menu.

Theo seemed to come into the house even less, appearing for meals but otherwise spending all his time outside. He and Maddie rode out most days, taking it in turns to ride Firebird, whose legs were fine a couple of days after the dramatic leap over the hedge. When she was put into the field to graze, Lady Ella's retired hack, Dora, was put out with her for company. The two mares seemed to get on quite well, and Firebird hadn't jumped out of the field since.

As far as Maddie was concerned, Theo was a thousand times easier to be around when he was outdoors with the horses, except when Maddie had used a stiff brush on Firebird's tail by mistake. Theo took it out of her hand at once and told her to use a soft-bristled body brush or better still, her fingers, to ease out the tangles. While he was explaining this, Firebird rested her muzzle against Maddie's back in a gesture of silent affection that almost made her sink onto the straw in gratitude. She loved the chestnut mare with a ferocity that far outweighed how she felt about Charlie or even Starling. She recalled what Theo had said about his best friend Jonathan, how he had loved horses as if they were people, and suddenly she wished she'd had a chance to meet him.

On the morning of the ball, Maddie was awakened by the sound of tapping. Looking through her window, which overlooked the driveway at the front of the house, she saw two men hammering short wooden posts along the edge of the lawn— the fireworks! Maddie snatched her dressing gown from her chair and went through the bathroom to knock on the door of Louisa's bedroom.

"Come in."

Lou was sitting up in bed with a lace shawl around her shoulders. Her dark brown hair was pushed behind her ears and she looked very young—far too young to be getting married, Maddie thought. She was going to miss Lou so much.

"Hello there." Lou smiled, putting down the book she was reading. "You're awake early."

Maddie went over and perched on the edge of the bed. "What time is it?"

Louisa glanced at the clock on her nightstand. "Just past seven."

"Have you seen the fireworks people?"

"No, but I've been listening to them for the past half hour. I think Ella is determined that her display will outshine the Granvilles' by at least a dozen pounds of explosive," Lou remarked.

"Well, it's your display too," Maddie pointed out. "If you didn't want so many fireworks, you should have said."

"What, and disrupt Ella's plans? I don't think so."

"You do want to have this party, don't you?" Maddie said anxiously. "You could have insisted that you just wanted to announce your engagement in the *Times* if you really didn't want it."

Louisa pushed back the covers and swung her legs over the side of the bed. "The trouble with me is I don't know what I want."

Maddie stared at her in dismay. "What do you mean? What about George? You aren't going to marry him if you don't want to, are you?"

Lou rolled up a pair of stockings that had been draped over the back of an armchair. "George is a kind, sweet, gentle man who will look after me very well. Growing up isn't just about doing what you want to do, you know."

"That's not what Mother and Father would have said!"

Maddie argued. "They wanted us to follow our hearts and be happy."

Lou dropped the stockings back on the chair and came over to squeeze Maddie's hands. "Oh, Mouse, I will be happy. The most important thing I wished for has come true already. Theo came back to us, didn't he? It would be greedy to want anything more. Now shoo, and let me have my bath."

Maddie slipped off the bed and padded back to her own room. She told herself it was perfectly natural for Lou to feel a bit jittery about marrying George. Didn't all brides suffer from nerves?

There would be no time to ride today—she could already hear her grandmother issuing orders to the housekeeper at the foot of the stairs—so she put on a skirt and blouse rather than her breeches and riding habit. She ate a piece of toast as she stood at the window of the breakfast room, watching Toby and Theo help unload trestle tables and folding chairs from the cart that had brought them up the hill from the village hall. Dressed in near-matching breeches and shirtsleeves, it was hard to tell the men apart until they turned and Maddie saw Theo's scar, flushed dark red with the effort of lifting the heavy tables onto the ground.

After breakfast, she helped Pippa cover the tables with crisp white tablecloths, starched to the texture of cardboard. It was hot for early May, with a clear blue sky and just the hint of a breeze, perfect for eating outside. The tables had been set up in rows on the back lawn, leaving the front lawn clear for the jazz band and the fireworks display. When the tables had been covered, Maddie watched her grandmother supervise Fred cutting some early roses for the flower arrangements, making sure he left enough on the bushes for people to admire as well. Grandpapa's valet was hanging lanterns around the garden and putting candles inside to be lit later on. Maddie helped him by carrying the box of candles and handing him the matches to melt the end of each one and fix it into place. She couldn't stop grinning—it was as if Sefton Park was being transformed into a fairyland, with tiny twinkling lights and snow-white tables everywhere. Even Lou was starting to look excited as she swept past Maddie with the tray of handwritten place settings, the rolled-up seating plan tucked under her arm.

Faye and Pippa started laying out the best silver cutlery on the tables, and folding heavy linen napkins into boat shapes.

Maddie's grandmother came over. "Sharpen the creases on that napkin, Faye," she instructed, tapping the drooping square of linen with the handle of her lorgnettes. She caught sight of Maddie. "Madeline, Mrs. Kirby will be serving a light luncheon in half an hour. Could you fetch Theo, please?"

"Yes, Grandmama." Maddie flashed a sympathetic grin at Faye, who was patiently refolding the napkin, and walked around to the front of the house.

She turned as a motorcar crunched over the gravel and pulled up on the other side of the fountain, close to where Theo and Toby were building a stage for the jazz band. As the car halted beside him, Theo looked up, letting the hammer hang loosely in his fingers.

The driver of the motorcar stepped out, and Maddie recognized Colonel Day-Wilson, a friend of her grandfather's. He nodded to Theo and Toby. "Good day to you," he said, his bushy white mustache twitching.

Theo and Toby nodded politely. Maddie waited for Theo to introduce himself, but he said nothing, just watched the visitor with a curiously blank expression.

The Colonel clapped his gloved hands together. "I say, could one of you chaps park the car for me?"

Theo glanced at Toby, then jumped down from the half-built platform and walked across the grass, tucking the hammer into a tool belt that hung around his waist. "I can do that for you, sir," he offered.

"Good man, good man," said the Colonel, walking around the front of the car to help his wife out of the passenger seat. He looked across the roof at Theo. "Do you know where I'll find Sir Wilfred?"

Theo shook his head. "I couldn't say exactly, sir. The family are all over the place today, getting ready. But the butler will be able to help you if you go to the house."

Colonel Day-Wilson nodded, and bent down to give an arm to his wife, who was struggling to get out of the car, thanks to the size of her broad-brimmed hat.

Maddie frowned. Why had Theo let Colonel Day-Wilson treat him like a servant? Why had he talked about "the family" as if he wasn't part of it himself? She tried to catch his eye as he steered the Colonel's motorcar in a wide circle, back toward the garages, but he was concentrating on driving and didn't seem to notice her standing by the steps.

"Is everything all right, Miss Maddie?" Toby had come to the edge of the lawn and was calling to her across the sweep of gravel.

Maddie looked at the groom, shading her eyes from the sun. For a moment, she was tempted to ask him about Theo's strange behavior, but she decided she might sound over-curious and even a little foolish. "I'm fine, thank you, Toby," she called back. "My grandmother sent me to tell Theo that luncheon will be served in half an hour."

"I'll tell him," said Toby. "I expect he'll want to stay out here until the platform's finished. I've some bread and cheese he can share if he gets hungry."

"Oh, all right," Maddie said awkwardly.

Behind her, Matthew had come out to meet the Day-Wilsons, and Maddie was distantly aware of Theo returning from the garages, whistling and with the hammer swinging at his waist. Maddie supposed it didn't really matter if her brother had parked the Colonel's car for him; she just hoped their guest wouldn't be embarrassed later on when he found out who Theo really was.

After lunch, Lady Ella insisted that Maddie and Louisa rest for a couple of hours before the guests started arriving in earnest. Maddie lay on her bed with the latest edition of *Pearsons Crime Weekly*, but for once the journal of detective stories couldn't hold her attention. The sound of hammering, punctuated by quiet conversation and occasional bursts of laughter, drifted through her open window, and when she knelt on the window seat to look out she could see Theo and Toby working side by side on the bandstand, which was slowly taking shape.

Maddie shook her head. She couldn't help feeling puzzled, and even a little hurt, by the way her brother seemed happier around Toby and the other servants than around his own family. Was it the war that had changed him or being in Namibia or losing his best friend in the mining accident?

Maybe all three, she decided, as the clock downstairs chimed four, and she went into her bathroom to run her bath. Usually Mrs. Kirby, the housekeeper, or her grandmother's maid, Kate, did this for her, but today all the servants were busy, and it wasn't exactly difficult to put in the plug and turn on the taps so that water gushed noisily into the claw-footed tub. She added some of Louisa's rose-scented bath oil and sluiced herself energetically before drying herself with a clean towel.

She was just taking her dress out of the closet when there was a tap at the door, and Louisa put her head into the room.

"How are you getting on, Maddie? Would you like me to do your hair?"

"Yes, please," said Maddie. She held the coat hanger in front of her, running her hand down the front of the dress. "What do you think?"

"It's beautiful. No one will recognize you looking so grown-up and glamorous!"

Maddie grinned at her sister as she lifted the dress off the hanger and slipped it over her head. It was made of cream-colored silk, with a full, pleated skirt that ended just above her ankles.

Louisa came over to help her tie the pale pink sash around her waist. "I'm glad I caught you before you finished getting ready. Rosie will be here soon to help me dress, and I wanted to have some time with you, just the two of us." She put her hands on Maddie's shoulders to steer her over to the dressing table, and Maddie sat obediently on the padded stool. Lou began to brush her hair, making it fall in coppery waves almost to the bottom of her shoulder blades. Maddie passed her the hairgrips one by one, and watched her sister pin her hair so that it was held away from the sides of her face, making her look older and more elegant than she was used to.

"I hardly recognize myself!" she joked.

Lou bent down to give her a hug. "You look amazing. Do you have your mask?"

Maddie took it from the dressing table and held it up. It was made of pink satin to match her sash, and the dressmaker had sewn tiny diamanté beads around the edges. There was an elasticized strap to hold it in place around her head, and when she was wearing it, only her nose and mouth could be seen.

Louisa nodded. "Perfect," she said. Downstairs, the clock chimed five. "Heavens! I must go and run my bath. Could you send Rosie up when she arrives?"

"Of course," said Maddie. Holding her mask carefully in one hand, she went downstairs to find something to do that wouldn't crumple her dress. The fabric felt cold and shiny against her skin, and she shivered.

"Would you like me to send Kate to fetch you a wrap?" said a concerned voice.

Her grandfather was standing in the doorway to the library. "No, thank you, Grandpapa. I can always warm up by dancing later on." Outside, Maddie could hear the string quartet, the dinnertime entertainment, warming up, and a thrill of anticipation ran through her.

Sir Wilfred smiled. "You look lovely, my dear. Very like your mother, if I may say so."

Maddie looked at him in surprise. "Like Mother?" Usually it was Louisa who was compared with Amelia Harman, because they had the same slender frame and dark brown hair.

Sir Wilfred nodded. "She was a very beautiful woman. You all take after her in one way or another." He looked at her for a moment longer. "I'm very, very proud of my three grandchildren, do you know that?"

Maddie went over and put her arms around him. Her grandfather wasn't usually a demonstrative man, but he hugged her back, and she felt his chin rest on top of her head for a moment. "I know it hasn't been easy, Maddie," he murmured. "But now Theodore has come home, it feels as if we can all start this tricky old business of living again, doesn't it?"

She nodded, carefully, so as not to bang against his chin. Then there was the sound of a car outside, and voices calling excitedly, and Sir Wilfred straightened up. "The hordes have begun to arrive," he declared, with a wink at Maddie. "Shall we go forth and greet them?"

Laughing, she tucked her arm into his and they went to meet their guests.

Maddie hadn't realized her grandparents knew quite so many people. Lady Ella seemed to have invited everyone in the county and most of London. It was just as well they were eating outside, because Maddie didn't think they'd fit into the house even if they used all the downstairs rooms. Watching the guests milling about on the lawn, she found herself thinking of her grandfather's bird paintings, with the ladies' dresses looking like bright glossy feathers. Every so often the dresses would shift to reveal a splash of black dinner suit; in Maddie's mind, these were like penguins, standing guard among their gaudy companions.

As the stable yard clock chimed six, Louisa and George made a suitably dramatic entrance from the French windows of Grandmama's salon; George was handsome and smiling in his dark suit, and Lou looked startlingly beautiful in a crimson dress with a skirt made of layers of chiffon cut into points that hung like petals from her narrow waist. Everyone cheered and clapped when they appeared, and Maddie was relieved to see her sister was smiling under her sparkling red mask with no sign of her earlier nerves.

The dinner was magnificent, with platters of smoked salmon, cold chicken, salad, and strawberry ice cream for dessert. A few people took their masks off to eat, but most kept them on, which gave the party an air of glamour and mystery that made Maddie's fingers tingle as she looked around. She was sitting at the same table as Rosie Williams and Bertram Farnsworth, who asked her if Theo was going to enter Firebird for the King George V Gold Cup.

Hastily swallowing a mouthful of strawberries, Maddie said

it was too early to decide if Firebird was good enough for the competition, but the mare was settling in better and better, and they were working on building up her muscles to make her strong and fit. . . . She trailed off when she realized she had been talking for several minutes without stopping. Rosie and Bertram smiled indulgently at her from underneath their masks.

"Madeline, have you seen Theo anywhere?" Her grandmother bore down upon her, magnificent in a floor-length purple gown. "I sat him next to Algernon Ponsonby, but he's not at the table now. Really, he should be here. Your grandfather wishes to propose a toast before the fireworks display."

Maddie looked around. She'd caught sight of Theo just after the first guests arrived, nervously adjusting his mask in front of the mirror in the breakfast room. The plain band of black silk covered his eyes, but there was no mistaking the scar that stretched down one side of his face, however much he fiddled about. Maddie had slipped out of the room before Theo saw her, embarrassed that she had seen him trying to hide his injury.

"Shall I go and look for him?" Maddie offered.

"Yes, please," said Lady Ella. "Be as quick as you can. It's very important that you are both here for the toast." She turned away as Matthew appeared with a tray of champagne glasses and a tall green bottle with gold foil around its neck.

Maddie pushed back her chair and stood up. On the other

side of the table, Bertram Farnsworth stood up as well. "Good luck finding Theo," he said with a wink.

Maddie made her way between the tables, past the extraordinary ice sculpture of a swan that had been brought from Newbury in a crate packed with straw and more chunks of ice. Patrice had piled strawberries onto its back between the wings, and Maddie took one as she went past, feeling a little resentful that she hadn't been allowed to finish her dessert.

As she followed the path around the house, she heard a trumpet playing on the front lawn, its squeaky, cheerful notes echoed by a mournful-sounding bassoon. That was the jazz band warming up. Maddie grinned, already planning to ask Theo to dance with her. Lou had been teaching her the Charleston, and she was dying to try it out with a proper band.

She headed straight for the stable yard, guessing that was where Theo would have gone. There was a light on in Toby's quarters above the tack room, but all the stables were dark. It was very quiet, the noise from the party fading to a hushed murmur, and soft rustles and snorts came from the shadows as the horses settled for the night. Maddie's high-heeled shoes slipped on the cobbles, so she walked on tiptoe to Firebird's stable.

"Theo?" she whispered. "Are you in there?"

Two shining points of light blinked at her as Firebird turned her head and the light was reflected in her eyes.

"Theo?" Maddie said again.

A low voice said, "Yes. I'm here." He sounded resigned, as if he had known he couldn't stay hidden forever.

Maddie felt her way to the bolt and started to open the door. "What are you doing? Is Birdy all right?"

"Yes, yes, she's fine. Hang on, don't come in when it's so dark." There was the snap of a match and a flame glowed, becoming brighter and more steady as Theo lit the candle inside the lantern he had brought with him. The flickering light threw shadows onto his face. He was sitting in the corner, still wearing his dinner suit but with the bowtie loose around his neck, and his mask hanging out of his breast pocket.

Maddie closed the door behind her. "You can't stay here all night," she said, running her hand down Firebird's nose as the mare came over to greet her. The stable felt warm and sweetly scented with hay and horse.

Theo reached up to hang the lantern on a nail above his head and shrugged. "I don't see why not. This is George and Louisa's evening. No one will miss me."

The noise of talking from the back lawn died down, and Maddie knew her grandfather was about to start his speech. "Come on, Theo," she tried again. "Grandmama wants us to hear Grandpapa's toast."

Theo kept his eyes fixed on the piece of straw he was twisting in his fingers. "I'm not coming," he said. "I told you, I don't like being around that many people."

Maddie wound her fingers in Birdy's mane. "Being grown-up isn't about what you want to do," she said, echoing what Louisa had said to her that morning. "It's about what people expect you to do, as well. And right now, everyone expects you to join in with Lou's party."

Theo dropped the piece of straw and gave a short, harsh laugh. "Expectations, is that it?" he said. "Well, no one ever had any expectations of me when I was growing up, so maybe that's the problem."

Maddie opened her mouth to tell him to stop being so ridiculous; he was brought up exactly the same way as she and Louisa had been, with encouragement and love and, yes, expectations, but only that they should be polite and responsible for their actions, and brave enough to do what they believed to be right. But the words died before she could say anything. She stared at the man sitting in front of her, the good side of his face hidden in shadow so that he looked like a child's drawing of a person, with his mouth all stretched out of shape.

She felt as if there was a jigsaw puzzle raining in her head, and all the pieces were falling into place as they landed.

"You're not my brother, are you?"

He looked up at her and his gray eyes were full of pain, but also something like relief.

"No," he said. "Your brother is dead. I'm Jonathan Price."

CHAPTER
16

———∞∞∞———

AT THAT MOMENT, THE SKY exploded and the stable lit up with flashes of red, green, and blue. Firebird threw up her head and jumped to the back of the stall, the whites of her eyes showing.

"It's all right, Birdy," Maddie soothed. "It's only fireworks."

Another volley rang out, rat-a-tat, rat-a-tat, and Maddie saw Theo flinch; she wondered if it sounded like gunfire to him, and felt a stab of sympathy for her brother.

Except that he wasn't her brother. He was someone else, the man called Jonathan Price, who Theo had spoken about in his letters. Theo was dead.

Maddie rested her forehead against Firebird's mane as the sky crackled and flashed above them. The mare was as tense as a bowstring, rivulets of sweat springing out on her coat, her flanks lifting with quick, shallow breaths.

Stop! Please, stop! But the fireworks went on and on, punctuated by excited yelps and gasps from the people watching on the lawn.

After what seemed like an hour, the last volley faded away

and Birdy relaxed, stretching her head out to snatch a mouthful of hay. Maddie sprang toward the door as if her feet were on fire. She had to find her grandparents and Lou!

"Wait! Where are you going?" croaked a voice from the back of the stable, and it didn't sound like Theo at all.

Maddie shook her head despairingly. She didn't know what Theo would sound like now. She'd thought this was Theo!

"Don't go," said Jonathan. He stood up and gazed at her, his eyes pleading.

Shock and confusion turned Maddie's fingers to ice. "Did you kill my brother?"

"No, no." Jonathan looked horrified. "I would never have done that. Theo was my best friend. He . . . he didn't make it out of the mine after the accident." He rubbed one hand over his face. "I promise I didn't plan for any of this to happen."

Maddie pressed her hand against the cold strip of metal that Toby nailed over the stable doors to stop the horses from chewing the wood. "You lied to all of us," she choked. "Why? What did we do to deserve that?" She tried to ignore the tiny voice inside her that answered, *You wished too hard for Theo to come back.*

"You have to let me explain."

Maddie whipped her head around to glare at Jonathan, and he held his hands up in surrender.

"There's too much to be explained, I know. But I have a story too, you know. I . . . I'd like you to hear it first."

Feeling dazed, Maddie let go of the door. She ducked under Firebird's neck and sat down on the straw as far from Jonathan as she could. She would have preferred to stand but she didn't think her legs were going to hold her up for much longer. The mare broke off from pulling at her haynet to blow stickily into Maddie's hair, and she put up her hand to stroke Firebird's smooth chestnut shoulder, glad she was there.

Jonathan sat down with his legs straight in front of him. His trousers were covered in straw, but that didn't matter now, Maddie thought fiercely. The suit he was wearing, all the clothes that had been made for him, were nothing better than stolen.

"Everything Theo told you about me is true," he began. "I know, because he used to read his letters to me before he sent them. I don't have any family of my own, so it was a bit like someone writing to me, you know?" He glanced up at Maddie but she stared stonily back at him, so he dropped his gaze and went on. "I was born in the Black Mountains in Wales. My dad was a coal miner, and my mam took in washing. They died when I was six, and I went to live with my grandparents in a place called Knighton, on the Welsh border. My grandfather was an ostler, in charge of the stable yard at an inn called The Spotted Flag. That's where I learned about horses, riding every minute I wasn't asleep or in school. That thing I said about loving horses like they're people? That's true."

He looked at Maddie again and this time she nodded, because she believed him.

"I joined the army in 1914, soon as war broke out. My grandmother had died two years before, and my grandfather not long after, so there was nothing to keep me in Wales. Even though I wasn't educated like some of the other men, they made me an officer because I'd spent a year down the mines and knew about digging tunnels, which meant I could teach people how to build trenches." He rubbed his hand over his scarred face, as if remembering made him tired. "That's how I met Theo, when we were both Captains. I'd already heard of him because people kept mistaking us for each other. We looked so alike, see."

At the mention of her brother, Maddie caught her breath. How was she ever going to tell Louisa, or her grandparents that Theo was dead? Lou had said it didn't matter what she wanted, because she had her brother home again, and Grandpapa had said that he could finally start living again. *What would happen to her family now?*

"We got on straightaway," Jonathan continued, his eyes focusing on something far away. "All those long nights keeping watch over No Man's Land didn't seem so bad when Theo was there, telling me about this wonderful family of his, how his grandparents lived in a big house in the country, and his sisters were the best girls you could ever meet. He was right, too."

Maddie didn't say anything. There was a lump in her throat, hearing her brother spoken about with such affection; at the same time, she was jealous of Jonathan because he seemed to know Theo a thousand times better than she ever had. And now she would never get to know her brother for real, because he was dead, and would never come home. . . .

"We both got invalided out in the same gas attack, and were sent to a hospital in Norfolk. Theo had nightmares every night, even when we knew we weren't going back to France. I didn't have nightmares, not then. I thought maybe I wasn't so nervous as he was, but now I think I was just lucky." He paused and swallowed. "I heard about this company looking for diamonds in Namibia and decided to go out and try my hand at digging a different sort of tunnel. Back to mining, for something a sight more valuable than coal. There was nothing for me back here. I didn't mean for Theo to come too—I thought he'd want to come back to his family—but he insisted on coming with me. We were a team, mismatched like a pit pony and a thoroughbred, but both pulling in the same direction." He smiled. "We had some good times, even if we didn't make our fortune." His voice cracked, and he buried his face in his hands.

Maddie fought down an urge to reach over and comfort him. They had both loved Theo, one as a brother and the other as a friend, and they had both lost him. But only one had taken his identity and lied his way into someone else's family.

"How did Theo die?" she asked, and her voice rang harshly in the quiet stable.

Jonathan lifted his head. His face was tearstained. "It . . . it was in the mine accident. I was in a different tunnel than Theo when the explosion happened. All I remember is a big bang, then the roof fell onto my head. Next thing I knew, I was in the medical hut. They'd dug me out because I was closest to the surface, but they didn't find anyone else. Six men we lost that day, including Theo." He blinked. "When I woke up, all the nurses were calling me Theo. I tried to say they'd made a mistake, but they told me I'd taken a bump on my head and was confused. Mind you, it was hard to talk much, with all the bandages." He traced his fingers along the scar. "They said I was lucky to be alive, and I shouldn't try to talk in case it stopped my jaw from healing. So I just lay quiet and let them go on thinking I was Theo. I thought he must be badly hurt like me, and not able to tell them his name either. Our foreman, Mr. McNicholas, would have known us at once, but he was injured too. Every day I thought the nurses would come in and tell me they'd realized who I really was."

"But why did they think you were Theo in the first place?"

"Remember that knife? The one you gave him, with his name on it?" Maddie nodded. "He lent it to me that morning because I'd lost mine. When they carried me out, my face was all bashed up, and the knife was the only thing I had with a name on it. Except it wasn't my own name."

"You didn't have to let them think you were Theo!" Maddie protested. "You could have told them who you were!"

Jonathan picked at a loose thread on his trouser leg. "By the time I could talk properly, they'd given up searching for the last person trapped by the explosion. They thought it was me, but I knew it had to be Theo. I couldn't believe it. My best friend was dead! I knew he had a family waiting for him in England, so I decided to go back and see them, tell them what a good friend he'd been to me. When I was leaving the hospital, the doctor handed me Theo's passport and all the wages he was owed—same as I would have been owed—and told me he'd written to the family to let them know I'd be coming home. It seemed too late to say I wasn't who they thought I was. It made no difference to him if I was Jonathan or Theo."

Maddie stared at him in utter disbelief. When she tried to speak, the words came out as a croak, and she had to swallow hard before going on. "It might not have mattered to the doctor, but what about us? We had a right to know he was dead. You should never have let us think you were Theo!"

Jonathan's face twisted with pain. "I promise I meant to tell you the truth, all the time I was coming here. It felt so strange, seeing all these places that Theo had described over and over. It was as if Theo was with me, showing me his home like he always promised he would."

"But he wasn't with you! He was dead."

"Do you think I didn't know that?" Jonathan flashed back. "I'd lost the only friend I'd ever had. I would have died instead of him if I could have, knowing he had a family who'd grieve for him when there was no one who'd even notice if I died. If you had realized at once that I wasn't him, that would have solved everything, wouldn't it? I could have said who I really was, and left."

"But we thought you were Theo," Maddie whispered. "We called you Theo, and you didn't tell us we were wrong."

Jonathan gazed back at her, his gray eyes steady. "And I saw how much that meant to you, to *all* of you. What would you have rather happened, Maddie? Be honest. To have your brother back, just like you wanted, or to hear that he was dead, lost in some mine thousands of miles away? Maybe I can't live up to all these expectations of yours, but at least I made you happy for a while."

Maddie kept silent, trembling with fury. Jonathan may have saved them from the grief of knowing Theo was dead when he first arrived at Sefton Park, but he'd made everything a thousand times worse by letting them think Theo was alive. The truth was going to ruin everything.

"Maddie! Theo!"

Louisa was running across the yard, her skirt flaring behind her like a scarlet butterfly's wings. She stopped, panting, by the door.

"There you are! You missed the fireworks!"

"We heard them," Maddie said flatly, going over to the door. She felt as if she was wading through water that sucked at her legs, threatening to pull her under and fill her nose and mouth, choking her. . . .

"Is everything all right?" Louisa peered at her. "You look very pale."

"I'm fine." Behind her, she heard Jonathan stand up and duck under Firebird's neck to join her.

Lou smiled at him. "You really don't like crowds, do you, Theo? Don't worry. Grandmama will stop rampaging once she realizes what a success this party has been. Everyone says her fireworks were much more impressive than the Granvilles'!" She unbolted the door and held it open, and Maddie saw that she looked tired and strained. "I almost envy you, being able to escape out here. It's been like swimming in a goldfish bowl, having everyone looking at me all evening. Goodness knows what the wedding's going to be like!"

She linked her arms in each of theirs as they walked out of the stable. "Can you imagine what Mother and Father would say if they could see us now? Their daughter having a grand ball to announce her engagement to the future Lord Edwards!" She tipped her head back and stared up at the sky, where thousands of stars gleamed like fairy lights.

Maddie bit her lip. How could she tell her sister that the evening was about to be spoiled?

Louisa glanced at her and smiled. "Don't look so solemn, Mouse. Everything is going to be all right. How can it not be? Theo has come home, and we have each other, the three of us together again, forever. Nothing else matters."

Maddie shut her eyes. She couldn't tell Louisa that this man wasn't her brother. It would turn everything they had wished for to dust.

She squeezed Louisa's arm. "That's right," she whispered. "The three of us together again, forever."

17

MADDIE DIDN'T SLEEP AT ALL that night. She lay awake and watched the sky grow light through a gap in the curtains. Theo was dead! And the man she thought was her brother, the man who had made her family happier than they had been for as long as Maddie could remember, was nothing more than a thief who had stolen Theo's name and lied to them all. How could this impostor, this man called Jonathan Price, have deceived them so cruelly?

Because we let him, answered a voice inside Maddie's head. It was as if they had all been treading water since Maddie's parents died, holding their breath and waiting for a reason to start living again. Theo was that reason. And if Maddie told them who Jonathan Price really was, and that Theo had been dead all along, what would happen then? Her grandparents would be devastated, and the scandal would make it impossible for Lou to get married to George. Maddie twisted her fingers into her bedclothes. If she knew how much grief her announcement would cause, yet still told her grandparents, did that make her even crueler than Jonathan for lying in the first place?

When she heard the clock at the foot of the stairs strike five, Maddie jumped out of bed and pulled on her riding habit. Suddenly the only company she wanted was Firebird's.

Outside, the grass was still wet with dew, and the air spilled over with birdsong. The lawns were deserted, the chairs and tables stacked neatly on the drive. In the stable yard, the curtains were still drawn at Toby's window. Maddie let herself into the tack room and took down a sidesaddle and Birdy's bridle. Even though she'd never ridden on her own before, she'd tacked up enough times under Theo's watchful eye to know what she was doing.

A sharp pain stabbed at her and she bent double, gasping for breath. *Not Theo—Jonathan!* Breathing carefully, she straightened up and heaved the saddle onto her hip before tiptoeing across the cobbles to Firebird's stable.

The mare looked surprised to see her this early, and her ears pricked so sharply that the tips almost met above her forelock. Maddie balanced the saddle on top of the door and slipped into the stable. "It's not breakfast time yet, beautiful girl," she murmured as Firebird sniffed curiously at her hands. The saddle seemed heavier than Maddie remembered, perhaps because she felt light-headed and achy after her sleepless night, but the mare stood patiently while she slid it into place, then fastened the girth. The bridle was much easier, Firebird helpfully lowering her head and opening her mouth so Maddie could push the bits over her teeth and hook the headpiece behind her ears.

She closed her eyes for a moment, one hand resting on Firebird's forelock. She hadn't known anything about saddling a horse before Jonathan came to Sefton Park. She would miss him so much if he had to leave.

Then don't say anything, whispered a voice deep inside her.

Maddie gasped. She couldn't let her family go on thinking Jonathan was Theo!

Could she?

Maddie shook her head. These were questions she couldn't answer—questions she shouldn't even be thinking about. There was no way Jonathan Price could stay at Sefton Park!

There was no puzzled shout as she rode out of the yard, nothing to suggest that Toby wanted to know why Maddie was taking one of the horses out at this hour. She guided Firebird onto the lane and down the hill that led past the church, turning back into the estate just before the canal.

She concentrated on letting the mare walk freely, with her neck arched and the lightest contact on the reins. When she thought Firebird's muscles were warmed up, she steered her onto the grass beside the track. Maddie didn't want to risk Firebird getting a stone in her shoe because if she got off to fish it out, she wouldn't be able to get back on again. Firebird tossed her head, enjoying the feel of the grass under her hooves, and

Maddie sat deep in the saddle to let her canter. The estate looked as if it had been washed clean overnight, every leaf carved in shining green glass, and the lake gleaming like a giant mirror.

She reined Firebird to a halt beside the water and watched circles appear on the surface of the lake where fishes came up in search of bugs. The mare snorted when a fly landed on her nose and, laughing, Maddie let her walk on. She couldn't imagine how she'd ever found it hard to figure out which rein went between which fingers. Jonathan had explained to her that the top rein, the curb, was the fiercest one, so it had to be held between her bottom fingers. The other rein was attached to the gentler bit, called the bridoon, and that went between her middle fingers where she could keep a firm contact and listen to the messages that Firebird sent back to her.

Jonathan had taught her all this as if he had spoken directly to Firebird, listening to how she wanted to be ridden and what would make her most comfortable. *He couldn't do that if he was a bad person, could he?* Maddie thought desperately. If the truth came out, he would be punished—maybe even arrested and put into prison! Did Jonathan really deserve that?

Firebird shied at a blackbird flying out of a hedge, startling Maddie out of her thoughts. She leaned forward to put her hand on the horse's neck. The track curved to the right around the top of the lake but Maddie turned left along a grassy path.

Firebird lifted her head and brought her quarters underneath her, sending Maddie a clear signal that she wanted to pick up the pace. Maddie leaned forward and closed her left leg against Firebird's side. The mare sprang into a gallop almost from a standstill, racing over the grass until it was just a pale green blur beneath her hooves.

Maddie urged her faster and faster, as if she could leave everything behind and forget she had ever discovered Jonathan's terrible secret. Suddenly she saw a fallen tree blocking the path, its trunk smooth where the branches had been cut off and stacked to one side, ready to be chopped into firewood.

It was too late to pull up, and for a moment Maddie panicked, convinced they were going to crash straight into it. But then Firebird's ears flicked, just once, and the mare slowed down, gathering herself until she was cantering more steadily. Maddie felt the strength in the mare's hindquarters and remembered the way she had flown over the hedge. She knew the mare could jump this tree trunk easily. She sat up straighter and kept a gentle pressure on the reins, letting Firebird know she was there. *Fold to the left,* she whispered to herself.

Nearer and nearer they came, until the tree trunk was right in front of them, and Firebird's head was lifting up, up, and Maddie found herself leaning forward and sideways, left shoulder over right knee. She saw Firebird's front hooves snatch up under her chest and felt her hind legs push against the ground, springing her into the air. Then they were on the other side, and the empty path stretched out in front of them. They had done it!

Maddie ran her hand down Firebird's mane. "Good girl!" she cried, letting the mare slow to a trot and then to a walk. She turned her in a circle and looked back at the tree trunk. It wasn't as high as the hedge—perhaps four feet, no more—but it looked bulky and unforgiving. Maddie shuddered, knowing that if Firebird had rapped it with one of her hooves, she could have hurt herself or worse, somersaulted right over the tree.

But she hadn't! She'd grown invisible wings and flown over as if it was nothing more than a stick on the ground. She had to jump in the King George V Gold Cup, she just had to!

Maddie stopped. If she told her grandparents about Jonathan Price, he wouldn't be the only one to leave Sefton Park. Firebird would go with him.

Maddie couldn't bear the thought of losing the desert-gold mare. Nor of saying good-bye to the man she thought was her brother, the man who had taught her so much about riding and horses, and made Sefton Park feel like a proper home for the first time. She blinked hard, forcing away the tears that scorched her eyelids. Jonathan hadn't hurt anyone, had he? He didn't deserve to be punished; after all, he had lost Theo too. And in a way, it was worse for him, because he *knew* Theo was dead, and he had to live with that sadness every day. Whereas

Maddie's grandparents and Lou all thought Theo was alive and well and home again, just as they had wished for seven long years.

"I can't say anything," Maddie said out loud, and Firebird's ears twitched. "How can I? This isn't only Jonathan's fault. We wanted Theo to come home so badly, we saw him in the first stranger that turned up on the doorstep. If my grandparents knew the truth, it would ruin everything."

She turned Firebird toward home, hoping with all her heart that she was doing the right thing.

She was the one who had guessed Jonathan's secret, and she would be the one to help him keep it.

Toby was letting himself out of Thor's stable when she arrived back at the yard. "Early ride, Miss Maddie?"

Maddie nodded, kicking her left foot out of the stirrup and jumping lightly down.

"Shall I send Ollie to take the mare?" Toby offered.

"I can manage, thank you," Maddie said. She led Firebird across the yard to her stable and was just undoing the girth when a shadow fell across her. She turned, expecting to see Toby with Firebird's morning feed.

It was Jonathan. "Hello," he said, running his hand nervously along the top of the door. "Good ride?"

Maddie looked at him, trying to see a man who wasn't her

brother. But she had been too young to know Theo properly before he went away—the only brother she knew was the one who had come back, the one who was someone else. It would be harder to believe this wasn't Theo than to pretend that he was. Unable to think of anything to say, she turned away to wrestle with the girth buckle. Firebird was breathing out, and the girth was pulled tight against the clasp.

"Here, let me help." Maddie stepped back and watched Jonathan tug the straps until the buckle loosened and the girth fell away. He lifted the saddle off Firebird's back and looked at Maddie, his eyes solemn.

"You haven't told anyone yet, then."

Maddie's heart started thudding so loud that she was convinced Jonathan would hear it. "No. I'm not going to."

He stared at her. "What do you mean?"

"Look, what you did was wrong, utterly wrong. But Theo's dead. If I tell my grandparents who you really are, everything will be even worse than it was before. We wished for Theo to come home, and in a way, he did. I just don't think I can take him away from my family again."

Jonathan's mouth twisted. "I know I'm not Theo," he said quietly. "And I promise I never thought I could be, however much people called me by his name. He was the finest person I ever met. But this feels like my home now, and I'd like to stay."

Maddie looked away and smoothed a tangle out of Firebird's mane. "I might not be the only one who figures out the truth," she warned him. "But I'm not going to say anything. It would cause too much hurt, and we've had more than enough already." She turned to face him. "If I think you're trying to steal any of my grandfather's money, or if you hurt my family in any way, I will tell my grandparents everything. Is that clear?"

Jonathan nodded. "I understand. I never wanted your money, I promise."

Feeling a little embarrassed by her threat, Maddie started to unbuckle the bridle. "Birdy jumped again today. A tree trunk, near the lake." She remembered the feeling of flying through the air, Firebird's hindquarters pushing them powerfully up, and she spun around to face Jonathan. "She's amazing! I really think we should enter her in the Gold Cup. I know it's only two months away, but she jumps so well already, she wouldn't need much more training. Please say that you think she's good enough!"

Jonathan glanced down at a piece of straw he was twisting in his fingers. "Oh, she's good enough, all right. The reason I said no before was because, well, because it would mean lying to even more people about who I am."

"I don't think the people at the horse show are more important than my family," Maddie pointed out icily.

Jonathan went red. "I suppose not." He lifted his head and gazed earnestly at her. "All I ever wanted was a home and a family. You, Louisa, Sefton Park—you mean everything to me now."

"And Firebird," Maddie prompted, running her fingers through the mare's silky orange mane.

"And Firebird," Jonathan echoed; his voice was so solemn that it sounded like a holy vow, and Maddie let out a long, shaky breath, hoping with all her heart that she was doing the right thing.

18

LIFE QUICKLY RETURNED TO normal after the ball—at least, as normal as it would ever be now that Maddie knew the person they thought was Theo was an impostor. When she heard her grandfather call him "Theo" for the first time, she flinched and watched Jonathan's face for some sign of guilt. But he answered as easily as he had ever done, so easily that Maddie wondered if Jonathan sometimes forgot that he wasn't Theo.

They had been forgiven for missing the speech and the fireworks, since the rest of the party had been such a success; and from the wariness in their eyes, Maddie suspected her grandparents didn't want to push their grandson too far in case he disappeared again.

The tables and chairs were taken back to the village hall, and there was only a neat row of holes in the front lawn to suggest there had been a fireworks display. Stan the gardener put little felt shoes onto the hooves of his patient pony, Jenny, and hitched the heavy roller to her harness. Then he led her up and down the lawn, back and forth until all the footprints had been smoothed away and the grass was flat enough for croquet again.

Lady Ella turned her attention to the wedding with the same vigor she had tackled the ball. She had already ordered so many wedding catalogs that Maddie thought an entire forest must have been cut down to provide all the pages.

But Louisa made it clear that she and George were in no hurry to get married and weren't going to consider setting a date for another few months, even though Lady Ella frowned and fretted about booking the church and organizing the menu. Louisa calmly looked at her grandmother and pointed out that Hamstead Marshall wasn't big enough to provide brides for every weekend of the year, so there would be no problem finding a spare date in the church calendar; and as for menus, she'd done a splendid job with the ball after just a few weeks' planning, so the wedding would hardly be a bigger challenge. Lady Ella seemed pleased by Lou's praise, but Maddie noticed that they still had some rather unusual meals—spiced quails one night, and salmon en croute the next—as if her grandmother was running through options for the big day.

Much more important than any talk about weddings, as far as Maddie was concerned, was Firebird's training. To her delight, Jonathan seemed set on keeping his promise to enter her for the Gold Cup. Two days after the ball, he examined her legs to check that they hadn't swelled up from jumping the tree trunk. Maddie stood in the stable and watched him run his hand down each of Firebird's legs. He beckoned her over to do the same, and the slender stems of bone and muscle felt smooth and hard under her fingers. That meant her tendons were much stronger, Jonathan explained.

"So we can start jumping her now?" Maddie said excitedly, and Jonathan nodded.

"I've been reading that article you showed me, about Nightwatchman. The course for the Gold Cup will be four upright fences, and one triple bar or a water jump. We know Birdy can jump hedges and tree trunks, but these will be very different. Easier to knock down, for a start."

Maddie frowned. "Will we be able to build them in the paddock?"

"I think so. I can make some stands to put the rails on, and there's plenty of wood for the poles."

"I can help you with the stands if you like, Master Theo." Toby was looking over the door, and Maddie froze. How long had he been standing there? She couldn't remember if she had called Jonathan by his real name.

"I had to tell Toby about the competition," Jonathan explained. "He'll need to start feeding Birdy more oats and bandaging her legs at night."

Maddie nodded. Much as she'd like to keep the Gold Cup a secret between her and Jonathan, they had enough secrets already—and he was right, it would be impossible to train the mare without Toby noticing something was different in her routine.

"Can we try jumping her today, Theo?" she asked. Her brother's name felt thick and scratchy in her throat, but she couldn't risk rousing even a whisker of suspicion in front of Toby.

Jonathan glanced at her as if he guessed she had used her brother's name deliberately. "I don't see why not," he said. Giving Firebird a last pat, he followed Toby out of the stable and headed for the tack room.

Maddie went over and rested her cheek against Birdy's. The mare blinked, and her eyelashes brushed softly against Maddie's forehead. "You're going to be brilliant, aren't you, little one?" she whispered, and Firebird blinked again.

Jonathan reappeared with a saddle slung over his arm. Maddie felt a stab of disappointment when she realized it wasn't a sidesaddle. He followed her gaze and guessed what she was thinking.

"It makes sense for me to jump her first, I think," he said. "But you can have a go later on, once she knows what she's doing."

Maddie was tempted to reply that so far Firebird had seemed to know exactly what she was doing, and that Maddie had been the only one to jump her at all, over the hedge and the tree trunk. But deep down she knew Jonathan was right; he was much more experienced than her, and he'd be riding her in the competition.

"I can still help, can't I?"

He grinned. "Of course! I need someone to watch and tell me how she's going, and what I'm doing wrong." He draped the reins over Firebird's head and turned to look at her. "I've not tried anything like this before, Maddie. I'm in the dark as much as you are, but I've never seen a horse jump like Birdy. We've just got to trust this little lady to help us out." He ran his hand over Firebird's nose, and she snuffled against his palm.

"She'll look after us," Maddie agreed.

They led Firebird into the schooling paddock, and Jonathan swung himself into the saddle. The mare danced skittishly when she felt his weight in the saddle, clamping her tail against the cold wind.

"Easy, girl," Jonathan soothed.

"What are you going to do first?" Maddie asked.

"I'll start by warming up with some circles, then you could put up some fences, if you like." Jonathan looked at her from under the peak of his cap, and Maddie could tell he was feeling nervous.

She nodded confidently to reassure him. "One course of jumps coming up! Just let me know when you're ready."

He smiled. "I think we'll start off with a couple first, rather than a whole course." He shortened the reins and turned

Firebird away to trot along the hedge. Halfway along, a rabbit shot out, closely followed by Charlie. Firebird stopped dead, then reared up and wheeled around.

Maddie gasped, but Jonathan sat as still as a statue and closed his fingers around the reins, keeping Firebird from going into a flat-out gallop.

"Charlie, you bad dog!" Maddie shouted, and the setter gave up on the rabbit, which had already vanished into the other hedge, and loped across the grass with her ears flying.

Jonathan pushed Firebird into a canter, keeping her at a slow, rocking-horse pace with her hocks tucked under her. He circled in the top half of the field, then turned her to go the other way. As he shifted in the saddle to face the other direction, Firebird gathered herself and gave a little skip to strike off on the other leg.

"That was neat!" Maddie called, impressed.

"It's called a flying change," Jonathan explained, reining to a halt beside her. "She'll need to be able to change legs quickly when we're jumping the course, rather than slow down to a trot every time we go around a corner."

Maddie nodded. "Shall I put up some jumps now?"

"Yes, please. I'll help you—some of those poles are heavy." He jumped down from the saddle and looped the reins over his arm. "Let's start with a rail over there," he said, pointing to the far hedge.

Maddie held Firebird while he carried a pole across the field, and then heaved four bales of straw over to support the rail. It looked very flimsy compared with a hedge or a tree trunk, Maddie thought. She looked around as a deafening rumble came from the stable yard. Firebird's head shot up and she leaped backward, with Maddie only just keeping hold of the reins.

"Steady, girl," she said, reaching up to stroke her neck. Firebird lowered her head and blew softly into Maddie's hair, making her smile.

The rumbling noise grew louder, and Toby appeared in the gateway, rolling a large metal drum. "I thought this'd do to put a rail on. There's a pair of them been standing empty in the garage for months," he puffed as he pushed the drum over to them. Firebird watched it with her eyes bulging, and Maddie rested one hand on her neck.

Toby heaved the drum onto its side and rested the end of a pole on top. It was a little less than four feet high, and Jonathan studied it approvingly. "Thanks, Toby."

Maddie led Firebird away and let her snatch a few mouthfuls of grass while Toby went off to fetch the other drum. Thor and Wayfarer stuck their heads over the fence from the neighboring paddock and watched curiously. When the second drum was in place, Maddie led the mare back to Jonathan. He cantered her in a wide circle before facing her at the first rail.

The breeze picked up as he approached, and the pole rolled on top of the straw bales.

Firebird's ears twitched and her stride faltered. Maddie clenched her hands. "Come on, Birdy," she whispered.

The pole swayed again, and Firebird skidded to a halt right in front of the fence, peeling back strips of turf with her front hooves. Jonathan lurched forward up her neck and only just managed to push himself back into the saddle.

"That wasn't a very good start," he muttered, going red.

"Never mind, try again," Maddie called encouragingly.

He shortened the reins and turned Firebird away from the fence. The mare spooked at a piece of bramble waving in the hedge, and Maddie saw Jonathan's mouth tighten in a straight line. Firebird seemed determined to make this difficult.

They cantered toward the fence again, and this time Jonathan drove her on with his legs, not giving her a chance to stop. Firebird flattened her ears, and just when Maddie thought she was going to jump the rail, she put in an extra stride so that she took off much too close and knocked the pole with her forelegs. It bounced off the straw bales and clattered to the ground. Jonathan steered her determinedly toward the second rail, the one on the oil drums, but Firebird fought against him, tossing her head.

A few yards from the rail, Jonathan pulled her up, shaking his head. "She doesn't like knocking them down," he said.

"Well, isn't that a good thing?" Maddie pointed out hopefully. "We don't want her to knock them down, do we?"

Jonathan pulled up and bent down to check the girth was tight enough. "True," he said, his voice muffled, "but she can't get upset by one fence falling. What if it's the first jump of the course? She has to be able to jump the rest."

Maddie stared helplessly at the mare. Firebird was looking around with her ears pricked, her tail streaming behind her like a golden flag. She looked as beautiful as ever, with her dished face, and her nostrils flaring quickly in and out. "She doesn't look upset now," Maddie said.

Jonathan gathered up the reins again. "No. I'll have another try. Come on, girl." He closed his legs against her sides and trotted in a wide circle before asking her to canter. Firebird tucked in her nose and bucked, then pricked her ears and picked up speed when she saw the rail. Jonathan sat very still, letting her stretch her neck forward, but Maddie could tell she was going too fast. Firebird took off yards away from the fence, her body flat in the air like a fish, and brought the pole crashing down with her back hooves.

Jonathan didn't look back as the rail hit the ground. Firebird kept going toward the next fence, even faster than before. Her head shot up and she took a funny little half stride before heaving herself into the air. She clipped the pole without knocking it off and it banged against the top of the drums, making a hollow clanging sound. As soon as she landed, Firebird dropped her head and bucked, flicking out her back hooves.

Jonathan pulled her up, looking exasperated. "It's no good," he puffed. "She just doesn't respect these fences like she did the hedge. She knows she can knock them down, so she's not even trying to clear them."

Maddie opened her mouth to protest that there must be something else they could do, but Jonathan was shaking his head. "I'm sorry, Maddie. I don't think this is going to work. We just don't know enough about training a horse for the Gold Cup."

19

MADDIE STARED AT HIM in dismay. "You can't give up! We've only just started trying."

Jonathan shrugged. "I really am sorry," he said again, running his fingers along the reins. "I wanted this to work as much as you did."

Maddie snatched the reins from him. "Really? That's not what it sounds like. I can't believe you're giving up so easily, not after . . . after everything." She clicked to Firebird and started to lead her across the field. The mare shied as they went past the drums, and Maddie yanked angrily at the reins before realizing she had no right to take it out on her.

"I'm sorry," she murmured, stroking Firebird's hot, damp neck. "It's not your fault if you don't want to jump today." She led her back into the stable, feeling relieved when Jonathan stayed in the paddock and left her to untack Birdy alone.

Toby appeared with a bucket of water and cloth just as she was putting the saddle on top of the door. "Shall I wash her down for you, Miss Maddie?"

Suddenly bone-tired, Maddie nodded. "Thank you, Toby. Did . . . did you see what happened?"

"Aye, but don't take it too hard." He let himself into the stable and ran one hand down Firebird's shoulder. "I've never met a chestnut mare that wasn't a handful."

"She's not a handful!" Maddie insisted. "We just weren't doing it right. She can jump those fences easily, I know she can."

Toby looked at her, his pale blue eyes serious. "Maybe she can," he said. "But Master Theo's one of the best horsemen I've seen, and I think you can trust his judgment."

Feeling thoroughly deflated, Maddie opened the stable door and trailed across the yard. Through the archway, she could see Jonathan stacking the poles at the side of the paddock. She glanced back and saw Firebird watching her with her ears pricked. Maddie felt a wave of affection for the beautiful mare. She couldn't have known how much it meant to Maddie that she jumped well today. Perhaps Jonathan was right, and they had been hoping for too much, to be able to turn her into a top-class show-jumper in just a few weeks. Surely what mattered most of all was that Maddie was keeping Jonathan's secret, and Firebird was going to stay at Sefton Park forever.

"I'm sorry, Birdy," she whispered. "It's not your fault. It should be enough just to have you here. I have to learn to stop wishing for more than I already have."

The next morning, Maddie came downstairs to find Jonathan having breakfast with her grandfather. Sir Wilfred was talking about an article in the *Times*. "Labour may be the second biggest party, but I can't see the Conservatives losing, I must say." He grunted and noisily folded the paper on to a new page.

"Would it be such a bad thing if Labour did win?" Jonathan ventured.

Sir Wilfred lowered his newspaper and stared at his grandson. "By Jove, Theo! You can't have been away long enough to turn into a Labour supporter!" His cheeks reddened above his bushy-white whiskers, and he lifted the paper again. "For a moment there, I thought you were serious, old boy."

Jonathan opened his mouth as if he was about to argue, and Maddie shot him a warning glare.

Her grandfather pushed back his chair. "I'll be in the library if anyone wants me," he said. "Theo, have you had a chance to think about Ponsonby's offer? You could do worse than to join him in the bank, you know."

Maddie narrowed her eyes, watching to see how Jonathan reacted.

"I've not thought about it yet, Grandfather," he replied carefully. "As you say, it's a generous offer."

Sir Wilfred nodded. "In your own time, lad," he said. "I'm in no hurry to send you away again, you can be sure of that. Even London seems a dashed long way off, though I suppose it's only a hop and a jump compared with Africa." He nodded to

Maddie. "Good morning, my dear."

She smiled at him as he went out of the breakfast room. Opposite her, Jonathan's fingers flicked nervously at a magazine that was folded beside his plate. He looked as if he was waiting for Maddie to point out the web of lies that was spinning endlessly around him.

"Theo used to call Sir Wilfred Grandpapa," was all she said, keeping her voice light as if they were having an ordinary conversation. "Not 'Grandfather.'"

He studied her for a few moments. "Theo would have changed too, Maddie. Don't forget that."

She opened her mouth, ready to lash back that he couldn't possibly know how Theo would have acted when he came home. Then she realized Jonathan probably knew better than anyone. She shrugged and reached over to help herself to some toast.

"What's the magazine?" she asked.

Jonathan's eyes lit up, and he unfolded the journal. Maddie saw it was the one that Rosie had lent her. "I've been reading that article about Nightwatchman again. It says that his trainer, a man called Dick Stillwell, has a yard near Oxford."

Maddie frowned. "But we couldn't possibly afford to send Birdy there." She guessed it would be like a more expensive version of piano lessons. Then she stopped. "Wait a minute. I thought you said we weren't going to enter Firebird in the Gold Cup."

Jonathan rubbed his finger along the edge of the magazine. "I know. I was in a temper, with myself more than the mare," he added. "I guess I'm not used to failing with horses." He smiled lopsidedly. "Anyway, I think we should keep trying—if you want to, that is."

Maddie stared at him in amazement. "Of course I do!" Then another thought struck her. "I wasn't going to tell Grandpapa, you know. I wouldn't do that just because you changed your mind about Firebird."

He blinked. "I . . . yes, I did think you might. Sorry, that wasn't fair. But I do want to try again with Birdy," he said earnestly. He held out the magazine to Maddie. "Look, there's a photograph of Stillwell's yard. I know we can't afford to send her there, but we want to train her ourselves anyway, don't we?" Maddie nodded, and he went on, "I thought if we could go to the yard and watch him training one of his show-jumpers, we could work out what to do with Firebird."

"It's a great idea, but how would we get to Oxford?" Maddie pointed out. "There isn't a train from Newbury."

"Who's going to Oxford?" asked Louisa, coming into the breakfast room.

"Theo and I were thinking of visiting someone," Maddie explained.

"Really? Who?" Lou started to spread jam onto a bread roll.

"There's a horse trainer there who might be able to help us with Firebird," said Jonathan.

Louisa swallowed her mouthful of roll. "Do you know whereabouts in Oxford? Rosie and I are driving up there next week to see Lily Farnsworth—do you remember her, Maddie? She's Bertie's sister. She went up to read Law at St. Hilda's College last September. Anyway"—she took a sip of tea and went on—"I'm sure Rosie wouldn't mind giving you a lift, if it's not too far out of our way."

Maddie grinned at Jonathan across the table. "That would be brilliant!"

Jonathan studied the article again. "It says here the yard's in Blewbury."

"Oh, that's easy. It's a village just outside Oxford, we drive right through it on the way."

As soon as she had finished her breakfast, Maddie ran outside to tell Firebird. The chestnut mare was in the paddock, and she trotted over when Maddie stood on the bottom rail of the fence and called to her. "We're going to find out how to train proper show-jumpers," she whispered into Firebird's velvety golden ear. "You're going to jump in the Gold Cup, you really are!"

20

⎯⎯⎯⎯⎯

THE JOURNEY TO BLEWBURY took a little less than an hour, which was quite long enough for Maddie. She and Jonathan were squeezed into the back of the Baby Austin, so close that their knees banged together every time the motorcar went over a pothole, and when they went around a corner, Maddie had to brace herself to avoid sliding into Jonathan's lap. Rosie was very excited to hear about their plans for Firebird, especially when Jonathan warned her not to give anything away to the owner of the yard.

Maddie stared at him in surprise. "Why does it have to be a secret?"

"Because Mr. Stillwell is hardly likely to tell us how he trained Nightwatchman if he finds out we're going to be competing against him!" Jonathan pointed out.

Blushing, Maddie realized he was right. "So what shall we tell him?" she asked. "He's bound to want to know why we've come to his yard."

Louisa twisted around in her seat. "I know! Maddie, you can pretend you've just started riding, and your father has promised to buy you a pony for your birthday. If you act as if you don't know the first thing about horses, the trainer will never suspect what you're really up to!"

"What about Theo?" Maddie said. "It's easy for me to act like I don't know anything."

"He'll have to be even more cunning," Rosie chipped in, without turning around. "He can be your bored elder brother who isn't the slightest bit interested in his little sister or her precious pony. Theo, do you have a pipe?"

Jonathan looked puzzled. "No."

"Well, fish around in the pocket inside the door. I think there's one of Bertie's in there. I've always thought men look a thousand times more bored if they have a pipe to fiddle with." Rosie drummed her fingers on the steering wheel. "Oh, this is so exciting! It's like being secret agents!"

Maddie was about to agree, already imagining how she could make a show of ignorance at Mr. Stillwell's yard, when she caught Jonathan's eye.

"Not quite as dramatic as secret agents," he said quietly. "It will save some awkward questions, that's all."

His gray eyes were unexpectedly solemn, and Maddie felt a stab of guilt. This was what he did all the time, wasn't it? Let people believe he was someone else, lie to everyone about where he came from and how much he knew. Pretending not to know about horses seemed like such a little lie in comparison. Maddie shook her head in confusion. Was there a sliding scale of deceit that made some lies all right?

Mr. Stillwell's yard was easy to find, with tall stone gates right in the center of Blewbury. Rosie pulled into the side of the road to let Maddie and Jonathan climb out. "We'll be back in a couple of hours!" she called, driving away again.

Maddie brushed out the creases in her skirt. "Well, do I look like a spoiled little girl?"

Jonathan studied her. "Absolutely!" he said cheerfully, and Maddie pulled a face at him, grateful that he had lightened the mood. Jonathan fished in his pocket and drew out Bertie's pipe. "And I'm ready to look suitably bored," he announced. "Right, let's go and learn how to train show-jumpers."

He offered her his arm and they walked up the drive to a very impressive stable block, horseshoe-shaped like the one at Sefton Park but with at least forty stables, nearly all with horses looking out of them. Stable boys ran everywhere, pushing wheelbarrows, carrying tack, or leading beautiful thoroughbreds with glossy coats.

Maddie stood at the edge of the yard and stared. "I've never seen so many horses!" she breathed.

"Come on," said Jonathan. "We need to find Mr. Stillwell."

A short, skinny lad with curly red hair stopped beside them. "Can I help, sir?"

"We're looking for Dick Stillwell," Jonathan told him.

"That's right," Maddie piped up. "Daddy's promised to buy me a pony, you see, and I thought Mr. Stillwell could help me find a nice pretty one. My brother didn't want to come because he doesn't like horses at all." She winced at how pathetic she sounded, but the stable boy didn't seem to notice.

He pointed to a path that led around the stable block. "He's teaching just now. If you go along there, you'll come to the schooling ring. Don't interrupt his lesson till he notices you're there, mind! He don't like to be disturbed, does Mr. Stillwell." He picked up the handles of his wheelbarrow and hurried away.

Maddie glanced at Jonathan. "Mr. Stillwell sounds a bit of a tyrant."

"You'd need to be, to organize all this lot." He looked around at the busy yard, then smiled at Maddie. "Ready for a spot of snooping?"

She nodded, trying hard not to think about different shades of lying, and they followed the path out of the yard to a large training arena enclosed by wooden rails. A dark brown horse was cantering in a circle at the far end of the arena.

"That's Nightwatchman!" Maddie whispered excitedly, recognizing the handsome gelding from his photograph in the magazine article. His rider looked tiny, but Maddie reminded herself that Nightwatchman was nearly seventeen hands high, a good six inches taller than Firebird.

"He's magnificent, isn't he?" Jonathan murmured, and Maddie nodded.

The horse was circling a sturdy man wearing a tweed jacket and breeches. A flat cap was crammed onto his white hair, and he carried a short hunting cane that he thwacked against his riding boot in time with the horse's stride.

"Come on, Phil, gather him up! You're a floppy disgrace up there today, boy! Call yourself a jockey?"

Maddie gulped. Suddenly she was even more determined that Mr. Stillwell didn't find out the real reason for their visit.

"All right, take him over the fence," snapped the trainer. "You're going to wear a ditch in the sand if you canter him much more." He jabbed his stick toward a fence in the center of the arena. A single rail was balanced on two wooden stands, with movable cups so the jump could be made lower or higher.

The horse snorted and snatched at the reins but his rider, who looked barely older than Maddie, sat very still and crouched low over his withers as the horse sprang into the air and cleared the rail by miles.

"Rubbish!" Mr. Stillwell bellowed from the end of the arena. "If I want you to take off two strides too early, I'll tell you. Bob!"

A broad-shouldered lad jumped down the fence at the edge

of the ring. "Yes, Mr. Stillwell?"

"Put down some canter poles in front of the jump. Four paces apart, mind you. I know we normally put them at three paces, but this horse has legs the length of a giraffe's."

Beside her, Maddie heard Jonathan mutter, "Canter poles in front of the fence, three paces apart."

"What are the poles for?" she whispered.

"I think they're a way of helping the horse measure his stride before the fence, so he takes off in the right place," Jonathan replied. "Birdy could have done with some of those the other day!"

"But you won't have them in the competition, will you?"

"No, but I think once you'd ridden over them a few times, both you and the horse would know how to approach the fence from the right distance."

Maddie nodded and turned back to watch Bob stagger across the ring with an armful of poles that he dropped on the sand at regular intervals, taking big steps in between. Four steps, pole, four steps, pole, until there were four poles in all, just visible on the deep sand.

When the poles were in place, Mr. Stillwell tapped his cane against his boot and told Phil to take the horse over the fence again. The gelding's hooves thundered on the sand, and the poles kept his stride perfectly even until he leaped over the jump.

"Better," called Mr. Stillwell. "Right, we'll try the triple bar now. Bob!" He looked around for the other lad, and spotted Maddie and Jonathan standing beside the fence.

"Hey, you there! Who the devil are you?"

21

MADDIE GASPED. WERE THEY about to be unmasked?

Mr. Stillwell strode over the sand. "Who said you could come and watch this lesson?"

Maddie glanced at Jonathan. He had stepped away from the fence and was gazing around him, tapping the bowl of his pipe in his hand as if he would rather be anywhere else. Right then, Maddie felt the same way. "I'm looking for a pony," she blurted out.

Mr. Stillwell stood in front of her and puffed out his mustache. "Looking for a pony, eh? Well, you've come to the right place. Ridden much, have you?"

"Yes, twice," Maddie said enthusiastically. In spite of the knot in her stomach, she was beginning to enjoy herself. "Daddy says I can have one for my birthday. That's not my father," she added, looking at Jonathan. "That's my brother. He doesn't like horses." She felt Jonathan glance at her, and wondered if she was overdoing it.

Mr. Stillwell raised his eyebrows. "You've ridden twice, have you? Well, you won't be interested in this one, then!" He nodded toward Nightwatchman, who was circling in a slow trot on the other side of the ring, his head low and his massive hooves barely skimming the sand. "I thought you might be some sort of spy, come to see how a real champion is trained!" Mr. Stillwell joked, his blue eyes twinkling at Maddie.

"Oh no," she stammered. "I'd be much too scared to jump anything as high as that. In fact, I don't want a pony who can jump at all." In case Mr. Stillwell shooed her away because she seemed too uninterested, she went on, "But I love watching show-jumping. Is that really Nightwatchman? Didn't he win the King George the Fifth Gold Cup last year?"

"It is indeed," Mr. Stillwell declared. "And all set to win it this year, I don't mind telling you. Would you and your brother mind waiting until I've finished? I've got one or two cracking little ponies that might be just what you're looking for."

"No, we don't mind waiting at all," Maddie said politely. "Thank you, Mr. Stillwell."

The trainer walked back into the middle of the ring, and Maddie let out a sigh of relief. "That was close."

"Well played." Jonathan grinned, coming to stand beside her. "I'd no idea you were such a good actor."

Maddie looked at him, letting an unspoken sentence crash into the air between them: They already knew Jonathan was a good actor, because he had been playing a role ever since he came to Sefton Park. With a pang of physical pain, Maddie wondered if he found it as exciting as she had when talking to Mr. Stillwell. She thrust the flicker of doubt away. She couldn't believe that Jonathan enjoyed deceiving her family, she just couldn't.

She turned back to the arena, resting her hands on the top rail. Bob was dragging three more pairs of stands into place, close together to make a single jump. The pole at the front was about three feet off the ground, and the back rail looked high enough for Maddie to walk underneath on tiptoe.

"That's a triple bar," Jonathan explained quietly. "There'll be one of those or a water jump in the competition."

The triple bar had been set up directly after the single rail, and Mr. Stillwell walked between the two fences with big strides, saying something under his breath.

"What's he doing?" whispered Maddie, puzzled.

Jonathan didn't answer until Mr. Stillwell reached the triple bar. Then he turned to Maddie and said, "Stillwell took seventeen paces between the two jumps. I think that means there's enough room for Nightwatchman to take proper strides between them."

Maddie remembered how Firebird had jumped the two fences they had set up, with an awkward little half stride before the second one. "So if the jumps are that close together, we need to measure the distance between them?"

"It looks like it," said Jonathan. He frowned. "I hadn't realized it was going to be so complicated."

Maddie touched his sleeve. "Don't worry. At least we've found all this out in time to get Birdy ready!"

He met her eyes and smiled. "I suppose so."

Phil cantered Nightwatchman in a small circle, then turned him toward the upright fence. Over the poles they bounced, two, three, four, and the horse flew over the upright rail with a flick of his heels. Four more strides to the triple bar, but this time he clipped the back pole and it thudded onto the sand.

"Stop!" shouted Mr. Stillwell, making Maddie jump. "Wretched boy, you know full well why you didn't clear that."

"Not enough impulsion, sir."

"Not enough impulsion, the boy says!" echoed Mr. Stillwell. "And if you knew that, why didn't you do something about it?"

"Sorry, sir. Shall I try again?"

"Unless you want to waste everyone's time, then yes, I think that would be a very good idea. Or shall I ask that young lady over there to have a try?"

To Maddie's horror, Mr. Stillwell pointed his cane in her direction. For one dreadful moment, she thought he was really going to order her to ride Nightwatchman.

But Phil was cantering in a circle again, and Maddie let out a long breath when she realized Mr. Stillwell had just been making a point.

"He had you worried there, didn't he?" Jonathan teased, and she pulled a face at him.

"What did he mean by 'impulsion'?" she asked.

Jonathan pointed at the horse, who was bounding over the canter poles. "See how his hocks are right under him, pushing him forward?" Maddie nodded. "Well, that's impulsion. It's like having lots of energy under control."

The gelding popped over the single rail, which looked easy compared with the triple bar. As soon as he landed, Phil kicked hard for the next four strides, quickening Nightwatchman's pace but sitting up and keeping the reins short so that the horse didn't stretch out his neck or flatten his body like Birdy did when she was galloping. The extra speed meant Nightwatchman pushed himself into the air harder than before, this time leaving a handspan of sky between his heels and the back rail.

"That's more like it," said Mr. Stillwell as Phil brought the horse back to a trot, patting his neck. "Right, we'll just pop him over a pair of uprights, make sure he doesn't flatten after all that fun, then we'll call it a day."

Bob ran out to dismantle the triple bar, taking away two of the poles to leave a single rail, just like the first. The trainer measured out the distance between the jumps again, dragging the second fence forward until it was exactly seventeen paces from the first.

"Right, lad," he called to Phil, who was gathering up

Nightwatchman's reins. "Nice and steady now, we don't want him to get carried away. He should be able to jump these out of a trot, but we'll let him canter today. And one and two, and one and two . . ." He tapped his cane against his boot, and Phil nudged the horse into a canter, slow and rocking-horse bouncy like Firebird's.

"He doesn't look like he's going fast enough to jump those fences!" Maddie whispered to Jonathan.

"You don't need speed to jump uprights," he replied. "It's all down to impulsion again. As long as the horse has his hocks underneath him, he just has to spring straight up in the air."

As he spoke, Nightwatchman bounced over the row of poles and leaped over the first rail. Phil sat up very straight as soon as they landed, holding the horse even though he was clearly fighting to go faster, anticipating the triple bar. Four slow, springy strides, and they flew over the second fence.

Mr. Stillwell tucked his cane under his arm and clapped. "Good work, lad. Cool him down with a few minutes' walking, then take him in and wash him down. I want every inch of him dried afterward, mind you." He opened the gate of the school and came over to Jonathan and Maddie. "Right then, shall we see about a pony for you? I've got a neat little cob called Trumpet Major. He couldn't jump a stick if his life depended on it, but he's got a super temperament."

Maddie glanced anxiously at Jonathan. She didn't want to

waste Mr. Stillwell's time by making him show her a horse she had no intention of buying. Jonathan stepped forward to help her out.

"That would be awfully kind of you, sir," he drawled. "My little sis doesn't have time to ride today, but I'm sure she'd like to have a look at this four-legged friend of yours."

Maddie caught his eye and stuffed her gloved hand into her mouth in an effort not to laugh.

Mr. Stillwell nodded, and led them back to the stable yard. It was quieter now, with only two stable boys in sight, sitting on upturned buckets surrounded by heaps of dismantled bridles.

"Most of the boys are at lunch," Mr. Stillwell explained. He walked briskly over to a stable at the end of the block. "Here's Trumpet Major."

A chunky pale gray head appeared over the stable door. He looked a bit like Wayfarer, but about a hand shorter. Maddie thought he had kind eyes, and she liked the way he snuffled his lips against her hand, looking for treats.

"He's a lovely little fellow," said Mr. Stillwell, rubbing the pony between his ears. "A bit too short in the leg for hunting, but you won't mind that if you don't want to jump."

"Er, no," Maddie agreed, studying the pony's solid-looking head and short, sturdy neck, looking even sturdier where his mane had been hogged. "He's very sweet," she added.

"Shall I get him out of the stable for you?" Mr. Stillwell

offered. When Maddie shook her head, he frowned. "You won't be able to choose a pony if you don't have a look at him first," he said sternly, and Maddie winced. She was going to have to put a little more imagination into her role.

"Oh I know," she said. "But this one isn't the right color."

Mr. Stillwell raised his eyebrows. So did Jonathan, who was standing behind him.

"That's right," Maddie went on. "You see, I have a dark green riding habit, and I just don't think it would look very striking against a gray pony. What do you think?" she added, beaming at Mr. Stillwell as if she genuinely wanted his opinion. When he stared at her in astonished silence, she gazed around the yard as if she was in a dressmaker's boutique.

"That color would be much nicer!" she announced, pointing at a tall horse with a coppery-brown coat and a jet-black mane. "Please could I see that one instead?"

Mr. Stillwell coughed. "I don't think that's a good choice, young lady. Duke's more of a gentleman's horse. But if it's a bay pony you're after, how about this one?" He strode along the row of stables and stopped with one hand resting on a door. "This is Fly. She's a nice little mare, six years old, done one season of hunting, but very steady." He addressed his comments to Jonathan with a hint of desperation in his eyes, but turned back to Maddie when Jonathan just stared blankly back at him.

Maddie stood on tiptoe to peer over the door. A short-legged bay pony gazed at her from a deep straw bed. Maddie pretended to think hard for a moment. "Well, she's the right color," she said, "but I'm not sure about her mane. It's a bit tufty. Have you got one with a nice smooth mane, this long?" She turned to Mr. Stillwell and held her hands about eight inches apart.

The trainer puffed out his mustache with barely concealed frustration. "Now, miss, you can't judge a pony just from the length of its mane. I'm thinking that maybe you should ride for a bit longer before you buy a pony. There's a fair bit more involved than the right color, you know."

Maddie felt a twinge of guilt and knew that she had played her role for long enough. She beamed at him, unable to resist one last mischief. "You're right, Mr. Stillwell. I might get a new riding habit in a few months' time, and then the gray pony could be best after all! But thank you for showing us the ponies."

Mr. Stillwell nodded, relief showing in his eyes. "Well, you know where they are if you decide you want to come back and try them. Either of them would make a fine pony for you."

"I'm sure they would," said Maddie earnestly.

Jonathan raised his cap to Mr. Stillwell, looking too bored to say good-bye, and they hurried back down the drive to wait for Rosie. As soon as they were out of sight of the yard, Jonathan let out a shout of laughter. "I can't believe you said that mare's mane was too tufty!"

Maddie grinned. "I know! And that Trumpet Major wouldn't go with my riding habit!"

The tiny cherry-colored car whizzed around the corner as they reached the gateway, and Louisa wound down the window to wave.

"Poor old Lily, we cut short our lunch because we couldn't wait to hear how you got on!" she called.

"Sssshhh!" Maddie hissed, climbing into the back of the car. "Someone might hear!"

Lou went red. "Oops, sorry."

"So?" Rosie demanded, snatching a glance over her shoulder as she pulled away.

Maddie grinned. "It was amazing! We saw Nightwatchman being schooled—can you believe our luck!—and we learned about uprights and triple bars and canter poles. . . ."

"Steady on!" Lou laughed, holding up her hands. "You're speaking a different language!"

"That's exactly what it's like!" Maddie agreed excitedly. "Jonathan was brilliant, too!"

"Jonathan?" echoed Louisa, sounding puzzled.

Maddie clapped her hand to her mouth. What had she done?

"That's what Maddie called me," Jonathan explained

smoothly. "We didn't want to use our real names, you see."

"What a splendid idea!" said Rosie. "Goodness, you'll be recruited by the government if they ever hear about this, Maddie. Don't you think secrets are such fun?"

But Maddie stared out of the window, feeling sick. Secrets weren't fun at all. All her excitement about watching Nightwatchman being trained ebbed away, and she watched the fields whiz past in a greenish blur, wishing everything could be less complicated, and that the man sitting next to her really was her brother.

After the visit to Mr. Stillwell's yard, preparations for the competition seemed to speed up, which Maddie found both exciting and a little bit daunting. After all, they still didn't know if Firebird could jump an entire course! First, Jonathan sent away for the forms that would enable him to register with the British Show-Jumping Association and enter the Gold Cup. Then, to Maddie's relief, her tutor, Miss Finnigan, announced that she was going to spend a month with her sister in Bognor Regis. This meant Maddie was free to ride every day, with only the occasional piano lesson looming like a little black cloud on the horizon.

Three days after the trip to Blewbury, Jonathan decided to have their first training session. When Maddie went down to the yard, he handed her a piece of paper on which he'd written a list of everything they'd learned from watching Mr. Stillwell.

Maddie leaned against the stable door and studied the list while Jonathan saddled Firebird. "Your handwriting's nothing like Theo's," she commented.

He stopped buckling the girth and turned to face her. "I know. I tried to copy a letter of his, but . . . I'll be careful, I promise."

Maddie folded the piece of paper and tucked it into her jacket. "You'd better be," she said lightly. "You can't let Birdy down now!"

There was a scraping noise behind her, and she looked over her shoulder to see Toby crossing the yard with a wooden jumping stand under each arm.

"Your brother and I made these yesterday," he explained breathlessly, propping them on the cobbles next to Maddie. "We thought they'd be better than straw bales."

Maddie ran her hand down the smooth, white-painted wood. "They look perfect!" she said.

Jonathan tied Firebird to a ring inside the stable and came out to help Toby carry the jump stands into the paddock. Maddie brought over some poles from the stack by the hedge and dropped them onto the grass with a satisfying thud.

"I think we'll start with an upright first," said Jonathan. "And four canter poles, like Mr. Stillwell put out for Nightwatchman."

Maddie nodded. "But only three paces apart, not four. Birdy's legs are a lot shorter than Nightwatchman's, so her strides will be shorter too."

"Good idea," Jonathan agreed. He smiled at Maddie. "Do you want to measure out the canter poles?"

"Yes, please!" While Jonathan and Toby heaved the jump stands into position, Maddie picked up a pole and held it in front of her like a tightrope walker. With her back to the jump, she counted three strides, then laid the pole carefully on the grass. She did the same with three more poles, laying each one a little farther from the jump.

"That looks great!" declared Jonathan. "Right, there's just the fence to put up now." He slid out the nail that held the cup in place and moved it to the top of the stand.

"I hope you're not going to start off that high," Maddie warned. It was well over her head, at least five and a half feet above the ground.

Jonathan grinned and fixed the cup about halfway down the pole. "Not yet, anyway."

Maddie stayed in the paddock while Jonathan and Toby went back to the yard. She had butterflies of excitement in her stomach at the thought of trying out what they had learned from Mr. Stillwell. *Please let this work,* she whispered to herself.

Jonathan rode Firebird right up to the jump stands first to let her sniff at them. Then he circled away, trotting and cantering until she had warmed up. Maddie held her breath as they approached the canter poles. Firebird looked in a much better mood today than last time, but she might still object to the poles lying half-hidden in the grass.

She pricked up her ears in surprise when she saw the first, but Jonathan closed his legs against her and kept her cantering steadily. Maddie noticed the mare's stride shorten and become bouncier, two, three, four, before she popped neatly over the rail.

"Bravo!" she cried, jumping down from the fence and clapping her hands.

Jonathan circled Firebird close to Maddie. "Not bad for a first try. But I think the poles might be a bit close together. She had to shorten her stride to get over them, didn't she?"

Maddie nodded. "Shall I roll them apart?"

"Yes, please. Not too far, though."

She jogged over, wishing she could take off the apron from her riding habit to save her legs from melting under all the layers of cloth. She kicked the poles so that they were three and a half paces apart, and stepped back to let Jonathan ride over them again.

This time Firebird's strides landed her perfectly in between the poles, and she cleared the rail by miles. Maddie let out a cheer. The canter poles were working perfectly!

"Do you want to make it higher?" Jonathan called, so

Maddie tucked the end of the pole under her arm while she took out the nail and fixed the cup three holes above the first one. She did the same for the other end of the pole, and watched as Firebird bounced over the poles and sprang up over the fence as if it was no bigger than before.

"She's brilliant!" Maddie exclaimed, and Jonathan grinned at her.

"I don't think we need to make the upright any higher," he said. "But I'd love to see what she makes of a triple bar."

"Have we got enough stands?" Maddie asked.

Jonathan slid off Firebird and led her over to the jumps. "Toby and I only had time to make one set yesterday. But we can put the other pair of stands next to the oil drums," he suggested, handing the reins to Maddie. "I'll measure the distance first, though." He counted seventeen paces from the upright rail and dropped the pole on the ground. Then he rolled the oil drums over and rested the pole on top, leaving the drums lying on their sides. He heaved the stands into position behind them and put the second rail about ten inches higher than the first.

"There," he said, stepping back and dusting off his hands. "Our first double bar!"

Maddie held the right stirrup while he climbed onto Birdy again. The mare swished her tail and sidestepped as if she knew what was coming.

Jonathan turned her away and nudged her into a brisk

canter. "I'm not sure about the distance," he confessed as he passed Maddie. "Seventeen paces might be right for Nightwatchman, but Firebird has different length strides. Still, let's see what happens."

He brought her into the first fence, and this time she hardly seemed to notice the canter poles, except that yet again they put her in exactly the right place to take off over the upright rail. Maddie watched closely as they cantered toward the spread fence. Two strides, three, four . . . and a jerky little fifth stride before Firebird heaved herself into the air, knocking the front pole with her forelegs.

Jonathan reined her to a halt beside Maddie. "I think we need to shorten the distance and make her stick to four strides," he said. "That would have been four faults there, because she knocked the rail with her front legs. It's two faults if she hits the fence behind, according to the Show-Jumping Association rule book."

Maddie frowned. "Why only two faults if she knocks it with her hind legs?"

"I think it's to do with hunting. If a horse hits a fence with its front legs, it's more likely to turn a somersault and injure the rider. I guess it's not so bad if they drop their hind legs. And if they just touch the fence without knocking it down, that's half a fault."

"This is starting to feel like a maths lesson," Maddie joked.

She heaved at the oil drums to inch them forward, then moved the wooden stands into place behind the drums. Jonathan took Firebird through the whole combination again, poles, then upright, then four neat strides and the double bar, sailing over the rails as if they were no higher than Maddie's shoe.

She watched the chestnut mare canter around the field with her tail streaming behind her, and laughed out loud in delight. Firebird was brilliant, Jonathan was brilliant, and everything felt perfect.

"Thank you, Mr. Stillwell!" she shouted, tipping back her head. "Birdy's going to win the Gold Cup!"

22

A FORTNIGHT LATER, Firebird was jumping so high that Maddie could hardly reach to put the poles on the cups. She had started taking away the canter poles so that Jonathan had to rely on his own eye to measure the distance before each fence, although she put them back if Firebird started taking off too far away again. Toby and Jonathan had made three more sets of stands and painted them dazzling white, just as they would be in the competition. They were so bright against the green grass that Firebird spooked and slid into the fences a couple of times, sending the rails flying, but she soon got used to them.

There was a chance they'd meet a water jump in the competition instead of a triple bar, so Jonathan jumped Firebird over a broad stream that led into the fishing lake. The mare seemed to find this easier than the upright fences because she could gallop as fast as she liked, stretching out her neck and flattening her body as she sprang into the air.

Finally Jonathan decided that the training was going well enough to fill in the official entry forms for the Gold Cup.

Maddie helped him, writing *Firebird* where it said *Name of horse*, and *Major Theodore Harman* for the *Owner* and *Rider*.

Jonathan stared at the name as if it had been written in blood. Maddie guessed he was feeling guilty about using Theo's name in black and white. "You traveled with Theo's passport," she pointed out. "That was much more serious."

"It's not that," Jonathan said. "I just wish I could be riding her in my own name."

Maddie ran her finger along the edge of the form. "Well, *I'll* know it's you," she said. "And I couldn't be prouder of you if you were my real brother, I promise."

Jonathan reached over and squeezed her shoulder. "Thanks. I couldn't think of anyone I'd rather have as my sister than you." She grinned at him, and folded the form to slide it into the envelope.

"King George the Fifth, here we come!" she declared.

"Not before a few more training sessions," Jonathan warned. "But I thought we'd try something different today. Would you like to have a go at riding her?"

Maddie stared at him. "Really? Over the jumps?" She'd ridden Firebird around the estate lots of times because Jonathan said they shouldn't jump her more than three times a week, but she hadn't schooled her over the fences yet.

"Why not?" Jonathan led the way out to the yard and carried a sidesaddle over to Firebird's stable. Above the stable block, the sun was hidden behind thick yellow clouds, and a cold wind stirred the leaves of the beech trees at the edge of the drive.

There was a faint rumble of thunder, and Jonathan glanced up at the sky. "Sounds like there's a storm coming. Let's hope we don't get caught in it."

When he lifted Maddie into the saddle, she was shaking so much at the thought of jumping Firebird that she could hardly hold the reins.

"Come on," coaxed Jonathan. "You know as much as I do about riding over those fences."

"Not in a sidesaddle!" Maddie protested.

"Don't think about being in a sidesaddle, just think about riding." He checked the girth was tight enough, then stepped back to let her walk across the cobbles.

Toby looked over the door of Matchstick's stable as they went past. "Good luck, Miss Maddie!" he called.

Maddie felt her cheeks burn. "Have you told everyone?" she hissed to Jonathan.

He grinned. "Only Toby."

She looked at him for a moment. "What else have you told him?" She understood now why Jonathan was so relaxed in Toby's company; they came from almost identical backgrounds, both growing up around horses. But had he confided in him that he wasn't Theo? For a second, Maddie felt jealous, as if Jonathan's secret should be hers alone to keep.

Jonathan didn't reply while he opened the gate to the schooling paddock. Then he stood with his hand on the latch. "I've not told him anything," he said, so quietly that Maddie had to strain to hear. "I'm not proud of this, you know."

"I didn't think you were," she said. "It's just strange, that no one else knows."

Jonathan swung the gate closed. "I thought it would get easier, but it hasn't," he confessed. "I . . . I don't know if I can keep lying like this. It's not fair on your grandparents or Louisa."

"You can't tell them yet! What about the Gold Cup?" Maddie didn't care if she was being selfish. Firebird was too important to her. If her grandparents found out the truth, there was no way Jonathan would be able to stay at Sefton Park.

He shrugged. "After the competition, then. I want Birdy to win as much as you do, I promise, Maddie."

She gathered up the reins and nudged Firebird into a smooth, swinging walk, concentrating hard on sitting straight. She didn't want to think about saying good-bye to Jonathan ever.

"Trot her on," he called from the middle of the field. Birdy tossed her head and sprang forward, taking Maddie by surprise. She bounced in the saddle as she scrambled to shorten her reins.

"You're a wobbly disgrace!" Jonathan teased, echoing Mr. Stillwell's words.

Maddie grinned and tucked her right leg closer into Birdy's shoulder, feeling her grip tighten on the top pommel. She let Firebird extend her stride as they trotted across the paddock, encouraging the mare to flick out her front hooves and arch her neck. "Dance, little one, dance," Maddie whispered under her breath.

As she circled at the top of the field, she saw Jonathan laying out canter poles in front of the first upright fence. He had lowered the rail so it was about three feet off the ground. He'd also taken the poles away from the second set of stands, leaving just one fence.

"Take her over this first, then I'll put up the others," he called.

Maddie nodded and squeezed Firebird into a canter. A gust of wind buffeted them as they turned away from the shelter of the hedge, and Firebird skittered sideways. "Easy, girl," Maddie soothed, running one hand down her mane.

Firebird's ears flicked back as another clap of thunder growled, closer this time. The clouds above the hills on the horizon were dark gray, with pale yellow streaks slanting down to the ground. It looked as if it was already raining on the flat-topped ridge known as Coombe Gibbet.

"Come on," Jonathan called. "We'll get a soaking if you don't hurry up."

Maddie turned Firebird toward the fence. Her pace quickened when she saw the rail, and Maddie was about to check her when she remembered that the canter poles would do that. Sure enough, the mare's ears twitched when she saw the first one, and she shortened her stride to bounce over each one. Maddie sat very still, just as she had seen Jonathan do, and let the poles put Firebird in the right place to take off over the jump. *Fold to the right,* she reminded herself, and this time it seemed easy as Firebird gathered her hindquarters under her and sprang over the rail with the glorious soaring feeling Maddie remembered from the hedge and the tree trunk.

"That was brilliant!" she exclaimed as she slowed to a walk. She wished Louisa was there to see her, but Lou had gone to London to stay with Rosie for a few days.

"You look like you've been doing this for years," Jonathan remarked, smiling. "Do you want to try again?"

Maddie nodded. This time she counted the strides more carefully, keeping Firebird steady before they reached the poles and closing her left heel against her when she felt the mare drifting off-center.

"Good work," Jonathan commented when she had cleared the jump, and Maddie went bright red with pride. He put up a second fence three strides from the first, and Maddie found that she had to kick as soon as she landed to keep Firebird cantering strongly enough to clear the second. When Jonathan made the second fence into a spread, Maddie kicked too hard and Firebird flattened, knocking the front rail with her forelegs.

"Rats!" she cursed, reining the mare to a halt.

"Don't worry," said Jonathan. "Try again, but this time sit up straight after the first jump and keep her quarters underneath her."

Maddie turned toward the fences again. The nerves in her tummy had vanished, replaced by a feeling of excitement that seemed to make her think more clearly than usual. She loved having to figure out the best way to approach the fences, how to balance Firebird's speed against the spring in her hindquarters. This time they sailed over the second fence, and Maddie clapped her hand against the mare's neck in delight.

"It's like flying!" she cried.

The wind threw a handful of icy rain at her face, and Firebird swung her quarters into it with a snort. The sky was almost black now, and the leaves rattled in the hedge. Suddenly a blaze of lightning lit up the sky. Firebird whipped right around with a terrified whinny, and Maddie caught sight of a dark-clad figure standing beside the fence. She gasped, then realized it was Matthew, her grandfather's butler. He raised his hand and called something but his words were lost in a deafening clap of thunder. Maddie tried to urge Firebird closer but the mare stood stiff-legged with fear.

Jonathan jogged over to them. "You'd better go and see what Matthew wants," he said, raising his voice above the wind. "I'll take Birdy for a walk around the paddock to cool her off." He held out his hand to help Maddie jump down, then looped the reins over the mare's head and clicked encouragingly at her. Firebird moved off with a jerk, her eyes rolling as lightning flashed again, followed almost at once by a sharp-edged crack of thunder.

Maddie wrapped the apron of her riding habit around her and held it with one hand as she ran across the field to Matthew. With her other hand she clutched her bowler hat, afraid that the wind would whip it away.

"Your grandmother sent me to fetch you in from the storm," the butler said when she reached the fence. Maddie nodded, too breathless to speak, and ran along the fence to let herself out of the gate. Rain had started to fall, fitfully at first, then harder, pattering on the sunbaked ground. On the far side of the paddock, Jonathan was leading Firebird beside the hedge, keeping close to her head as she danced on tiptoe with her tail streaming out.

"Are you ready, Miss Madeline?" said Matthew, and she turned to see him opening a large black umbrella. Sheltering underneath it as it was buffeted by the wind, they struggled across the lawn to the side door. Much as Maddie had been enjoying the jumping lesson, she couldn't help feeling relieved when they were out of the rain. She knew Jonathan would soon have Firebird in her warm stable, with a rug to help her dry off.

She went to thank her grandmother for sending Matthew out with the umbrella.

Lady Ella was sitting on the sofa in her salon with Pompidou beside her. "Oh good, you're out of that dreadful weather," she greeted Maddie, beckoning her into the room. "Shall I ring for some tea?"

"Thank you, Grandmama," said Maddie, realizing that she felt chilled to the bone under her rain-soaked riding habit. She sat carefully on a spindly-legged chair beside her grandmother and watched Jonathan and Firebird disappearing under the arch that led to the stable yard on the far side of the paddock.

The bell rang loudly at the front door, and Maddie heard Matthew walking across the parquet floor to answer it. From her grandmother's frown, Maddie guessed that she wasn't expecting visitors.

There were hushed voices in the hall, then a tap at the salon door.

"Come!" Maddie's grandmother called.

Matthew entered, looking rather red in the face. "Lady Ella, there is a gentleman here. Would you like to see him while I fetch Sir Wilfred?"

"Is my husband expecting anyone this morning?" asked Lady Ella.

"No, I don't think so, ma'am. Shall I show the gentleman in?"

Lady Ella looked surprised. "Well, yes, of course." The butler ran his fingers around his collar as if it was strangling him. "Is there something the matter, Matthew?"

The butler coughed. "It's the visitor, ma'am. He says his name is Theodore Harman."

23

MADDIE CLOSED HER EYES. The salon dipped and swirled around her, sending her stomach leaping into her throat.

"There must be some mistake," Lady Ella insisted with a small shake of her head. "Please, call Sir Wilfred."

"Ella?" said a voice from the hall. The door opened wider, pushed by an unseen hand, and a thin young man walked into the room. He had Louisa's dark brown hair, and the same gray eyes. It was Theo.

Lady Ella stared at him, openmouthed.

"Madeline," said Theo, looking at Maddie, and his voice was flat as if he was just stating a fact. She didn't know what to say, so she nodded.

There were rapid footsteps in the hall, and Matthew stepped back with relief in his face as Sir Wilfred came in. "What's going on?" he demanded.

The visitor turned to face him, and Sir Wilfred went white.

"Hello, Wilfred," said Theo. He made no attempt to shake hands, but kept his arms by his sides. His long gray coat had a tear down one sleeve that had been mended with thread a shade darker than the fabric. He wore battered leather boots, and his head was bare. His face was tanned as deeply as Jonathan's, but without the scar.

Maddie dug her nails into her palms. *Why had Jonathan told her Theo was dead?*

"There's someone else here, isn't there?" Theo said quietly, and his voice was unfamiliar, deeper than Maddie remembered and with a hint of an accent.

Sir Wilfred walked over to stand beside his wife and rested one hand on her shoulder. "Someone came," he agreed, his words falling like stones into water. "He said he was Theo, and we had no reason to doubt him."

Theo's mouth twisted. "His name is Jonathan Price. I told you about him in my letters." He shook his head, looking utterly bewildered. "I . . . I don't believe he really did it," he murmured. "After everything that happened . . ."

Sir Wilfred took a step forward. "Now look here," he said sternly. "Are you saying we've had a stranger living here for the past four months? Why should I believe you any more than him?"

There was a flash of desperation in Theo's eyes. He spun around and stabbed his finger at a silver-framed photograph on top of the piano. It showed Maddie's parents posing on a sunny riverbank; her mother was wearing a striped dress and holding a parasol, and her father stood with one foot on an upturned boat.

"That photograph was taken at Godstow, near Oxford," he said. "I was seventeen, Lou was fourteen, and Maddie was seven. There was another picture taken of all of us, but you decided not to frame it because Maddie was pulling a face. Our dog, Jester, had jumped into the river and splashed her new dress." He whirled back to face them. "How would I know all that if I hadn't been there? You have to believe me!"

"Theo could have told you about the photograph," Sir Wilfred pointed out, though it sounded as if the words were choking him.

Theo drew in his breath with a hiss. "And that one," he said, pointing to another photograph, "was taken at Christmas in 1913." Maddie didn't need to look to know which photograph he meant. That had been the last Christmas they'd had at Sefton Park before the war; all her family, including her grandparents, were sitting around the table in the dining room, about to divide the plum pudding.

Theo rubbed his hand over his eyes, suddenly looking bone-weary. "Whatever that man has said to convince you he's part of this family, he's lying."

Maddie felt sick.

Lady Ella clasped one hand to her throat. "I don't understand," she whispered. "How can this have happened?"

Theo spread his hands helplessly. "I don't know. I spent every moment of my journey home hoping he hadn't done anything more than steal my passport and my wages. But he did a lot more, didn't he?"

Sir Wilfred let go of his wife's shoulder and lowered himself heavily into a chair. "Start at the beginning, and tell us everything," he ordered.

Lady Ella stirred, and held out one hand. "Wait," she said, speaking in barely more than a whisper. She looked pleadingly across the room at the visitor, and her lips moved as if she was trying to say his name, but no words came out. Then she gestured to the sofa. "Please, sit down. Matthew, fetch some tea and take the . . . the gentleman's coat. He's soaked through."

The butler bowed and stepped forward as Theo shrugged off his rain-spattered overcoat, then lowered himself onto the sofa. He looked wary and hunted, and Maddie felt a pang of sympathy for him.

"The last time I saw Jonathan was the morning before the explosion in the mine," he began. "I presume he told you about that?"

Lady Ella nodded, leaning forward as if she wanted to hear every word clearly.

"The tunnel I was in was a long way from the main shaft. When the roof collapsed, I was knocked out. If anyone dug near enough to call out to me, I didn't hear them." Theo's voice was oddly expressionless, as if he was describing something that had happened to somebody else.

"One of the roof beams had fallen on my leg and I could feel my ankle was broken, so even when I woke up, I couldn't move. I don't know how long I stayed down there. When my water bottle ran out, I knew I had to get out. I dragged myself free and dug my way along the tunnel, away from the main shaft. I knew it would be harder to get out that way, closer to the explosion. Eventually I got to one of the air shafts and climbed up to the surface. Some bushmen found me and took me to their village where they looked after me until I was well enough to walk back to the mine. That was nearly a month after the accident, and when I got back, I found that Theodore Harman had already been rescued and sent home to England." He looked down at his hands.

"Everyone was astonished to see me. They'd all long given me up for dead—or at least, they'd given Jonathan Price up for dead. The foreman, Gerald McNicholas, recognized me at once. He hadn't seen Jonathan when he was in hospital, so he didn't know the wrong man had been given my name by the rescuers. Or that someone had stolen my identity."

"You knew what Price had done, then?" said Sir Wilfred.

Theo looked up, and Maddie winced at the pain in his eyes. "The doctor at the hospital told me he'd booked a boat ticket to England in the name of Theodore Harman, and given the man my passport. It could only have been Jonathan. We always used to joke about how much we looked alike. I don't think he meant to make trouble for me. As far as he knew, I was dead. There wouldn't be anyone else needing that passport."

"Why didn't you send a telegram from Africa, warning us about the mistake?" asked Lady Ella.

Theo blinked. "Because I never thought Jonathan would take it this far. It wasn't his fault that the people in the hospital thought he was me, and maybe it was easiest for him to use my passport to come back to England, but to keep lying? To come here and pretend to be me?" His voice rose, and he took a deep breath before going on more quietly, "I spent the last three months refusing to believe that the man I thought was my best friend would steal everything from me—even my name and my family. But I was wrong."

Maddie felt a surge of protectiveness toward Jonathan. He'd taken nothing that they hadn't been willing to give! She jumped to her feet, and her grandparents looked at her in surprise, as if they'd forgotten she was there.

"I . . . please, excuse me," she stammered, and her grandmother nodded vaguely.

Maddie pushed past Theo—the real Theo—and blundered out of the salon. How could this be happening? She blinked away tears and kept running, through the lobby and out of the side door. The rain had stopped, but water dripped off the roof and the lawn was shiny with puddles.

"Jonathan! Jonathan!" she shouted. She pelted around the

corner to see him coming out of Firebird's stable with her saddle over his arm. His jacket was drenched and clung to his body, and his hair was slicked down over his forehead. The color drained from his face when he realized she had called him by his proper name.

"He's alive, Jonathan!" Maddie sobbed breathlessly. "Theo's come back!"

Jonathan opened his mouth to say something, then shut it again and stared past her. Maddie spun around and saw Sir Wilfred and Theo marching into the yard.

"You're alive!" Jonathan whispered, putting down the saddle. "Thank God, you're alive!"

"It would seem that I am." Theo's words were like chips of ice. "But I guess that was the last thing you were expecting."

Maddie stood between the two men and looked from one to the other. They were uncannily alike in appearance—slightly built, not tall, with narrow heads and short dark hair, and eyes the color of water under a rainy sky.

Jonathan looked down at the ground, his arms hanging loose by his sides. "I never—"

Maddie realized that her grandfather was studying her closely, his forehead creased in a frown. "You called him Jonathan, and you tried to warn him," he said. "You knew all along, didn't you? How could you do something like that? Let an . . . an impostor into our house, steal our name—"

"Wilfred, stop it. You can't blame Madeline," said a voice from the edge of the yard. Lady Ella stood there with a shawl clutched untidily around her shoulders. Her lips were so bloodless they looked transparent. She walked forward unsteadily and reached out a hand to Theo, but let it fall back before she touched him.

"I'm sorry," she whispered. "How could I not know my own grandson?"

"None of this is our fault," Sir Wilfred broke in robustly. "Please, Ella, don't distress yourself."

Lady Ella turned to him, and her eyes were wild. "Don't distress myself? We brought a stranger into our home, when all the time our real grandson had been left to die!"

Theo held up his hand. "Ella, stop. Wilfred is right. This isn't your fault." He shot a furious glare at Jonathan. "How could you do this to me? Didn't you stop to think what you were doing?"

Jonathan pushed his hand through his hair. "I didn't think at all," he confessed, so quietly he could hardly be heard above the dripping gutter.

"Tell them you didn't plan to take Theo's place," Maddie begged. "Tell them we called you Theo first, and made it too difficult for you to say who you really were."

Sir Wilfred took a step toward Maddie, his face thunderous. "You cannot defend this man!" he roared. "Toby!"

The head groom was standing in the doorway to the tack room, his eyes on stalks. "Yes, sir?"

"Send Ollie to fetch the police."

"No, Grandpapa!" Maddie cried. "You can't!" She turned to Theo. "Tell him, Theo. There's no harm been done, nothing's been stolen. Please!"

Her brother shook his head. "This man is a liar and a thief, Maddie. How can I forgive him? He has been my best friend for the last seven years, but now I don't feel as if I know him at all."

Tears poured down Maddie's face, and she wiped them away crossly. Behind Theo, she saw Ollie wheel a bicycle out of the garage behind the stable block and start pedaling furiously down the drive. It wouldn't be long before the police were here, and Jonathan was arrested.

Maddie ran over and grabbed Jonathan's hands. They were icy cold, still wet from leading Firebird in the storm. "You have to go now, before the police come. Do you understand?"

He started to shake his head, but she gave him a little push. "Please," she begged.

Out of the corner of her eye, she saw Theo take a step forward. Maddie shoved Jonathan harder. "Run!" she hissed, and he spun around and raced for the archway that led to the paddocks.

"Jonathan, stop! This isn't going to help!" Theo took off

after him, his long coat flailing behind like a torn sail. He ran unevenly, favoring his left leg, and Maddie guessed his ankle hadn't fully healed from the accident in the mine.

She watched Jonathan vault over the gate into the schooling paddock, gripping the top rail with one hand and swinging his legs up without breaking his stride. Then he took off across the field, head down and arms pumping. His wet clothes didn't hamper him as much as Theo's lame ankle. He was barely halfway across when Jonathan reached the far gate and vanished into the neighboring field.

Limping heavily now, Theo stumbled to a halt beside the gate on the other side of the field and leaned against it, resting his head on his arms.

Maddie felt her grandfather come to stand beside her. She glanced at him and flinched when she saw that his face was black as thunder. "I will not forget this, Madeline," he said quietly. "The police will catch that man, you do know that, don't you?"

She nodded miserably.

Theo started to walk back across the field. Lady Ella went to the archway to meet him, holding out her arms. Theo looked at her for a long moment, then walked past her into the yard.

Maddie felt a pain in her chest that made her want to kneel down. Suddenly she knew what writers meant when they said someone's heart was breaking.

"Come inside, Madeline," said her grandmother.

Maddie stumbled after her, trying to picture how far Jonathan might have run. Was he at the lake yet? He should turn left along the track with the fallen tree, and head for the pine plantation at the edge of the estate. The trees stretched all the way down to the canal, and he might be able to get onto a barge going to London. . . . Maddie tried to remember if she had shown Jonathan the path through the plantation on one of their rides.

She was taking off her shoes in the cloakroom before she realized that she had run outside in her house shoes in the first place. Putting them back on, she walked into the hallway. Her grandparents and Theo were in the salon and Maddie paused by the door.

"You should rest, Theo," Lady Ella was saying. "I'll have one of the maids make up a bed for you."

"I'm fine, Ella. The police will want to speak to me when they arrive."

There was the sound of footsteps behind Maddie. "Excuse me, Miss Madeline," said Matthew. She turned to see him holding a tray with a decanter of brandy and three small glasses. "I thought this might be needed more than tea," he explained, and Maddie nodded.

"Madeline? Are you there?" called her grandmother, and reluctantly Maddie pushed open the door and went in.

She felt three pairs of eyes burn into her.

Theo spoke first, but when he did, he didn't sound angry. Instead he sounded bewildered and tired. "When did you find out who he really was?" he asked.

There was no point lying. "At the ball," Maddie replied. "He didn't tell me—I guessed." She wondered if that made it any better.

"Why didn't you tell us?" gasped her grandmother, ignoring the glass of brandy that Matthew held out to her.

Because he made us all happy again! Maddie wanted to scream. *Grandfather told me you had started living again because of him. How could I take that away from you?*

"I . . . I don't know. It seemed better not to."

Her grandfather frowned. "Better not to tell us? Better that we should let a stranger live in our home, trick his way into our family? No, Madeline, that was not better, not in any way."

Maddie couldn't bear the disapproval, the aching disappointment, the barely contained anger in his voice. But she still couldn't believe that she had done the wrong thing. Jonathan wasn't a criminal, and he didn't deserve to be hunted down and taken to jail.

"I'm sorry!" she blurted out, and spinning around, she ran out of the salon.

She made her way blindly to Firebird's stable, seeking comfort from the one thing that hadn't changed, when nothing else would ever be the same again.

At first she thought the stable was empty because the mare didn't come over to the door to greet her like she usually did. "Birdy?" she called softly.

There was a strange sort of grunt in the shadows, and Maddie stiffened. Something was wrong! She unbolted the door and slipped inside. Firebird was standing at the far side of the stable with her head hanging down. Her coat looked as if it was still wet from the rain, but when Maddie laid her hand on the mare's neck, she realized it was slippery with sweat, and the skin felt as if it was burning from inside.

"Birdy, what's wrong?" she whispered, staring in horror at the mare's half-closed eyes. In answer, Firebird twitched her head and groaned, and a spasm passed along her flank like a ripple in water.

Maddie rushed to the door. "Come quickly, Toby! Anyone! Firebird is sick!"

———◦◦◦———

MADDIE'S HANDS WERE SHAKING so much she could barely undo the bolt to let herself out. She fled across the yard, still calling for Toby. When he appeared around the edge of the stable block, she fell into his arms with relief.

"Steady on, now." He stepped back and held her at arm's length. "The police will be here soon. It's all being dealt with, miss," he added awkwardly.

"It's not that!" Maddie sobbed. "It's Firebird! She's sick!"

Toby ran to the stable door and looked over. When he turned around, his face was serious. "It's colic," he said. Maddie stared at him, not understanding. "It's like really bad stomach cramps," he explained. "She must have drunk too soon after the ride, when she was still hot. The shock of the cold water could have done this to her."

"Is she going to be all right?"

Toby glanced into the stable once more. "It looks like a bad one, I'm afraid," he said, and Maddie felt her knees buckle. "But there's something we can try," the groom went on. He hurried to the tack room and reappeared with a bottle in one hand and a halter slung over his shoulder. "We'll dose her with this drench," he said, nodding to the green glass bottle. "It won't be easy—horses don't like taking medicine at the best of times, so you'll have to help me. If we're lucky, it will ease the cramps in her belly."

Maddie followed him at a run back to the stable. The mare had sunk to her knees, her nose buried in the straw.

"We have to get her standing," Toby said. "If she rolls, she could twist her gut, and I won't be able to do anything for her then."

Maddie stared at him in horror. "She can't die! Please, don't let her die!"

Toby was slipping the halter over Firebird's head. "Come on, girl," he ordered, giving the rope a tug.

Maddie scrambled over to the mare, nearly tripping when her skirt twisted around her legs. With a hiss of exasperation, she wrenched at the buttons and unwound the heavy apron from her hips, dropping it in a corner of the stable. She was perfectly decent in breeches and short riding boots.

"Get up, Birdy," she pleaded, crouching by the mare's shoulder and leaning against her to rock Firebird's weight onto her forelegs.

Firebird grunted and her hind hooves scraped in the straw, but she didn't try to stand. Toby took hold of the halter and hauled on it. Firebird's head was twisted uncomfortably in the air, and her eyes rolled. A trickle of sweat ran down her shoulder.

"Please, Firebird," Maddie whispered. "You can't stay lying down."

With a huge effort, the mare stretched out her neck and heaved herself up until she was propped on her forelegs. Toby gave another tug on the halter and suddenly Firebird was on her feet, trembling the length of her body. Her coat was black with sweat, and her flanks were tucked up underneath her so that her ribs jutted out.

Toby whistled between his teeth. "We need to give her the drench"—he nodded to the bottle that was propped against the water bucket—"then keep her walking."

Maddie picked up the bottle and handed it to him. Toby forced Firebird's head up until her nose was higher than her ears. "Come an' hold her," he grunted to Maddie, shifting aside so she could stand under Firebird's chin.

The mare's head felt heavier than a rock, and Maddie blinked beads of sweat out of her eyes as Firebird wrestled against her, flicking her soaked mane into Maddie's face. Toby put one hand on Firebird's nose and tipped the bottle into her mouth. Firebird wrenched her head away as the glass knocked against her teeth, pouring bitter-smelling liquid onto Maddie's head.

"Oh!" she gasped, trying to duck and hold on to the halter at the same time.

Toby cursed under his breath and struggled to keep his footing in the straw. "Well, let's hope some went down. Come on, let's get her outside."

Maddie gave her arms a shake to bring back the feeling in her hands. Then she took the lead rope and clicked at Firebird to make her walk out of the stable. The mare stumbled forward with a groan, but halfway to the door she stopped and twisted her head to look at her stomach. She kicked at her belly with one hind hoof, then restlessly stamped a foreleg.

"Quick," said Toby, swinging open the door. "She's trying to roll."

Terrified, Maddie yanked at the lead rope. "Walk on, Birdy!" she cried, and to her relief the mare lurched toward the door and out into the air.

It was cold outside after the muggy stable, and Maddie gasped. Her legs felt very exposed in just her breeches, but she didn't want to put her skirt back on because she wouldn't be able to walk as easily.

The mare stood outside the stable with her head down and her front legs braced on the cobbles. Toby flapped his arms behind her. "Walk on, girl!" he ordered.

Maddie pulled the rope, and Firebird staggered forward, her nostrils flared and her eyes rolling. Another spasm flickered across her flank, and she stared straight at Maddie, her brown eyes pleading with her to take away the pain.

"Oh, Birdy, I can't," Maddie whispered. "You have to keep walking, please." She blinked hard and started trudging along the edge of the yard, around the corner and past Thor's stable toward the tack room. Firebird plodded beside her, every now and then snatching her head around to bite at her stomach or stopping to stamp uneasily, but Maddie urged her on until her throat was raw with pleading and her feet ached.

The clock on the dovecote above the archway chimed four, and Maddie realized she had missed lunch. Above the uneven rapping of Firebird's hooves on the cobbles, she heard the sound of a motorcar crunching down the drive, and she peered under the mare's neck to see who it was.

It was a large, gray vehicle that Maddie hadn't seen before, and when it rolled to a halt beside the fountain, two men in dark blue uniforms climbed out. The police! Maddie realized she had almost forgotten about Jonathan, fleeing for his life.

The policemen disappeared inside the house, and Maddie kept leading Firebird around the yard. The mare seemed to be getting slower and slower, and they were going around the corner by the garage when her knees suddenly buckled and she sagged toward the cobbles.

"Toby, help!" Maddie shouted as the lead rope went taut in her hands.

Toby rushed over. "Keep her head up!" he ordered, putting both hands on Firebird's quarters. He gave her a tremendous shove, almost pitching the mare onto her nose, and Maddie leaped backward as the lead rope slackened.

"Good girl!" she urged. "You can do it!"

With a grunt, Firebird stumbled forward. Toby walked on the other side of her neck, one hand resting on her mane, until it looked as if she would keep going. His eyes met Maddie's, and she swallowed hard when she saw the concern in them.

"She's getting worse," he said quietly. "I'll have to fetch the vet myself if Ollie doesn't get back soon."

Maddie nodded, not trusting herself to speak.

She turned at the sound of footsteps and saw her grandfather and Theo approaching with the two police officers. The taller one lifted his helmet to Maddie. "Good afternoon, miss," he said. "My name is Sergeant Walters. Do you mind if we ask you some questions?"

Maddie blinked. "I suppose not. But I have to keep this horse moving. She has colic." She was a bit surprised by how calm she sounded.

Toby reached out and took the lead rope from her. "Go on, Maddie," he said. "I'll keep walking the mare."

The sergeant's eyes narrowed as he looked at Firebird. He turned to Maddie's grandfather. "Is this the horse Price brought with him, sir?"

Sir Wilfred nodded. Sergeant Walters turned to his colleague. "Make a note of that, Burness." The other policeman nodded and flipped open his notebook.

Maddie let her fingers trail along Firebird's neck as the mare staggered away next to Toby. She looked up at Sergeant Walters, trying not to let him see how much she was shaking inside. Would she have to go to prison for what she had done? Her head spun and the cobbles swam, until she felt a hand grip her elbow and hold her upright. She turned and gazed straight into her brother's gray eyes.

"You have to tell them everything, Maddie," he said, and she nodded.

"I understand you knew that the man claiming to be Theodore Harman was, in fact, Jonathan Price," Sergeant Walters began.

"Y-yes, I did," Maddie stammered, feeling sick.

"When did you find this out?"

"About a month ago. At my sister's engagement ball."

The policeman raised his eyebrows. "But you said nothing to your grandparents?"

"No," whispered Maddie.

"And why was that?" Sergeant Walters pressed. "Did Price threaten you in some way? Did he say he would hurt you or your family if they learned the truth?"

Maddie shook her head vehemently. "It wasn't like that! Jonathan would never hurt me or any of my family. I didn't tell anyone because he told me Theo was dead, and I . . . I thought it would hurt everyone more to know the truth. Jonathan wasn't doing any harm."

The policeman with the notebook made a doubtful hissing noise through his lips.

"Well, miss, I hope you understand now just how serious this crime is and how much damage Price has done to your family." Sergeant Walters frowned at Maddie, and she wondered if he was about to arrest her. Her heart started thudding painfully.

"Your grandparents have been most insistent that you aren't punished for what you have done," he went on, and Maddie felt a rush of relief that she wasn't going to be put in jail, "but you need to tell us everything you know about Price. Have you any idea where he might go? Did he mention any friends who would hide him? Any places where he had a stash of money or connections to get out of the country?"

Maddie stared at the policeman in alarm. "I don't know! We never talked about that sort of thing. I promise, I don't know where he might go."

Sergeant Walters looked as if he didn't believe her, but Theo stepped forward before he could ask any more questions. "Whatever Madeline knew about Price's real identity, I don't think she'd do anything to protect a criminal," he said. "And surely Price wouldn't have told her anything in case the truth came out, and she was asked exactly this sort of thing. He's not lacking in intelligence—he'd have known Madeline would be questioned by the police."

Both policemen nodded thoughtfully, and Maddie shot a grateful glance at Theo, but he kept his eyes on the police sergeant. Behind her, she heard Firebird's step falter on the cobbles and she whirled around to see the mare standing stiff-legged on the other side of the yard, Toby tugging helplessly at her headcollar.

"Please, I have to see to the mare," Maddie blurted out, and when Sergeant Walters nodded she rushed over and put both hands on Firebird's shoulder. "Come on, Birdy!" she puffed, and the mare staggered forward with a lurch that nearly sent Maddie onto her knees.

"Well done, miss," said Toby. He waited until Firebird had made it to the corner of the yard before handing the lead rope to Maddie. "I'm going for the vet," he said. "You keep walking her."

Maddie nodded. Toby ran across the yard to the tack room, and a few seconds later she heard Thor's stable door open and close. Theo and her grandfather had left the yard with the policemen, and shortly afterward the motorcar started up and made its way down the drive again.

Maddie kept trudging around the yard, only stopping when she heard the clatter of hooves on the cobbles. Toby was swinging himself onto Thor's back. "I'll be back as quick as I can," he promised as he kicked the tall black gelding into a gallop.

Firebird shifted restlessly as Thor went past, and swung her head around to nip at her flank. At once Maddie pulled on the lead rope and clicked to make her walk on.

They had done another half dozen circuits of the yard when Ollie appeared, red in the face from his long cycle ride. "Those policemen didn't even offer me a lift when I asked them to come!" he grumbled, jumping off the bicycle and leaning it against the water butt. He stopped dead when he saw Maddie leading Firebird around.

"What's going on?" he demanded.

"Firebird's got colic," Maddie explained. "Toby's taken Thor to fetch the vet."

Ollie came over and laid his hand on Firebird's flank. "She's got it bad, too. Look, miss, you're both exhausted. It won't do you any good to keep on walking. Why don't you take her into her stable for a rest?"

"But she might lie down!" Maddie protested. She didn't care how much her feet hurt, there was no way she wanted to risk Firebird rolling and twisting her gut.

Ollie shook his head. "You'll do as much damage keeping her walking in this state. Look at her!"

It was true, Firebird looked on the verge of collapse. Her head hung lower than her knees, and her coat was matted with sweat.

"Go on, take her in," he urged. "Even if it's just for half an hour. I'll fetch a blanket to keep her warm. But don't let her eat anything, that'll just make the pain worse."

Maddie led Firebird wearily over to her stable. The mare stood in the middle of the straw, trembling, and Maddie leaned her forehead against Firebird's scorching, sticky neck. "Oh, Birdy, I don't know what to do!" she whispered, shutting her eyes and feeling hot tears pooling under her eyelids.

She straightened up as Ollie came into the stable with a horse blanket. "You all right to stay with her, Miss Maddie?" he asked, giving her a quick glance as he draped the blanket over Firebird's quarters.

Maddie nodded. "I'm not leaving her now."

"Right ho. I'll be feeding the other horses if you need me." Outside, the clock chimed eight. Ollie frowned. "The vet should be here by now. I 'ope Toby hasn't run into trouble."

Maddie bit her lip. That was all they needed. The vet had to come tonight!

Ollie let himself out of the stable, and she let her head rest on Firebird's neck once more. The mare seemed too tired to do anything but stand stock-still with her eyes half closed.

Maddie heard rapid footsteps approaching across the yard and turned, expecting to see Ollie, or someone from the house sent to call her in for dinner. Twilight had thickened to darkness outside, and Ollie had lit the lanterns that hung from the eaves of the stables, flooding the yard with pale yellow light.

When she saw who was looking over the stable door, Maddie nearly fell over.

"Jonathan!"

———— ∞∞∞ ————

"How bad is she?" Jonathan slipped into the stable and bolted the door behind him.

"Very," Maddie admitted. "I've been walking her, but Ollie said she's too exhausted to keep going."

"I think Ollie's right," said Jonathan. He ran his hand down Birdy's shoulder. "You poor old girl."

"Toby's gone to fetch the vet," Maddie explained.

Jonathan nodded. "I know. I'd got as far as Miller's Farm on the other side of the canal when I heard a horse coming up fast behind me. I . . . I thought it was someone chasing me so I hid in a barn. I heard Toby asking a farmworker if anyone knew where the vet was, and someone told him he'd been called out to the other side of Newbury. Toby stayed long enough to tell them what the trouble was back here before setting off again. When he said there was a horse with colic, I guessed it was Birdy." He untangled a knot in Firebird's mane. "It's my fault. I forgot to take her water bucket out of the stable until she'd cooled down properly."

Maddie grabbed hold of his sleeve. His clothes still felt

damp. "You shouldn't have come back!"

Jonathan looked at her, his eyes dark and unreadable. "I couldn't leave her," he said quietly.

"But if anyone finds you here, you'll be arrested!"

Jonathan shrugged. "I'll be gone by the morning, as long as we get this mare sorted out." He took off his jacket and rolled up his sleeves. Firebird let out another groan and swished her tail. "Right, it looks like we don't have much time. Has Toby dosed her with anything so far?"

"He tried, but I don't think much went in," said Maddie. She picked up the empty bottle where it was lying in a corner. "Here."

Jonathan sniffed at the top of the bottle. "Smells like paraffin," he said. "It's a start, but I think there's something else we can try."

"Have you cured horses with colic before?" Maddie asked.

He nodded. "Lots of times, back in Wales. Not so much in Africa, but the food's not so rich for them out there, and we didn't see much rain." He grimaced and started twisting a handful of hay into a wisp, plaiting the ends into themselves until he was left with a smooth, dense pad. "I'm going to rub her with this to keep her circulation going and relax her muscles," he explained as he wiped the wisp over Firebird's belly in quick, regular strokes. "And I want you to fetch me some things from the tack room. We're going to make up a different drench." He paused and looked at Maddie. "Do you think you can do that?"

She knew he was asking if she could do it without drawing the whole household down on top of them. She nodded. "But we'll have to be careful," she warned. "Ollie's in one of the other stables."

Jonathan went back to grooming Firebird with the wisp. "Right, we need linseed oil, vinegar, and a pinch of belladonna. There should be some in the tack room. And if you can find any Milk of Magnesia, that would be really useful."

Maddie stared at him in surprise. She knew her grandfather dosed himself from a little blue bottle of Phillips' Milk of Magnesia after a particularly rich meal, but she didn't see how she was going to get into the house and smuggle it out of his bathroom. Jonathan seemed to guess what she was thinking because he added, "We might have to do without that one. But the other things should help."

Linseed oil, vinegar, belladonna, Maddie repeated to herself as she hurried across the yard.

Ollie was in Canterbury's stable, emptying the gelding's evening feed into his manger. "Everything all right?" he called as Maddie scuttled past.

"Oh yes, fine," she called back, hoping he hadn't noticed how high and squeaky her voice sounded.

She reached the tack room and gazed helplessly at the row

of cupboards along one wall. It was going to take forever to search through all those!

"Miss Madeline?" said a voice behind her, and she spun around to see Matthew wrapped in his greatcoat, with a lantern in one hand. "Your grandmother sent me to tell you that it is time for dinner."

"Please, could you tell her I shan't be coming in?" Maddie said breathlessly. "The mare is still sick, and I want to stay with her until the vet arrives."

Matthew glanced across the yard toward Firebird's stable, and Maddie crossed her fingers behind her back that he wouldn't see Jonathan. When the butler looked back at her, his eyes were sympathetic. "I understand. Shall I send out some sandwiches?"

She was about to say no when she realized that Jonathan might be hungry. "Thank you," she said. "That would be kind."

Matthew nodded. "I am very sorry for . . . for everything that has happened," he said quietly.

"I know," Maddie said. She was determined not to sound too upset, in case anyone thought she might be sufficiently loyal toward Jonathan to help him escape—or hide him close by. "It's a rotten time. But at least Theo is safe."

"Indeed, Miss Madeline," said Matthew, and he walked away, quickly swallowed up by the shadows at the edge of the yard.

Maddie opened the first cupboard and searched along the shelves. She knew linseed oil was kept in a tin flagon in the feed room because she had seen Ollie adding it to the buckets of feed. She needed vinegar and belladonna from here—she didn't expect for a moment to find the Milk of Magnesia. To her relief, there was a half full bottle of vinegar on the bottom shelf. She put it on the ground beside her and opened the next cupboard.

"Belladonna, belladonna," she muttered to herself.

"Are you going to dose the mare again?" asked Ollie, coming into the tack room with a halter in his hand.

Maddie stood up awkwardly, dusting the knees of her breeches. "Er, yes," she stammered. "I . . . I heard that belladonna might help."

Ollie looked thoughtful. "Yes, it might. It's in the next cupboard along, second shelf down."

Maddie opened the cupboard and found a small paper bag with *Belladonna* clearly written on it. She tucked it into her jacket, then picked up the vinegar. "Thanks," she said, hoping Ollie wouldn't ask how she was going to dose the mare on her own. To her relief, the stable boy just nodded and went over to examine a snaffle bit that had been soaking in a bowl of water.

With her heart pounding, Maddie hesitated in the doorway and asked, "I don't suppose you have any Milk of Magnesia, do you?"

Ollie looked up at her. "He came back, didn't he? The chap that isn't Theo."

Maddie froze.

"I thought he would, if he knew the mare was sick," Ollie went on. "Never seen a horseman like him, I 'aven't. Did he tell you to fetch them things?" He nodded at the vinegar and the belladonna.

"Yes." Maddie didn't think there was any point in lying.

"An' he told you to get some Milk of Magnesia, too?"

"Yes. Are . . . are you going to tell my grandfather he's here?" Maddie forced herself to ask.

There was a long pause, then Ollie shook his head. He didn't meet Maddie's eyes as he fished the snaffle bit out of the bowl and lay it on a rag to dry. "I don't see that he's done any harm, not if he hasn't taken nothing from the house," he muttered. "You got yer real brother back, and that's what matters, don't it? Just as long as you make sure he's gone before morning, that's all."

"I will, I promise," Maddie whispered. "Thank you, Ollie."

He shrugged. "Get going, now. That mare needs dosing, soon as you can."

Maddie ran back to the stable, first stopping to collect the flagon of linseed oil from the feed room. It was heavier than she expected, and she felt some of it splash onto her boots as she hurried across the yard. Jonathan didn't say anything when she staggered into the stable with her armload, just picked up the empty bottle and started mixing the ingredients for the drench. Firebird watched him dully, flinching when a spasm racked her body. Before, the pain would have made her kick at her belly, or try to bite her flank, but now she seemed too exhausted to move.

Maddie rested her hand on the mare's nose. "It's all right, little one," she murmured. "We're here. Everything's going to be all right."

"I can't promise that," Jonathan said darkly, shaking the bottle. He came over and lifted Firebird's head. "Give me a hand, Maddie."

She stood underneath Firebird's chin like before and gripped the halter with both hands. This time the mare was too tired to struggle, and Jonathan tipped the whole bottle down her throat.

Maddie watched the mare swallow convulsively. "Good girl," she told her. "Drink it all up."

There was a strange rumbling sound as the mixture reached her belly, and Birdy stamped her foreleg. "Easy there," soothed Jonathan.

Suddenly a face appeared at the stable door. "I found that Milk of Magnesia," Ollie panted, thrusting a small blue bottle over the door. "Toby had some in 'is room."

Jonathan glanced at Maddie in alarm. "Ollie guessed you

were here," she said. "I thought he might be able to help find some of the ingredients. He promised he wouldn't tell anyone."

"And I won't, neither," Ollie said stoutly.

Jonathan reached out to take the medicine. "Thanks," he said.

"You can thank me when the mare gets better," Ollie replied. "She don't look any better, that's for sure."

"We're not giving up yet," Maddie insisted.

"No, we're not," Jonathan agreed, pouring nearly all the Milk of Magnesia into the dosing bottle. He lifted Birdy's head and slipped the neck of the bottle between her teeth. "Come on, lady," he muttered. She swallowed unprotestingly, and Jonathan stepped back.

"I'll leave you to it," said Ollie. "But I'll stay in Toby's room till he gets back, so call if you need me."

"We will," said Maddie. "And thank you, really."

Ollie walked away, pausing at Wayfarer's door to rub the cob's broad Roman nose before disappearing into the tack room. A moment later, a light appeared at Toby's window.

"What do we do now?" Maddie asked Jonathan.

"Nothing but wait," came the reply, his voice trembling with exhaustion and fear.

Maddie went over and laid her hand on his arm. It felt greasy from where the drench had spilled. "I'm so glad you came back. Birdy has to be all right now, she has to."

"She's not out of the woods yet," he said. He shook out his jacket and laid it on the straw next to the wall. "We may as well sit down, if we're going to be here all night."

Maddie held out her hand to silence him. She could hear someone walking along the gravel path from the house. It couldn't be Toby or the vet, because they'd come straight to the yard. It must be Matthew returning with her sandwiches. Flashing a warning glance at Jonathan, she let herself out and crossed the yard to meet the butler before he got too close to the stable. He was carrying a large plate of sandwiches and a thermos.

"Thank you, Matthew," said Maddie, taking the plate and thermos from him.

"How is the mare?" he asked.

"Still bad," Maddie replied.

"Shall I tell your grandparents that you'll wait out here until the vet arrives?" said Matthew. "I presume Ollie is waiting with you?"

"Oh, yes and yes," Maddie said quickly. "Please, tell them I'm fine. Are . . . are they all right?"

"As well as can be expected," was all the butler said before heading back to the house again.

Maddie watched Jonathan's eyes light up when she brought him the plate of sandwiches. "Thanks," he said, taking a big bite from one before pouring coffee into the cup from the top of the thermos.

Beside them, Firebird's belly let out another enormous rumble. "Is that a good sign?" Maddie asked.

Jonathan nodded. "It shows the drench has got her insides on the move again. She might like a warm bran mash now, if you can make one."

"Toby said she shouldn't eat," Maddie remembered.

"She'll be all right with something like a mash, but she shouldn't have anything hard to digest like hay." He explained to Maddie how to make up the mash, before picking up another sandwich.

Maddie went over and put her arms around the mare's neck. "I'm going to fetch you something to eat, precious girl," she murmured. "I won't be long." She looked at Jonathan over Firebird's mane. "Should we start walking her again?"

"Not unless she looks like she wants to roll."

Maddie went out of the stable again to make up the mash. She'd never mixed a feed before, but she knew where the bran was kept. She dug her hands into the fluffy brown flakes, her mind suddenly filling with a long-buried memory of burrowing for gifts in a tub of bran at a street fair. She heard her mother laughing beside her—"Dig deeper, Maddie! It's all right, you won't fall in!"—so clearly that she gasped and turned around, expecting to see her standing in the doorway.

There was nobody there, just the empty yard with shafts of

flickering light from the lanterns that Ollie had left burning. Angry with herself for being so fanciful, and missing her parents so fiercely it felt like a needle stabbing inside her, Maddie poured two scoops of bran into a bucket and added a dollop of sticky black molasses. Then she carried the bucket to the tack room where a kettle of water stood simmering day and night on the stove. The stove kept the tack room warm and dry, which was good for the leather and also for Toby, who slept upstairs next to the chimney. She added enough water to the bran to make a sloppy sort of porridge and took the bucket back to the stable. As she opened Firebird's door, the clock sounded the hour, and Maddie counted ten chimes.

She knew from the pungent smell inside the stable that Firebird's insides were definitely on the move. She wrinkled her nose, but Jonathan was smiling. "She's doing just fine!" he declared, rubbing his hand along Firebird's mane.

"If you say so," Maddie muttered, heaving the bucket onto the edge of the manger and tipping the mash in.

Firebird lifted her head and pricked her ears at the sweet, warm scent of bran and molasses. She took a few faltering steps toward the manger.

"Come on, little one," Maddie urged her. "This will make you feel even better."

The mare went over and dropped her nose into the manger. She gave a snort, and flecks of bran shot out and clung to

Maddie's jacket. She brushed them off, then beamed at Jonathan as Firebird started to munch noisily.

He smiled back. "We did it, Mouse!"

"*You* did it," she corrected him, but he shook his head.

"I couldn't have done anything without you." He reached down and picked up a small blue bottle. "And Toby's Milk of Magnesia, of course!"

Maddie laughed, then clapped her hands over her mouth. "Sorry. I'm just so relieved! I really thought we were going to lose Birdy today."

"I know you did. But she's not going anywhere. Look at her!"

They watched the chestnut mare tucking into her feed. Her coat was stiff with sweat, but it was dry now, and her eyes were bright as she glanced at them over the rim of the manger.

"She's perfect," Maddie whispered.

Jonathan leaned out of the door to pick up Firebird's haynet, which Toby had taken out of the stable. He tied it to the metal ring on the wall, then sat down on his jacket and stretched his legs out. "I'll stay with her tonight."

Maddie went over and sat down beside him. "I'm staying too." When he raised his eyebrows, she said, "No one will notice I'm not in bed until tomorrow morning, and it will be too late by then. There's no way I'm leaving Birdy now."

Jonathan shrugged and reached out for the riding apron that Maddie had taken off earlier. He spread it over their legs. "No point getting a chill," was all he said.

Maddie nodded and rested her head on his shoulder, feeling a black wave of sleep rising up to claim her. As she closed her eyes, all she could hear was steady munching as Firebird finished her bran mash, and the crackle of straw as she shifted her hooves.

CHAPTER

26

❦

MADDIE WOKE WITH A START as the cockerel let out a noisy cry from behind the stable block. Her first thought was *Where am I?*, then, *Birdy!* But the mare was standing on the other side of the stable with her head nodding gently, one hind leg resting underneath her. She had made it through the night without getting colic again. She was going to be all right!

Maddie turned to see Jonathan curled on the straw beside her, fast asleep. She bit her lip, knowing she ought to wake him so he could leave before anyone was about. A shadow fell across the straw in the middle of the stable, and she looked up with a start.

Theo was standing with his hands resting on top of the door, staring down at them.

Maddie scrambled to her feet. Beside her, Jonathan stirred.

"I won't let you take him!" Maddie said wildly, and Jonathan opened his eyes. He sat up as soon as he saw Theo.

"He only came back because Firebird was sick. Please let him go," Maddie begged her brother.

The two men held each other's gaze as if Maddie wasn't

there. Then Theo unbolted the stable door and swung it open.

"Go," he ordered. Jonathan opened his mouth to say something but Theo held up his hand. "Just go."

Jonathan jumped up, pulling on his jacket. He rested his hand briefly on Maddie's shoulder before he slipped out of the stable and sprinted toward the archway.

Maddie watched until he vaulted the gate on the other side of the schooling paddock and disappeared. She turned to Theo. "Thank you."

He didn't take his eyes from the paddock. "I didn't do it for you." Taking a deep breath, he turned to her. "How's the mare?"

"Sh-she's fine," Maddie stammered.

"Jonathan's the best horseman I ever met," Theo said quietly. "I'm not surprised he came back to help her."

"Did he really teach you to ride?" Maddie blurted out.

Theo nodded. His eyes narrowed as he looked at Firebird. "She came from the desert, didn't she? I'd guess she has some Arabian breeding."

"That's what Jonathan thought," Maddie agreed. "And he said she's the best jumper he has ever seen!" She was about to tell Theo about their plans for the Gold Cup when she noticed he was frowning at her.

"I didn't think you'd be interested in horses," he said. "You were always too scared to ride when you were little."

Maddie shrugged. "Things are different now." *Because of*

Jonathan, she added silently, picking at a splinter in the door frame. What was the point of telling Theo how much her life had changed since Jonathan came to Sefton Park? As far as the rest of her family was concerned, he was nothing but a criminal.

She looked over the door as hooves crunched on the driveway, and a trap bowled into the stable yard. Toby jumped down from the seat next to the driver. "Is the mare all right?" he called.

"She's fine," Maddie told him. She glanced at Theo, praying he wouldn't say anything about Jonathan coming back. "Ollie and I gave her another drench, and some of your Milk of Magnesia, and that seemed to do the trick." She glanced at the clock above the archway. It was six o'clock. If she was lucky, her grandparents would never know she'd spent the night in Firebird's stable.

The door to the tack room opened and Ollie came out, looking bleary-eyed and rumpled as if he had slept in his clothes. "Have you only just got back?" he asked Toby in surprise.

The head groom nodded. "By the time I caught up with Mr. Jackson, Thor had gone lame. I left him at a farm near Hermitage, and the vet brought me over this morning. But it looks like we don't need him after all, thanks to you and Miss Maddie."

Ollie glanced at Maddie and she gave a tiny nod, hoping he wouldn't give her away. "It was mostly Miss Maddie," he said.

The vet led his pony and trap over and handed the reins to Ollie. "Where's this mare, Chalk?"

Toby pointed to Firebird's stable. "Over there, but from the sounds of it, she's pulled through on her own. I'm sorry to have brought you out for nothing, sir."

"No need to apologize," said Mr. Jackson. "I'm sorry you had such a job tracking me down. I'll just take a look at her, since I'm here."

He strode over to Firebird's stable, and Theo stepped back. With a final glance at Maddie, he turned and walked out of the yard.

Mr. Jackson peered over the door. "No problems there," he said. He snapped open his black leather bag and took out something that looked like a tiny trumpet. "I'll listen to her insides and take her temperature, but I'd say she's well over the worst. Keep her in for a day or two, then put her onto grass that's not too rich for the next week."

He went into Firebird's stable. Maddie felt Toby staring at her with a puzzled frown. "Milk of Magnesia, did you say? I've not thought of using that on horses before."

"My . . . my grandfather takes it when he has stomachache," Maddie faltered. "I thought it might help Birdy too."

Toby nodded. "You did a good job. It's not often colic as bad as that gets better. We'll make a horsewoman of you yet, Miss Maddie."

The vet emerged from the stable, confirmed Firebird was

making good progress, and climbed back into his trap. Halfway down the drive, the cob swerved onto the lawn.

"Where's he going?" Toby wondered, shielding his eyes against the sun.

A moment later, a sturdy, snub-nosed vehicle appeared at the bottom of the drive. As it swung around the corner, Maddie saw that it was a large green truck with *Portman Stock Transport* painted along the side in black letters. It was followed by the gray police car that had visited the day before.

On the lawn, Mr. Jackson's cob wheeled in a nervous circle, scoring deep lines with the wheels of the cart. Once the vehicles had gone past, he headed for the gate at a brisk canter. The truck rumbled into the stable yard and shuddered to a halt. The police car pulled up beside it and Sergeant Walters climbed out.

He lifted his hat to Maddie. "Good morning, miss. We've come to collect the mare."

Maddie stared at him in horror. "Firebird?"

The sergeant glanced at his colleague, who looked at his notebook and nodded.

"She was bought with money that rightfully belonged to Mr. Theodore Harman, and that makes her stolen property," said Sergeant Walters.

"You can't take Firebird away!" Maddie gasped. "She belongs here."

"Not now she doesn't, and not ever, in fact," said the policeman.

"She needs to be returned to her rightful owners."

Maddie started trembling. She had fought so hard to save Firebird from the colic, and now she was going to lose her after all!

The driver of the truck climbed out and lowered the ramp at the back. It looked a bit like a stable inside, with wood panels on the walls and straw on the floor.

"Is the horse ready, sir?" said the driver, touching the brim of his flat cap to Toby.

"She's in her stable," Toby muttered, looking as if he didn't want this to happen any more than Maddie.

Maddie stood by the tack room, watching helplessly.

Toby led Firebird out of her stable, and Maddie saw the truck driver raise his eyebrows as if he couldn't understand why there was so much bother over this ragged-looking horse. Firebird's mane and tail hung in limp tangles, and her coat was blotchy with dried sweat. Her head shot up when she saw the truck and she snorted loudly. Toby patted her and clicked his tongue. She allowed him to lead her to the foot of the ramp, but then she stopped dead with her hooves jammed under the edge. She swished her tail crossly when Toby tugged on the lead rein.

The driver walked behind Firebird and flapped his arms. "Get on there!" he shouted. He rolled his eyes at Sergeant Walters. "Looks like we've got a difficult one here."

The police sergeant came over to stand next to the driver. "Up you go!" he said briskly.

Firebird snorted and tried to swing her quarters sideways. To Maddie's horror, the driver reached into the truck and took out a long wooden pole. As Firebird sidestepped toward him, he lifted it into the air, ready to bring down on the mare's back.

"Stop!"

Maddie jumped. Had she spoken out loud?

Theo was striding across the yard. "Stop that at once!" he said again. He caught hold of the driver's sleeve and wrenched the stick out of his hand. "There's no need to hit her."

"There is if she won't go up the ramp," the driver muttered.

Theo turned to Sergeant Walters. "What on earth is going on?"

"We're come to take the mare, sir," said the policeman.

"You're not taking her anywhere," said Theo.

Maddie nearly fell over.

Sergeant Walters looked harassed. "Sir, you don't understand. That horse is stolen property."

Theo raised his eyebrows. "I think you'll find she was bought in a fair transaction. Perhaps you should speak to her previous owners before claiming that she was stolen?"

Toby had stopped pulling on the lead rein and was standing next to Firebird at the bottom of the ramp, one hand resting on her nose.

"She was bought with stolen money," argued the police sergeant.

"Money that was stolen from me," Theo pointed out. "Which makes me her rightful owner, wouldn't you say?"

Sergeant Walters frowned.

Theo went on, "I may disagree strongly with the way Price lied to my family, but I have no complaints about how he spent my money. It's my decision what happens to the mare, and I don't want her taken away."

Maddie could have hugged him except she didn't trust herself to move without her legs giving way.

The policeman narrowed his eyes. "As you wish, sir. I shall consult with my senior officers and let you know if they agree with your decision."

"Thank you," said Theo. "But I shall be very surprised if they find there is any need to remove the mare."

"Shall I put her back in her stable, Master Theo?" asked Toby.

"Yes, that would be best."

Scowling and grumbling about time wasters, the driver heaved the ramp into place and went around to the front of the truck to start the engine. He gave the crank handle a savage wrench, and the engine roared into life, belching a cloud of black smoke into the stable yard. The two policemen climbed into their motorcar and followed the truck down the drive.

Theo watched Toby lead Firebird into her stable and bolt the door. Then he thrust his hands into his pockets and started to walk toward the house.

Maddie's legs came back to life, and she ran over to him, catching hold of his sleeve. "You saved Firebird!"

Her brother shrugged. "According to the law, she's mine. I wasn't lying to those police officers."

"No, of course not. But thank you anyway. She means a lot to me," Maddie faltered. "Jonathan would be really glad, too," she added.

Theo's face went dark. "I don't care what Jonathan thinks," he told her. "I will never forgive him for what he has done. Never."

A FEW DAYS AFTER THEO returned, a letter arrived for him with a West London postmark. Maddie saw it lying on the table in the hall and picked it up. On the back of the heavy white envelope was a stamp with the distinctive British Show-Jumping Association crest. For a moment her heart thudded with excitement, until she remembered that Jonathan had gone and Firebird would no longer be competing in the Gold Cup. She was on her way upstairs with the envelope—there was no point giving it to Theo, since it wasn't for him in the first place—when she met Louisa coming down.

"Is everything all right, Mouse?"

Maddie hid the envelope in a fold of her skirt. "I'm fine," she said.

Louisa looked tired and pale, as if she hadn't slept since learning the truth about Jonathan. She had been distraught to discover that she hadn't recognized her own brother, and had let a stranger lie his way into their home. Maddie hadn't been able to say anything to comfort her—she felt much too guilty for keeping Jonathan's secret, and besides, she still couldn't believe he had done anything wrong. Or at least, whatever he had done, they had been partly responsible, because they had so badly wanted Theo to come home.

Louisa turned and followed Maddie upstairs to her bedroom. She perched on the bed and folded the edge of Maddie's bedspread into tiny pleats. "It's strange, having Theo back twice, isn't it?"

Maddie nodded and sat down on the window seat, feeling the pane of glass cold against her shoulder blades. She caught her breath as the envelope rustled under her skirt, but her sister didn't seem to notice.

"Sometimes I forget that it hasn't been Theo here all along," Lou went on. "I can't believe that man ever thought he'd get away with pretending to be him."

"Jonathan. His name was Jonathan," Maddie said, and her sister looked up, startled.

"You liked him, didn't you? You must have done, seeing as you found out before the rest of us and didn't say anything."

Maddie looked out of the window. "I wished for my brother to come home, and that's what happened," she said quietly. "Jonathan thought Theo was dead, remember? He was saving us from knowing that by letting us think he was Theo."

"But he wasn't our brother! He was a complete stranger!"

"He was a lot nicer than the one we've got now!" Maddie burst out. She stood up, ignoring the envelope as it fell onto the floor. There was no use opening it anyway.

Louisa stared at Maddie in horror. "What are you saying? That . . . that man was no easier than Theo to have around, not when he first arrived. Have you forgotten that already? You have to make the same allowances for Theo. He'll settle in soon enough. After all, he does belong here."

Maddie clenched her hands at her sides. "Jonathan belonged here too. He loved Firebird as much as I did."

"That wretched horse!" Lou exclaimed. "Life's not just about riding horses, Maddie. Why can't you understand that?" She swept out of the room, shutting the door so hard that a silver photograph frame bounced off the wall and crashed onto the floor.

Maddie went over and picked it up, running her finger along the crack in the glass. Her parents smiled up at her, their arms around each other's shoulders as they stood on a path lined with trees. Was it Wimbledon Common? Or Richmond Park? Maddie couldn't remember.

"What's happening to us?" she whispered to her mother and father. "I wish you were here, then none of this would have happened. You would have known Jonathan wasn't Theo right away. Why can't Lou and my grandparents see it was our fault, too?"

Pausing to help herself to an apple from the sideboard in the dining room, Maddie headed for the stable yard. It was two days after her quarrel with Louisa, and yesterday Toby had announced that Firebird was well enough to be ridden again. Maddie hoped that going for a ride would clear away the miserable cobwebs in her head, tangled with thoughts of Lou and Theo and Jonathan and her grandparents. Discovering the truth hadn't made any of them happy, and Maddie felt as if she was stuck helplessly in the middle.

When she reached the tack room, she tossed the apple core to Jinx before lifting down Firebird's bridle and a sidesaddle. The yard was empty: Toby had gone over to Hermitage to collect Thor, who had recovered from his lameness, and Ollie was exercising the carriage horses.

Firebird kicked at her stable door when she saw Maddie approaching, expressing her impatience at being inside when the other horses had gone out to the paddocks.

"No grass for you yet, my lady," Maddie told her, heaving the saddle onto the top of the door. Firebird circled mutinously, churning the straw, and Maddie laughed. "You look like a spoiled child," she scolded.

The mare's coat was clean and glossy again after her illness, and her mane brushed silkily against Maddie's fingers as she lifted the bridle over Firebird's head. She danced sideways when Maddie led her out of the stable, arching her neck and flicking out her hooves. Maddie grinned and held her on a loose rein to let her get rid of some of the pent-up energy. She had left the paddock gate open so she could ride straight into the field, and Firebird whirled around as soon as her hooves touched the grass, her tail streaming out and her ears pricked.

Maddie took a deep breath to make the butterflies stop leaping in her stomach. She'd felt much safer when Jonathan was with her. *Pretend that he is,* she told herself. Right now, he'd be telling her to ride the mare forward so she didn't have time to jump around. Gritting her teeth, Maddie pushed Firebird into a trot, and although she spooked at one of the jump stands and bucked when a rabbit shot out of the hedge, she had settled into her stride by the end of the paddock. At the corner, Maddie let her canter and sat straight in the saddle as the mare floated across the field, her hooves hardly seeming to touch the grass.

Maddie reined her in. "Shall we try the jumps, Birdy?" she whispered, and the mare tossed her head as if to say yes. A little voice demanded to know why she was wasting time schooling Firebird over the fences when she wouldn't be entering the Gold Cup. The envelope from the British Show-Jumping Association had contained the showground passes and details on when the class began, neat cardboard badges for the owners to wear, and a map of the arena. Maddie had run her finger along the edge of a glossy scarlet badge, letting herself imagine for just one moment what it would be like to see Firebird sailing over the huge white fences, then stuffed everything back in the envelope and slid it underneath her mattress. She couldn't bear to look at it because it reminded her of what she had lost when Jonathan left, but she couldn't bring herself to throw it away either.

As Firebird sidled restlessly underneath her, she shook her head to get rid of the little voice, then scooped up the reins and cantered the mare in a wide circle before turning her toward the first jump. The mare's ears shot forward and she quickened her pace, but the canter poles steadied her and put her in the right spot to spring over the first rail. Three brisk strides, and they were over the spread fence without touching a single pole.

"Good work," a voice said quietly as Maddie cantered along the edge of the paddock. She looked around, startled. There was someone watching her from the back lawn, his arms folded on the top rail of the fence.

"Jonathan!" she gasped.

"Theo," her brother corrected her flatly.

Something flashed in his eyes that Maddie couldn't read, then his gaze shifted to the line of jumps. "You ride very well," he said.

"It's nothing to do with me," Maddie told him. She ran her hand along Firebird's mane. "You can see how good Birdy is. I hated riding until Jonathan told me what to do. We were going to enter her in the Gold Cup." She stopped awkwardly, waiting for her brother to tell her not to mention Jonathan again.

But Theo just nodded. "Jonathan always liked horses that could jump. In Africa, he was forever riding the horses over stock fences or garden walls. He landed in a vegetable patch once and had to spend the afternoon replanting a crop of maize!"

Maddie laughed. "I wonder where he is now?" she said suddenly.

Theo's eyes clouded. "Isn't it better not to know?"

"But why?" Maddie protested. "He hasn't done anything wrong, not now you're here." She broke off, knowing there was something not quite right with her logic. She just couldn't treat Jonathan like a criminal. "Don't you want to help him?" she asked. "He was your best friend."

"The man I was friends with wasn't a liar and a thief!"

"The brother I remember would have given his friends a second chance," Maddie flashed back.

"But which brother are you remembering?" Theo asked, and Maddie couldn't think of a reply.

"Maybe we didn't give Jonathan a chance to be honest," she said at last. "We wanted him—no, you—back so badly that we swallowed him up as soon as he arrived." Theo looked puzzled and she struggled on, "Not just me and Lou, but everyone at Sefton Park. Can't you see we only believed him because of how much we *wanted* to?"

Theo didn't say anything, just looked down at the rail beneath his hands.

"Of course he wasn't exactly the same as you had been before you went away," Maddie persisted, "but we always expected you to be different when you came back. It was easy to blame the war for the way Jonathan hated meeting people, or wouldn't talk about what he was going to do next. We never stopped to think that he might be different because he was really a different person."

"This is not your fault!" Theo hissed. "Jonathan knew how much you wanted me to come home. He read all the letters you sent, waited for the post even more eagerly than I did. He said it was because he didn't have a family of his own to write to him, but he just wanted to find out enough so that he could steal my name and come back instead of me."

"That's not true!" Maddie cried, and Firebird wheeled around in alarm. Maddie brought her back to the fence and glared at Theo. "Jonathan isn't like that. And how was he to know there'd be an accident in the mine? That wasn't his fault, for goodness' sake. People were calling him Theo before he woke up, because he had your knife in his pocket."

"The knife has nothing to do with this," Theo argued. "He should have told you who he really was."

"Why? So we could send him away? Where would he have gone? Have you forgotten that all his family are dead? He has no one, Theo, no one!"

Theo started to walk away.

"Jonathan is a good man!" Maddie shouted after him. "He thought you were dead!"

Theo didn't look back, and Maddie twisted her fingers in Birdy's mane. "He is a good man," she repeated hoarsely. She didn't care if Theo heard. "And I wish he were here instead of you."

28

MADDIE WOKE THE FOLLOWING morning feeling as if she had hardly slept at all. The atmosphere at dinner the night before had been icy, with neither Theo nor Lou joining in the conversation except to ask for the salt or to refuse more wine. Both their faces were pale and drawn, and Maddie's guilt for everything she had done sat like a lump in her throat, making it impossible to eat. Were her brother and sister going to hate her forever?

As the clock struck seven downstairs, Maddie jumped out of bed and scrambled into her clothes. It was too early for breakfast, so she decided to go to the library for an hour and read—anything to stop her head buzzing with thoughts of Jonathan and where he might be. There had been no word from the police, except to say that they were still looking for him. It was nearly a week since he left, and Maddie told herself she didn't mind not knowing where he was, as long as he was far, far away and safe.

"Good morning, Miss Madeline." Matthew was standing in the hallway, sorting through the morning post. A shaft of sunlight was slicing through the tall window beside the door, sending warm orange sunbeams bouncing onto the parquet floor. Sir Wilfred's Irish setter was stretched out blissfully, her body long and thin to fit into the ray of sun.

"Good morning, Matthew," said Maddie. She crouched down to run her hand along Charlie's silky back.

There were footsteps behind her, and she turned to see Matthew holding something out to her. "You have some post, Miss Madeline," he said.

Maddie stood up and took the brown paper parcel. It was not much bigger than an envelope, but bulkier, as if there was more than just a letter inside. Holding it, she could feel a hard, slim shape with rounded ends. Her heart started to beat faster. She had felt this shape before through scratchy khaki cloth, when she had hugged Theo good-bye before he went to war.

She looked up. Matthew was watching her, his eyebrows slightly raised. Maddie turned away, holding the package close to her chest. "Thank you, Matthew," she said. She pushed open the library door, resisting the urge to slam it behind her and rest her weight against it. She waited a few moments until she heard Matthew walk away. Then she sat heavily in her grand-father's wingback chair and turned the parcel over in her hands.

She recognized the handwriting at once, from the notes Jonathan had made after their visit to Dick Stillwell's yard. It was untidier than she remembered, and the blue ink had run in places as if the parcel had been caught in the rain. There was nothing to say who had sent it, just her name and the address of Sefton Park. Maddie tore open the parcel, her fingers trembling so much that the paper unfolded with a jerk and whatever was inside shot out and clattered onto the floor by her feet. She bent down and picked it up.

It was Theo's knife.

A crumpled sheet of white paper lay beside it, shaped as if it had been folded around the knife. Maddie smoothed it out so she could read the lines of uneven blue writing.

Dear Maddie,

I'm so sorry. Please believe that I never meant to hurt you, nor any of your family. I am as happy as you are that Theo is alive, so don't feel bad this is how things have turned out. You have your brother back, and nothing else matters.

I'm sending you Theo's knife because I didn't think he'd open a letter from me if he recognized my writing. Please tell him that I never meant to take anything from him, not one thing.

I will never forget you.

Jonathan

The lines blurred as Maddie's eyes filled with tears, and she closed her fingers tightly around the smooth silver penknife.

Wherever Jonathan was, at least he was safe enough to be able to send a parcel. Wherever he was . . . A thought struck her, and she snatched up the torn brown paper. Peering closely at the side where the address was written, she could just make out a faint, watery postmark. There were two words that she could read, the second one slightly shorter than the other, then underneath some letters that spelled *Cymru*.

Maddie frowned. Where was that? It didn't sound English—could Jonathan be overseas? She heard voices in the hallway and quickly folded the letter around the knife, then bundled them both into the brown paper. She slipped out of the library to find her grandfather talking to Theo. They looked at her in surprise.

"Good morning, Madeline! You're up early," said Sir Wilfred.

"I had to read a poem for my lesson with Miss Finnigan," Maddie lied, holding the untidy parcel behind her back.

Theo started to walk away, and Maddie hurried after him. She caught up with him as he was putting on his outdoor shoes by the back door. "Theo, wait!"

"What is it?"

"There's something I have to show you. Not here, though. Come to the stable yard." Maddie gave him a little push. For a moment, he looked startled, then opened the door. Maddie stuffed her feet into her galoshes and ran along the path behind him. She dodged past him and headed for Firebird's stable. "In here," she said.

Firebird twitched her ears as they came in, but didn't lift her nose out of the manger where she was tucking into her breakfast. Theo looked expectantly at Maddie, waiting for her to say something. Before she could change her mind, she thrust the parcel at him.

"Jonathan wrote to me. He asked me to give this to you. It's your penknife."

Theo unwrapped the knife and stood looking down at it without saying anything. Suddenly Maddie had a terrible thought. What if Theo gave the knife and the letter to the police, and they used it to track Jonathan down?

"Read the letter," she urged. "He says he never meant to steal anything, and he's glad you're alive. You have to believe him, you have to!"

Theo turned the knife over in his hands and ran his finger over the inscription. Then he unfolded the letter and read it. Behind Maddie, Firebird finished her breakfast and came over to blow stickily in her hair, brushing tiny fragments of grain onto Maddie's shoulders. Maddie reached up and stroked the mare's velvety nose. Theo still didn't say a word.

"Please don't tell the police," Maddie begged him. "You can't let them find him. He'd go to prison!"

Theo looked up, and Maddie's heart flipped over when she

saw that his eyes were full of tears.

"He was my best friend," he said. "He should never have betrayed me."

Maddie stepped forward and grasped Theo's hands. They felt bitterly cold. "Jonathan wasn't betraying you," she told him. "He thought you were dead. Please, we have to help him."

Theo shook his head. "How can we help him? We don't know where he is."

Maddie let go of her brother's hands and bent down to pick up the brown paper, which had fallen onto the straw. "There's a postmark," she said. "It's hard to read, but I think it says Cymru. Is that abroad? Might Jonathan have gone to France?"

Theo shook his head. "Cymru means Wales. If Jonathan was going to run anywhere, it would be to Wales."

"Do the police know that?" said Maddie.

Theo looked steadily at her. "Well, I didn't tell them."

Something like hope flared in Maddie's chest. "Are you going to tell the police about the knife?" she forced herself to ask.

Her brother rolled the knife on the palm of his hand. Firebird pricked her ears as the metal flashed in the sun, then went back to her haynet. Maddie held her breath.

"No," Theo said at last. "Nothing would be gained by Jonathan going to prison."

"Then let's go and find him!" Maddie burst out. "We know

he's in Wales because of the postmark."

Theo looked quizzically at her. "Wales is a pretty big place, Maddie. We can't just drive to the border and shout Jonathan's name."

Maddie clenched her fists in frustration. "There must be something we can do." Her shoulders slumped, and she gazed helplessly at her brother. "I can't leave it like this, not knowing where Jonathan is or if he's all right."

Theo turned away and reached over the stable door to open the bolt. When Maddie took a step toward him, he held up his hand. "I need to think, Maddie," he said. "Jonathan sending the knife back doesn't change what he did to us."

"No," Maddie agreed. "But it shows that he never stopped being your friend. And that has to mean something to you, I know it does."

She watched Theo walk across the yard with his shoulders hunched. It was impossible to tell what he was thinking. Suddenly, keeping Jonathan's letter hidden from the police wasn't enough for Maddie; she wanted to go to Wales and find him. But unless Theo agreed to help, there was nothing she could do.

MADDIE SAT UP AND PUSHED back her bedspread. Something had woken her. It had taken her ages to get to sleep, as she tried to imagine where Jonathan might be. All she could think about was going to Wales to look for him, but she hadn't seen Theo since he walked out of Firebird's stable. He had taken a pony and trap out, according to Ollie, and hadn't returned by dinnertime. Maddie had struggled against the cold suspicion that Theo had taken the letter to the police after all, and the net was closing around Jonathan even now. . . .

She held her breath, waiting to see if the sound came again.

Tap, tap!

Maddie slid out of bed, wincing as her feet touched the cold floorboards, and padded over to the door. "Who is it?" she whispered.

"It's me, Theo."

Maddie opened her door a little. Her brother was standing on the landing, fully dressed and etched in pale gray moonlight.

Maddie felt behind her for the dressing gown that was draped over the back of her chair. She shoved one arm into a sleeve and flipped it onto her shoulders, opening the door wider with her other hand. "What time is it?"

Theo came in and lit the candle beside her bed. "Four o'clock. Get dressed," he told her. "You'll need warm clothes."

Maddie stared at him in confusion. "Why?"

"We're going to look for Jonathan. You were right, we can't leave it like this. I'll wait for you downstairs." He went out of the room before Maddie could say anything else.

She stood still for a moment, her brother's words echoing in her mind. They were going to find Jonathan! She realized she was grinning and quickly started to pick out some clothes. She pulled on a thick skirt and found a V-necked woolen sweater to go over her blouse. Carrying her shoes in one hand, she ran downstairs in her stockinged feet and found Theo in the lobby, taking down a greatcoat from the row of pegs. He put his finger to his lips, warning her to be quiet, before slipping out of the door.

Maddie snatched Lou's heavy car coat and a long knitted scarf and hurried after him. An unfamiliar Baby Austin was parked outside the garages.

"Whose car is this?" Maddie whispered.

"I hired it from a garage in Newbury," Theo explained. He shut the door behind her and went around to the front to crank the starting handle. The engine clattered to life like someone dropping a stack of tin trays, and Maddie held her breath.

"What if someone hears us?" she whispered as Theo climbed in beside her.

"I left a note in the hall. They'll know that it's us and not someone making off with the silver."

He steered the car onto the lane that led past the church and over the canal. Maddie wrenched at her scarf to loosen it. "Are we going to Wales?" she asked, twisting around to look at her brother.

He nodded and slowed down to let a weasel scamper across the road. "I've been trying to remember what Jonathan said about his childhood, to see if there's somewhere he might go first. He grew up in Knighton, on the border, but I don't think he would go back there now that his grandparents are dead. He used to spend his summers on a sheep farm near a town called Builth Wells. I got the feeling that the man who owned it was the nearest thing he had to a father, aside from his grandfather. I think he'd go there, if he was going to head anywhere from his past."

Maddie pictured the faded postmark on the parcel. The two words that she couldn't read could have been Builth Wells. It sounded like a good place to start, anyway.

They reached the main road that ran from Newbury to Hungerford, and beyond that to Marlborough, Swindon, all the way to Bristol. Theo swung the steering wheel to the left and they headed west, leaving the thin strip of brightening sky behind them.

"What was the name of the farm?"

Theo shrugged. "I don't think he told me. But it was near a village called Hundred House, and the farmer's name was Rhodri."

"How long do you think it will take us to get there?" Maddie peered ahead at the strips of road illuminated by the thin headlight beams.

"We should be there by tomorrow lunchtime. We'll stay in Chepstow overnight." Theo reached behind him and felt around on the backseat. "Here's a map," he said, thrusting an untidily folded sheet of paper at Maddie. "We'll head north to Chepstow, then northwest to the Black Mountains. Can you see them on the map?"

Maddie ran her finger over the paper until she came to a shaded area just inside the Welsh border. "Yes, I've found them," she said. "And Hundred House, too!" She rested her finger on a cluster of tiny squares indicating a village. "What will we do when we find him?" She blinked as a tiny worm of dread burrowed into her stomach. What if Theo only wanted to look for Jonathan in order to hand him over to the police? "We . . . we are going to help him, aren't we?"

Theo glanced sideways at her. "Yes, we are," he said. "What you said was true. Jonathan was my best friend, and he would never have done anything to hurt me or my family. Sending back the knife was his way of letting me know that. I can't forgive what he did, but he doesn't deserve to be punished. I know him. Being found out has been punishment enough."

"He wanted to tell everyone the truth," Maddie confessed. "But I asked him to wait until after the Gold Cup." She fiddled with a corner of the map, suddenly feeling ashamed.

She felt Theo look sharply at her. "Was the competition really that important to you?"

"It was back then," she admitted. "Learning to ride Firebird, finding out she was a brilliant show-jumper, was the best thing that had ever happened to me. Without Jonathan, I wouldn't have had Birdy, and that felt like too much to lose." She bit her lip. "But that wasn't the only reason I wanted to keep Jonathan's secret. He told me you were dead and I . . . I wanted my brother back so badly that it was enough to have him there, even if he wasn't really you." She broke off, wondering if she was making any sense.

Theo was silent for a while, watching the road slip steadily beneath the front of the motorcar. "I don't think I can say that I wouldn't have done the same," he said at last. "But secrets don't make people happy, Maddie. Remember that."

"I don't think I'll ever forget," she murmured. She stopped crumpling the corner of the map and started to smooth it out, wondering exactly where Jonathan was amid the lines and shadows. "Do you really think we'll find him?" she said.

"I don't know," Theo admitted. "But we have to look."

"What about the police? Won't they keep on looking for him?"

Theo shook his head. "Not if I ask them to drop the charges. They can't prosecute him if I say I won't give evidence against him. I'll speak to the officer at Newbury when we get back."

"If we manage to find him at all," Maddie put in.

"If we manage to find him," Theo echoed. "Look, why don't you try to get some sleep? I know the way as far as Swindon."

Maddie folded the map, leaving the Black Mountains face up, and burrowed inside her coat. She closed her eyes and let the murmur of the engine lull her. *We're coming to find you, Jonathan,* she promised silently. *We're coming to find you.*

They drove all day, until Maddie felt as if she'd never be able to walk upright again. At first, the roads were smoothly paved, but as they left the major route from London to Bristol and headed into the Gloucestershire countryside along smaller roads, the surfaces became rutted and stony, and sometimes a thick line of grass stretched down the center of the road. When they arrived in the pretty market town of Chepstow, Theo pulled up outside an inn. The sign swinging outside announced that The Gray Goose was open for lodging and fine home-cooked food.

"Perfect." Maddie sighed, climbing stiffly out.

The landlord's wife showed them to a pair of tiny rooms

side by side, with narrow beds that looked suspiciously lumpy under the shiny pink bedspreads. The landlady left them to wash before dinner, and Theo put his head around Maddie's door. He pulled a face at the busy floral wallpaper and frilled lampshades. "My room's the same," he said. "I feel like a flower shop has exploded on top of me."

Maddie laughed and shooed him away so she could finish washing. She hadn't brought any spare clothes with her, but Theo had stopped in Swindon so she could buy soap and a flannel. She poked at her hair, frowning at her reflection in the mirror. It was more tangled than Firebird's mane had ever been, and Jonathan's voice suddenly echoed in her ears, telling her to use her fingers instead of a hard-bristled brush. She closed her eyes, trying to imagine where he was right now. She hoped he was safe and warm, and not too scared.

The bed was indeed lumpy, but Maddie was too tired to notice. As she dressed the next morning, she felt a knot of anxiety in her stomach like a stone. Today was the day they'd reach Hundred House, but what if Jonathan wasn't there?

They had been driving for about an hour when Maddie spotted a sign that said *Croeso i Cymru*.

"Welcome to Wales," Theo translated, and when Maddie looked at him in surprise, he explained, "Jonathan put it on a sign outside the first mine shaft he ever dug."

"He said you had taught him to speak Welsh," Maddie said, then stopped. "I mean, that Jonathan had taught him, when he was pretending to be Theo. Did you? Or he?"

"You mean, did Jonathan teach me to speak Welsh?" Theo interpreted. "A little, but it's a very tricky language to learn. Wait till we get to Hundred House, then you'll see what I mean. I mostly picked up swear words, when he hit his thumb with the hammer."

Maddie grinned. They were driving along the side of a tree-lined valley now. A shallow river sparkled at the bottom, and Maddie wished she could dip her feet in the water. The road was little more than a stony track, only just wider than the mirrors on either side of the car, and tufty weeds grew in a pale green stripe down the center of the pebbles.

They reached a junction, and Maddie peered at the wooden signpost, half-hidden by ferns. "Builth Wells one mile," she read on the board pointing to the left. "And Hundred House is two miles the other way."

She felt a tremor of excitement as they turned right. The road swept between high walls and broad fields where sheep grazed with their tails turned to the wind. Less than a mile away, the land rose up sharply to form a ridge of low mountains, mostly covered in grass and bracken except for the very tops, which were exposed craggy rock. Even though the sky was blue and the sun shone directly overhead, a cold wind buffeted the sides of the car and rippled the bracken like the fur of a shaggy prehistoric animal. The only sign of human life was a tiny white cottage at the foot of the ridge, half-hidden by a stunted ash tree. Maddie shivered. This would be a bleak, lonely place to live, especially in winter.

The road dipped down to the left, and the ground flattened out to reveal a tiny hamlet. Maddie counted less than a dozen houses clustered around a fork in the road, one branch continuing along the foot of the ridge, and the other narrower road swerving right to head straight for the mountains. A lopsided sign announced that they had reached Hundred House.

Theo drew up in front of the largest building, a white-painted two-story house with a slate roof. A wooden sign hung above the door with a picture of something a bit like a cloud on legs. Crooked letters underneath informed Maddie that this was *The Ram Public House, proprietor Dai Gruffyd.*

"I'll go in and ask Mr. Gruffyd if he knows of Rhodri," said Theo, opening his door. He pronounced the name "Griffith."

Maddie fumbled with the handle on her door. "I'm coming too." She swung her legs out, glad of the chance to stretch them.

A hay cart rumbled past, pulled by a sturdy gray cob with its forelock falling over its eyes. Maddie's fingers twitched, longing to untangle the horse's mane and brush its stone-colored coat. A thin, wiry man was walking beside the horse. He stopped when he saw Maddie and Theo, and the horse halted too, nodding its head with the effort of bringing the heavy cart to a standstill.

"*Bore da,*" the man called to them.

"Good day to you," Theo replied, lifting his hat.

"English, are you?" said the man. His voice rose and fell as if he was half talking, half singing.

Theo nodded. "We're looking for a farmer named Rhodri."

The man frowned. "Rhodri ap Huw, would that be? His farm's on that hill over there." He pointed toward the ridge of mountains.

"Thank you very much," said Theo, opening the door of the motorcar again.

"Wait a minute," said the man. "You'll not find Rhodri there now. He died five year ago, not long after the war. Lost all four sons, he did, so he had nothing left to live for, not with his wife dying an' all."

"Who runs the farm now?" Theo asked.

The man with the hay cart shrugged. "No one. You think we've men to spare for an empty farm? There's barely enough of us left to look after our own land. Rhodri's place has been going to ruin these past four year, more's the pity."

Maddie realized she was clenching her fist around the handle of the door. Had they come all this way for nothing? But Theo was thanking the man and getting back into the motorcar. He leaned across the seat and spoke to her through the window. "Come on, Maddie. We'll try the farm anyway." She nodded and climbed in.

Theo turned the car around, and they headed back out of the village. The road that led to the mountains was little more than a stony track with deep hollows that made the motorcar lurch, the engine whining in protest.

Theo brought the car to a stop. "Do you think that's it?" He pointed to a stand of ash trees half hiding a gray stone wall. Maddie peered and realized it was the front of a house that had lost its roof. There were some crumbling piles of stone beside it that might once have been outbuildings. The man with the hay cart hadn't been exaggerating when he described the farm as a ruin.

Theo steered the motorcar onto the driveway and put on the hand brake. The track was too deeply rutted for the Baby Austin's narrow wheels. In silence, they climbed out and began to walk toward the trees. The wind played with the branches, first lifting them aside to reveal the outline of the old house, then dropping them again so that barely a gleam of stone showed through the leaves.

Maddie's heart began to pound. Could Jonathan really be here? Only the walls of the farmhouse remained. The roof had long since fallen in and spars of wood stuck up at angles above the walls. The glassless windows looked like blind eyes, staring unseeing at the visitors. If Jonathan had made it this far, how must he have felt? The one place he thought he could run to was nothing but a heap of stones.

"There's nothing here," said Theo, echoing her thoughts. "We may as well leave."

Maddie went over to the nearest window and looked in, more from curiosity than anything else. She'd never seen a ruined house before. There was a large black range against the far wall, covered in dust and bits of rubble. This must have been the kitchen. The flagstone floor was dotted with broken stones and pieces of wood, and here and there a shattered roof slate. A single wooden chair stood just below the window, and in the far corner, someone had left a pile of dirty rags on the floor.

Maddie stared at the rags. Then she ran to the front door and squeezed through, the wood protesting as it scraped over the stone.

"Jonathan!" she cried. "Jonathan, it's me, Maddie!"

CHAPTER

30

⁓⁓⁓

THE MAN IN THE CORNER of the kitchen stirred as Maddie flung herself down beside him. She felt one of her stockings rip on a stone, but she didn't care. She reached out and put her hand on Jonathan's forehead. It felt colder than the flagstones under her knees.

Jonathan opened his eyes and looked at her for a long moment. *"Annwyl Maddie, mae'n flyn gen i,"* he murmured. He twitched his head impatiently, as if consciously making the change to English. "Maddie, I'm so sorry."

Theo crouched beside Maddie and put one hand on Jonathan's shoulder. "Come on, old chap, let's get you out of here."

Jonathan sat up, looking wary. His face looked gaunt as if he hadn't eaten much since he ran away from Sefton Park, and his scar was a taut scarlet slash across his cheekbone. "Have you come to take me to the police?"

"No!" said Maddie. "We've come to help you."

Jonathan's eyes clouded in confusion. "Is that true?" he said to Theo. "After what I did?"

"Yes," Theo said gruffly, and the two men stared at each other.

"I am sorry," said Jonathan.

Theo stood up. "I know you are."

Maddie looked from one to the other. The similarities between them were less striking now—perhaps because Jonathan looked tired and thin, perhaps because she knew Theo, her real brother, better than she had before. She shook her head. Something felt wrong; they had found Jonathan, so why didn't she feel like turning cartwheels for joy? She stared at Theo's hunched shoulders and realized she had expected some sort of happy reunion between him and Jonathan. She should have known that would be impossible, after everything that had happened.

Theo turned away. "What are you planning to do now?" he asked over his shoulder.

Jonathan stood up and brushed down his clothes. They hung loosely on him, and one of the straps on his gaiters was broken. "I don't know," he admitted. "I only got here yesterday." He glanced awkwardly at Maddie. "I walked most of the way, in case anyone was looking out for me. I wasn't expecting to find the place like this. Poor Rhodri. If I'd come back sooner, I could have helped him run the farm, maybe given him something to hang on for."

The sadness in his voice made Maddie's heart twist with

pity. "Couldn't you stay here and run it now?"

He shook his head. "I've no money to buy livestock, and this place needs more work than I could do on my own." He smiled crookedly. "Looks like I really have lost everything, doesn't it?"

On the other side of the room, Theo reached inside his jacket and brought out an envelope. He stood looking down at it for a few moments, turning it over in his hands. Then he thrust it toward Jonathan.

"There's one hundred pounds in here, and the address of a company in Wrexham. They use ex-servicemen to cut and polish diamonds, and I've heard they're looking for a foreman."

Jonathan took a step back. "I don't need charity, Theo. I can manage for myself, you know."

Theo's mouth twisted in frustration. "Just take it, will you?" Suddenly he smiled. "You always were too proud for your own good."

Maddie felt herself smiling too. The friendship between the two men was still there, still burning away like a stubborn flame.

Jonathan stared at Theo without taking the envelope. "Why are you doing this for me?"

Theo looked down. "Because you're my friend, Jonathan. You saved my life more than once in the trenches, and I owe you for that a hundred times over." He lifted his head and held

Jonathan's gaze. "If I had died in the mine, you would have been a good brother to Maddie. According to her, my family wanted you to be me even more than you might have wanted it yourself. I can't blame you for that."

Jonathan stared at him, his eyes wide. "Does that mean you've forgiven me?"

Theo nodded, and Maddie had to hold her arms tight by her sides to stop herself from going over and hugging him.

"You took nothing from me," Theo said quietly. "You didn't need to send back the knife for that to be true. But it meant a lot to me that you did." He held out the envelope again. "Getting out of that mine alive was like a second chance for me. This isn't charity. It's your second chance. Don't turn it down."

"I won't," Jonathan promised. "Thank you, Theo."

Theo shivered as a gust of wind swept into the room. "You'll freeze to death if you stay here. Come on, we'll take you to the nearest station."

"What, now?" said Jonathan.

"Why not? The sooner you get to Wrexham, the sooner you'll find out about this job. I know it's not farming or horses, but it's a start."

"Will I be safe?" Jonathan asked, his eyes serious, and Maddie knew he was thinking about the police still looking for him.

"I'll go to Sergeant Walters and explain that we're dropping all charges," said Theo. Jonathan started to thank him, but Theo held up his hand to stop him. "We've been friends long enough for me to know what this means to you," he said. "I wouldn't have done it if I didn't believe it was the right thing to do." He turned and walked out of the kitchen.

Maddie was about to follow when Jonathan caught hold of her arm. "Thank you for coming to find me," he said.

Maddie knew she couldn't put what she was feeling into words—joy at finding him safe, relief that Theo had forgiven him, even a twinge of envy at the intensity of the bond between the two men. "Like Theo said, it was the right thing to do," she said.

Outside, they heard Theo crank the engine of the motorcar, and they hurried out of the farmhouse to join him. Jonathan climbed into the backseat behind Maddie. "The nearest station is at Llandrindod Wells," he told them. "It's the other side of Builth Wells, just north of the Brecon Beacons."

Maddie quickly found the town on the map. She directed Theo back along the road to Hundred House, then through Builth Wells and across a windswept stretch of open moorland.

Jonathan leaned forward. "How's Birdy?"

"She's fine." Maddie couldn't help smiling as she pictured the chestnut mare. "She's completely recovered from the colic. And she's jumping out of her skin!" She hesitated, wondering if Jonathan would want to know what was happening at Sefton Park. "I jumped her in the paddock, and she went brilliantly."

"You did a good job schooling her, Jonathan," Theo put in.

Jonathan shrugged. "She was a good horse to start with. And Maddie's a natural rider, you know."

"No, I didn't know," said Theo. "Not until I watched her the other day." He glanced at Maddie, and she felt herself go red.

She was saved from having to say anything else by a large sign beside the road, telling them they had reached Llandrindod Wells. It was a surprisingly big and prosperous-seeming town, with streets lined by tall Victorian terraces and a busy market square. The station was just beyond the square, and Theo parked next to a large town carriage like Sir Wilfred's.

A timetable in the ticket office informed them that there was a train leaving for Wrexham in fifteen minutes. Jonathan used some of the money from the envelope to buy a ticket, and Maddie and Theo followed him onto the platform. They stood in a little circle, rather awkwardly as if there was nothing left to say, and waited for the train to arrive. A cold wind swept along the platform, stirring a page of newspaper, and Theo slapped his hands against his sides to keep warm. Maddie looked at the other people on the platform and wondered if any of them would guess in a thousand years the story behind the two men who looked so similar.

At last the train wheezed alongside the platform, spewing gritty smoke. Jonathan climbed into a carriage and pushed down the window to lean out. His hair was lifted by the wind and he looked exactly as he had when he first came to Sefton Park. Hopeful, hesitant, a little bit scared. Not knowing what the future would bring. Maddie hoped he would have better luck this time—and no need to lie.

Suddenly he beckoned to her. "Look after Firebird," he shouted above the noise of the steam engine. "She's a grand little mare. It would be a shame to let all that training go to waste."

Maddie stared up at him, puzzled. "But she can't jump in the Gold Cup now! I can't ride her!"

"Maybe you can't, but Major Theodore Harman can."

"Really?"

Jonathan nodded. "Your brother's a natural rider, like you. He'd need to practice, but you've a few weeks before the show. Firebird deserves a chance to prove how good she is. Please, Maddie. I know I don't have the right to ask you anything, but I know you want to see Birdy win that cup as much as I do."

He started to say something else but his words were drowned by the shriek of the guard's whistle and the roar of the train, building up steam. Maddie stepped back, blinking as smuts pricked her eyes. She knew this was good-bye forever, that the three of them would never see one another again. For a moment, it hurt so much she could hardly breathe.

Jonathan waved to them as the train pulled slowly out of the station. Theo lifted his hand too, his expression unreadable as he watched his friend leave.

"Good-bye, Jonathan," Maddie whispered. "Good luck."

31

"No."

"Please, Theo! Jonathan says you could do it."

"I'm not going to argue about this, Maddie. I'm not riding Firebird in the Gold Cup."

Maddie dug her fingers into the map, crumpling the edges of the paper. How could Theo be so stubborn?

"Don't do that to the map," Theo said testily. "We need it to get home."

Maddie was tempted to fling the map on the floor and tell Theo to find his own way. She had waited until they crossed the border into England before telling him what Jonathan had said, about the real Theodore Harman taking Firebird in the Gold Cup. To her surprise—after all, he'd seen Birdy jump and knew how much Jonathan thought of her—he said no at once.

"Why not?"

Theo half turned to look at her. "What's the matter with you, Maddie? Don't you listen to people anymore? I've told you I'm not going to do it."

Without warning, he swerved off the road in front of a café.

A large sign declared that it served *Teas for Travelers*. "We'll stop here for something to eat. We should reach Sefton Park by tomorrow morning if we don't stop overnight."

Maddie leaned forward to open her door, but sat back when she realized Theo hadn't moved.

He rested his hands on the steering wheel. "I know you're disappointed that I won't ride Firebird," he said. "But let's get one thing straight before we go any farther. I'm not Jonathan. I'm Theo. You can't expect me to be like him." His hands clenched into fists around the wheel, then relaxed. "Jonathan and I are completely different people, whatever we look like. If people expect me to be like him, it's as if he really has stolen my life. Do you understand?"

Maddie nodded. She wanted to tell Theo that she didn't want him to ride in the competition for Jonathan's sake, but for the sake of Firebird herself, because she deserved to show everyone how brilliant she was. But Theo was already striding toward the tearoom, his head down against the wind.

I'm sorry, Birdy, Maddie thought gloomily. *You won't be jumping in the Gold Cup after all.*

"We're home."

Maddie fought her way up through foggy layers of sleep to hear the sound of tires crunching over gravel. She pushed back the coat that Theo had draped over her and sat up. They were rolling up the drive to Sefton Park. Theo stopped the motor-car outside the front door. There was a light burning in the window of the library, but the rest of the house was in darkness.

He opened his door. "Come on."

Maddie struggled out. The clock in the yard was chiming three. She glanced at the stables, but Theo laid a hand on her arm.

"You can see the mare tomorrow," he said, and his voice was kind.

"Are you going to tell Grandpapa where we've been?" Maddie asked. She didn't need to add, *And what we've done?*

"Yes," said Theo. "I don't want there to be any more lies. Wilfred will understand. Nothing has been lost, and we can put this all behind us now."

Except you've lost your best friend, and I've lost the man I thought was my brother, Maddie thought.

The front door opened as they were walking up the steps, and Sir Wilfred stood there with a lamp in his hand. "I thought it would be you," he said. "Would you like me to ring for some tea?"

Theo shook his head. "No, thank you, Wilfred. We should all go to bed. I'll explain everything in the morning."

"Did you see Price?"

"Yes." Theo made his way toward the stairs. "As I said, we can talk in the morning. I promise everything is going to be all right." Suddenly he sounded older than Sir Wilfred, as if he was in charge of the family now. Maddie touched her grandfather lightly on his arm as she went past, before following Theo up the stairs, too tired even to notice the birds watching her from the paintings.

Her ears drummed all night as if they were still driving, and when she woke she felt as if she had traveled a hundred miles more in her sleep. A shaft of sunlight sliced through the curtains like a spotlight for a troupe of tiny dancing dust motes. Maddie stumbled through to the bathroom to wash her face. Lou's dressing gown was lying on the wicker chair beside the bath, which meant she was here and not in London.

There was no sound from Louisa's room so Maddie left her to sleep and tiptoed downstairs. It was nearly ten o'clock, and she could hear Pippa clearing away crockery in the dining room. Maddie knew she could have a late breakfast if she wanted, but she didn't feel hungry.

Pippa came out of the door carrying a laden tray and almost dropped it when she saw Maddie. "Heavens, Miss Maddie, you startled me!"

"Sorry, Pippa," said Maddie, bending down to pull on her riding boots. "If anyone asks where I am, would you tell them I've gone for a ride, please?"

Pippa nodded. Maddie opened the side door and headed for the stable yard. A half dozen pale brown rabbits scattered to the edge of the paddock as she crunched along the path.

Toby was sitting on a wooden trunk outside the tack room, cleaning a bridle. "Morning, miss," he called.

"Morning, Toby. I'd like to take Firebird out. Would that be all right?"

"Aye, she's long since finished her breakfast."

Maddie fetched Firebird's tack and was on her way to the mare's stable when Toby asked quietly, "Did you see him?"

She stopped, resting the heavy saddle on her hip. There was no need to ask who Toby meant. "Yes. He's all right. He's going to North Wales to look for work." She took a deep breath. "Toby, did you know? That he wasn't Theo, I mean?"

For a few moments, the groom concentrated on rubbing soap onto the noseband in his lap. "I knew he weren't the same Theo that left," he said at last. "But then none of us came back from the war the same. Did I know he was a completely different person? Maybe sometimes I thought he might be."

"Then why didn't you say something?" Maddie asked.

He stopped rubbing and looked up at her. "We've all changed since that war, Miss Maddie. You, your grandparents, everyone that got left behind as well as those of us who went to France. It wasn't for me to say one of you had changed more than he should. An' I could see how happy you were to have him home." He bent down to pick up the bucket, slopping water onto the cobbles. "Those are probably the reasons you said nothing, too."

Maddie knew he was right. Somehow, it was enough to remember how much Toby and Jonathan had liked each other. Of all of them, Toby was the nearest thing he'd had to a real friend at Sefton Park.

She went over to Firebird's stable. The mare greeted her with a rumbling whicker, like a giant cat's purr, and Maddie leaned against her warm neck. "He's gone, Birdy," she whispered. "I'm so sorry."

Firebird reached around to brush her muzzle against Maddie's hair. Her lips pulled against a couple of strands, and Maddie twisted away, laughing.

"Don't eat me, daft girl!" She unbuckled the cotton sheet and slid it off Firebird's gleaming golden back so she could put on the saddle.

They headed down the lane past the church and through the gate into the estate. The air was filled with birdsong, competing with the loud and tuneless singing that was coming from a maroon-painted barge moored close to the bridge. A woman with curly black hair popped her head out of the cabin door and waved to Maddie as she trotted past. She waved back and pushed Firebird into a canter. The mare's hooves drummed lightly on the grass. Sir Wilfred's stockman had turned out some cows to graze alongside the track, and every so often Birdy swerved to avoid one of the tawny-colored cattle, snorting in mock fear.

Maddie urged her faster until they were galloping, then turned along the track where the tree had fallen. She didn't try to slow Firebird's stride—the tree trunk was lower than the jumps in the paddock, and Maddie knew she'd need extra speed to clear the width. The mare soared over on her invisible wings and tried to put her head down afterward to flick up her heels, just for the joy of it.

Laughing and breathless, Maddie sat up straight and kept hold of the reins. She didn't mind Firebird having fun, but she didn't want to end up on the ground. She slowed her to a walk as they reached the pinewoods. The air felt cool and damp under the trees, and a pair of deer leaped, startled, through the trunks ahead of them, their white tails bobbing a warning. Maddie let the reins slip through her fingers so Firebird could stretch her neck. She wondered where Jonathan was and what he was doing. Had he reached Wrexham? Would he be able to get a job with the diamond company? Would there be any horses for him to ride? Maddie couldn't imagine him being happy unless there were.

When she rode back down the drive, she saw George's motorcar parked by the front door. She unsaddled Firebird and sponged her down, then went indoors, unpinning her hair and shaking it away from her neck.

Voices were coming from her grandmother's salon. Matthew appeared in the hall with an empty tray. "I think your grandmother would like you to join her, Miss Madeline," he said.

Maddie went over and opened one of the double doors. She hoped George hadn't brought his parents with him. She was still wearing her riding habit and her hair was sticking up like a gorse bush. Lord and Lady Edwards were not in the salon, but everyone else was. Maddie's grandmother was in her usual seat, with Sir Wilfred standing behind her. George and Louisa were on the sofa opposite them, and Theo was standing by the fireplace, one hand resting on the marble mantelpiece. Maddie wondered if they were about to get into trouble for going to find Jonathan.

"Come and sit down, Madeline," Lady Ella ordered, beckoning her to an empty chair. Her cheeks were faintly pink and her hands were clasped in her lap, the knuckles showing white through her papery skin. Maddie braced herself. Her grandmother was clearly agitated about something, and it could only be the news that Theo had helped Jonathan to escape.

"George has something he wants to tell us," Lady Ella went on.

What did George have to do with Jonathan? Puzzled, Maddie looked at her sister, but Lou was staring at the floor, two dark wings of hair falling forward to hide her face.

George put down his teacup and smiled. "Thank you for humoring me like this. What I have to say is mainly for Louisa's ears, but I thought it might be easier if you all heard it together."

So this wasn't about Jonathan. Maddie breathed out in relief and looked expectantly at her future brother-in-law, wondering what on earth he was going to say.

George took hold of Lou's hand and twisted around to look at her. His false leg stuck out at an awkward angle, but his back was ramrod straight.

"My dear Lou," he began, and Maddie watched her sister's cheeks go red. "You did me a great honor by agreeing to marry me. But I know that it's not what you want, not in your heart. I . . ." His voice faltered. "I think we should call off the wedding."

Maddie stared at him in astonishment.

Lady Ella gasped. She reached out to clutch her husband's hand, knocking her teacup off the table beside her. Tea splashed across the rug but she didn't even look down. "You don't mean that, George! Louisa, tell him he's wrong! Of course you want to marry him."

Louisa turned to look at her grandmother, and to Maddie's surprise she seemed quite calm. "No, Ella. George is right." She touched his hand lightly. "That is the kindest, most loving thing you have ever done for me," she said. "I can never thank you enough."

Sir Wilfred cleared his throat. "I say, George, old chap. I'm not sure about all this. Is it fair on Lou, calling off her engagement so suddenly? What will everyone think?"

Louisa stood up, her eyes blazing. "Who cares what people think?" she demanded. "They'll be more interested in the fact that we let a complete stranger into our home for four months. A broken engagement is hardly a scandal on that sort of scale!"

Maddie winced and at the same time felt a stab of guilt that she had failed to realize that her sister never really wanted to get married. She had been too caught up with Jonathan and Firebird, and suddenly she felt as if she had let Lou down.

George put his hand on Louisa's arm. "Steady on, my dear. Sit down, it's all right." As if Lou was a startled horse, she allowed herself to be steadied and sat back on the sofa, smoothing her skirt with trembling fingers.

George looked solemnly at Maddie's grandparents. "I don't see this is any sort of scandal. I could not admire Louisa more, I promise. She is brave, intelligent, and strong-minded—all excellent qualities for a modern young woman," he added, as Lady Ella pursed her lips at "strong-minded." "I also know that she would like to go to Oxford University and read Law. If she wishes to marry me afterward, I would be very happy indeed to make her my wife, but if her life takes her in a different direction, then so be it."

Maddie's grandmother frowned. "This is all because of those rallies, isn't it? I knew something like this would happen if you spent too much time in London, Louisa."

"Something like what?" Lou challenged. "Like me discovering what I really want to do with my life? Why can't you accept me for who I am, Ella?"

"I think you should be extremely proud of your granddaughter," said George. "I am, and I know her parents would be."

Maddie swallowed. George was right—right to be proud of Louisa, and right to break off their engagement if it wasn't what Lou wanted most. "I'm proud of you too, Lou," she said shakily, ignoring the angry glance from her grandmother. She stood up and went over to put her hand on Lou's shoulder.

Her sister looked up at her with a faint smile. She obviously didn't bear Maddie a grudge for not noticing how she really felt. "Thank you, Maddie. Don't worry, we'll get through all this. Everything will be all right, you'll see."

The atmosphere in the house crackled as if a storm were about to break, so Maddie went back outside, leaving Louisa and George telling her grandparents how they would take care of all the announcements to break off the engagement. Maddie ran across the lawn, light-footed with relief by the time she reached the fence. She liked George, she really did, but Lou shouldn't marry him if it wasn't what she wanted. She still felt bad for not realizing long ago, but then she remembered the night of the ball, when her sister had seemed genuinely excited to be celebrating her engagement, and she told herself this was one thing she couldn't feel responsible for. It was enough that George had known how Lou felt, and had the courage to break off their engagement.

Firebird was grazing in the paddock, swishing her tail at flies. She lifted her head as Maddie reached the fence and ambled over, her neat leaf-shaped ears twitching in time with her strides.

Maddie reached out and ran her fingers down Birdy's white-striped nose. Suddenly Firebird pricked her ears and looked over Maddie's shoulder. Theo was walking across the grass. He came up to stand beside her, resting his hands on the top rail.

"Well, that was quite an announcement," he said, whistling through his teeth.

"Better for Lou to go to university if that's what she wants, though," said Maddie.

Theo nodded. "Oh yes. We only get one crack at being happy."

"What did Grandpapa say when you told him about Jonathan?" Maddie asked.

"He's still very angry, but I think he understands why I don't want Jonathan to go to prison. I . . . I did have to promise that I'd never see Jonathan again."

Maddie glanced sympathetically at her brother. She had seen the echo of the friendship they had shared for the last seven years. However much she missed Jonathan, Theo would miss him a hundred times more.

An engine growled on the other side of the hedge, and Firebird wheeled away, kicking up her heels. Maddie knew she was only pretending to be scared for the sheer delight of being able to leap around. She watched the mare gallop to the far side of the paddock, then spin on her hindquarters and canter back, shaking her mane.

"She's a real beauty, isn't she?" Theo commented.

"Yes, she is," Maddie agreed.

"Jonathan always had a good eye for horses," he murmured. He turned to face Maddie. "You really want Firebird to jump in the Gold Cup, don't you?"

She nodded. "Yes, I do. You've seen how much she loves jumping. It's even more amazing when you're riding her. It's like she's flying! I'm so proud of her, I want as many people as possible to see how brilliant she is."

Theo smiled. "You know what George said, about Mother and Father being proud of Lou? They'd be proud of you too, Maddie. The way you ride, how you trained Firebird over those jumps." He reached out and ran his hand down Firebird's neck. "When I said I wouldn't ride her in the Gold Cup, I was afraid you were trying to turn me into Jonathan. It felt as if you wished I hadn't come back."

"That's not true!" said Maddie. It was how she had felt to

begin with, but now, she wished she could have both of them.

Theo was looking at her with one eyebrow raised as if he could read her thoughts, and Maddie stumbled on, "Well, maybe it was hard at first because I was used to having Jonathan around. But I promise I didn't want you to ride Birdy just because Jonathan was going to. He's the one who said you should ride her. He would never have said that if he didn't think you were good enough."

Theo turned to watch Firebird, who had stopped cantering and was standing a little way off, grazing. "Jonathan always had faith in me, even when I didn't. He's right, she's a great little mare. And I will ride her in the Gold Cup, if that's what you want."

"If there's a water jump, you'll be fine. You just need to gallop her as fast as you can without letting her fall onto her forehand. It's the triple bar we need to worry about." Maddie kept pace with Theo as he walked Firebird around the paddock. The competition was less than three weeks away, and Maddie was struggling to remember everything Jonathan had told her when they had started Firebird's training.

She measured the distance between the canter poles once more, then beckoned to Theo. "Bring her over the upright to start with," she called.

He nodded and shortened the reins, his knuckles looking

taut and white against the chestnut mane. Firebird tossed her head, her hind legs skittering underneath her.

"Be good, little one," Maddie murmured. She knew Theo wouldn't relax until he found out for himself just how well Firebird could jump. "Don't worry about trying to see the stride before the fence," she told him, raising her voice. "The canter poles will put her in the right place."

He turned the mare toward the jump and her pace quickened. To Maddie's relief, Theo didn't try to slow her down, but sat still and let her find her own stride as she bounced over the poles. She sprang over the rail with a flick of her heels, clearing it by a good three feet.

Theo lurched backward, taken by surprise. He landed with a thud in the saddle and drew up breathlessly alongside Maddie. "She's got quite a jump," he panted.

"I did warn you!" Maddie told him with a grin. "At least you know what it's going to feel like next time." She walked over and lifted a rail onto the second set of jump stands. "You'll get two strides between these two fences," she explained. "But the distance might be longer in the competition, so we'll move them apart once you've jumped it a couple of times."

Theo smiled at her, his gray eyes warm under the brim of his cap. "You really know what you're talking about, don't you?"

She shrugged. "It doesn't feel like it. Mostly I'm just repeating what Jonathan said, or what we found out when we visited the show-jumping yard."

"Don't be so hard on yourself." Theo scooped up the reins and leaned forward to pat Firebird's neck. "Come on, my lady. Let's have another go."

This time he leaned forward as Firebird took off, pushing his hands up her neck to avoid catching her mouth. Four quick strides and they were over the second, but Firebird dropped a hind leg and brought the pole clattering to the ground behind them.

Theo pulled a face.

"Don't worry," Maddie told him as she hoisted the rail back onto the cups. It was a hot day, and she felt as if she was melting inside her riding habit. "Knocking a jump with her back legs is worth two faults," she explained. "It's worse if she hits it with her front legs, because that's four faults."

"That seems odd," Theo remarked.

"Jonathan said it's because of hunting. If a horse hits a fence in front, he's more likely to somersault over and hurt his rider. It doesn't matter so much if he knocks it on the way down."

Theo nodded. "Makes sense, I suppose. Right, let's have another go at those fences, then we'll try the triple bar." He nudged Birdy into a canter, keeping her nose tucked in and her quarters underneath her. Maddie smiled. The flame-colored horse was working her magic again.

They cleared the pair of uprights, and Maddie moved the

second fence a little farther away so that Theo would have to push Firebird on when she landed, encouraging her to take longer strides but without flattening her for the second rail. Then she set up the triple bar, which seemed big enough to house a family of pigs underneath it. Firebird's ears flicked as Theo cantered her toward it, and Maddie held her breath, but Theo kicked once, twice, then they were flying over the rails to land cleanly on the other side.

Maddie ran up and threw her arms around Firebird's neck. "You did it! You were wonderful!" she cried, meaning both Firebird and Theo at the same time.

Above her, Theo patted the mare over and over, grinning. "Jonathan was right," he agreed. "She's amazing! Next stop for us, the Grand Hall at Olympia!"

32

MADDIE RAN HER HAND down the bandage to smooth out any wrinkles, then stood up and looked at Firebird. A wave of emotion made her knees feel wobbly, and she rested one hand on the mare's flank, letting the warmth of Firebird's skin underneath the cotton rug soothe her. Her coat was the color of sunrise, glowing orange and gold, and her tail had been washed until every strand was soft and shiny. She looked small and vulnerable with her legs thickly bandaged and a clean blue-and-white-checked sheet buckled over her. Maddie fought down an urge to take off the sheet and the bandages and set Firebird loose in the paddock. What if Jonathan's early worries had been right, and she was too small to compete against thoroughbreds like Nightwatchman? What if she got hurt, or worse?

"All set?" called a cheerful voice behind her. Toby was leaning over the door in his shirtsleeves. "The van will be here in a few minutes."

Maddie nodded. Toby and Theo were taking Firebird to Olympia a day early to give her time to settle in. Maddie would have given anything to be able to go with them but they would be sleeping in the wagon like the other riders and grooms, and there wouldn't be any other girls around. She was going up the following day with George and Louisa, and would have to be content with watching from the seats around the arena. Lady Ella and Sir Wilfred had decided it was too far for them to travel in a single day, although they wanted to hear all about the competition afterward.

"I'll bring her out in a moment," she told Toby.

"Right you are. She looks grand, by the way. You've done a good job there."

Maddie smiled. "Thank you." Even if she couldn't be Firebird's official groom at the show, she would know that at least part of the shine in her coat was down to her. She rested her hands on either side of the mare's face. Firebird looked at her with liquid brown eyes and blew gently down her nose.

"You take care, my precious girl," Maddie whispered. "I'll be there tomorrow, I promise." She bent down and pressed her face against the broad white stripe that ran down Firebird's nose.

The mare pricked her ears as an engine rumbled into the yard. Maddie looked over the stable door and watched a large, pale green truck reverse over the cobbles. She was glad it wasn't the same truck that the police had sent to fetch Firebird, whose driver had tried to hit her. A short, stocky man jumped down from the cab and lowered the ramp.

Climbing into the back of the truck, he kicked a thin layer of straw over the wooden slats.

"Here goes, Birdy," Maddie said, untying the lead rope from the ring in the wall. Firebird snuffled her lips against her sleeve, leaving a faint smear of foam.

Outside, Theo was loading his overnight bag into the cab. He slammed the door and came over to Maddie. "Would you like to load her?"

The driver of the truck raised his eyebrows but stood back to let Maddie lead Firebird up to the ramp. The mare walked stiffly in her bandages, her neck arched and her nostrils flared. For a moment, she looked like a desert horse again, too wild to be ridden. . . .

Maddie shook herself. It was too late to change her mind now. She clicked her tongue as Firebird hesitated at the bottom of the ramp, knocking the tip of her hoof against the wood. "Come on, girl," she said encouragingly.

Firebird tossed her head and snorted. The truck driver glanced at Toby, but the groom held up his hand as if to say, *Wait, let her try again.*

Maddie reached up and rubbed the top of Firebird's neck, under her mane. The mare's ears flickered, then she lowered her head and put her front hoof flat on the ramp. "Good girl!" Maddie praised her.

With a grunt, Firebird cantered up the ramp in a couple of

strides, with Maddie running to keep up and trying not to trip on the wooden slats. Inside, the truck was like a low-ceilinged stable, with slatted sides to let in air. Firebird looked around, rolling her eyes. Maddie quickly tied her to a metal ring before the mare decided to run out again. She gave Firebird one last pat, feeling her coat already damp with sweat, and walked back down the ramp.

"Well done," said Toby, and even the truck driver looked impressed. Between them, they heaved up the ramp and slid the bolts into place. Firebird kicked the side of the truck, and Maddie winced.

"Don't worry, lass," said the truck driver. "She'll settle down once we're on the move."

Theo swung himself into the passenger seat, and Toby climbed in after him as the driver cranked the engine. There was a deafening roar as the engine started up and the yard filled with choking black fumes. Firebird let out a whinny of protest and kicked the side of the truck again.

Maddie watched the truck turn into the lane. It would take them about four hours to reach Olympia. Toby was going to lunge Firebird this afternoon to get rid of any stiffness from the journey, then Theo would jump her over a couple of practice fences. The competition was scheduled to start at two o'clock the following day, so Firebird would have plenty of time to rest before the competition.

The stable yard clock chimed eight, and Maddie stumbled indoors for some breakfast. She had been up since six, washing Birdy's tail and polishing her coat with a stable rubber until it gleamed. Now she had to wait a whole day and a night before she saw Firebird again—in the Grand Hall at Olympia, with the rest of the horses and riders competing for the King George V Gold Cup.

The noise was deafening, and Maddie's hands twitched by her sides with the urge to clap her hands over her ears. Someone trod heavily on Maddie's toe, and she let out a startled yelp.

Louisa touched her arm. "Are you all right?" she mouthed.

Before Maddie could say anything, the loudspeakers crackled to life along the crowded corridor. "Class Four, the High Jump, is about to start. Please take your seats, ladies and gentlemen," declared the announcer. The High Jump was the class before the Gold Cup, which meant they had about an hour to find Theo and wish him luck. They had only just fought their way into the outer hall at Olympia, and George had temporarily abandoned them in search of a program and a map of the halls.

"Got them!" called a voice, and Maddie looked up to see George fighting his way toward them. "I think I deserve an extra medal for that," he puffed, leaning on his stick to get his breath back.

"You're definitely our hero of the hour," Louisa teased, patting him on the arm. Maddie caught Lou's eye and grinned.

"Where to first?" George asked, as Maddie unfolded the map and tried to hold it flat.

"I'd like to go to the Collecting Ring and find Theo before the class starts," she said. "I think it's along this corridor, then left at the end of the Grand Hall."

George offered his arm to each of them, and they started to weave their way through the tide of people, all of whom seemed to be going in the opposite direction. Maddie hadn't seen this many people since she had lived in London. Louisa seemed quite comfortable with treading on other people's heels and hardly having space to breathe, but Maddie felt a stab of longing for the peaceful grassy paddocks at Sefton Park.

She heaved a sigh of relief as they turned the corner into the passage that led to the Collecting Rings. There were far fewer people here, mostly wiry-looking grooms with tweed caps and gaiters, and riders in military uniforms, or dark jackets and breeches if they weren't in the army.

A man wearing a brown suit stopped them halfway down the passage. "Excuse me, sir," he said to George. "Riders, owners, and grooms only beyond this point."

George drew the scarlet cardboard badge from his pocket. "We're owners," he said, and Maddie felt her stomach flip over with excitement.

The man nodded. "Very well, sir. On you go, but only as far as the gate, please. And good luck!"

"Thanks!" Maddie called over her shoulder.

The gate at the end of the passage was almost hidden behind a row of anxious-looking people. Maddie guessed they were the other owners. Letting go of George's arm, she squeezed between them and stared around the large sandy arena. Glossy, long-legged thoroughbreds were cantering around the edge, their riders serious-faced. Maddie looked for a little chestnut horse with a dished face, but the smallest animal was a dark gray gelding ridden by a man in a bulging navy coat.

Maddie's heart sank. What if something had happened overnight? Firebird could have been injured on the journey, or maybe she had tried to get out of her unfamiliar stable and hurt herself.

She felt Lou squeeze in behind her. "Can you see them?" she asked in Maddie's ear.

"Not yet." She leaned farther over the gate and nearly toppled into the arena altogether when there was a thunder of hooves beside her and a voice shouted, "Look out, there!"

Louisa grabbed Maddie's arm and yanked her back. "Be careful!"

"I just want to find Birdy," Maddie said, feeling her voice wobble treacherously.

There was the hollow sound of a rail hitting sand from behind a huge pair of doors at the end of the arena, and a few moments later the doors opened to let a bay horse canter out, shaking its head and sweating. Its rider was dressed in a dark blue uniform with a red collar.

"*Four faults for Capitano Bartelli and Noche,*" announced the loud-speaker.

A dark-haired boy ran up to the bay horse and took hold of its bridle while the rider jumped off, looking disappointed.

"*Competitor number twenty-eight for the High Jump,*" called a man with a megaphone in his hand. The man on the gray gelding trotted into the arena.

"*Next in the arena we have Mr. William Leigh riding Cloud,*" said the announcer as the doors closed again.

"The High Jump will be over soon," Louisa warned in a low voice. "We'll have to go and find our seats."

Maddie bit her lip. "We can't go without saying good luck to Theo!"

George patted her on the shoulder. "We've got front row seats, Maddie. We'll be able to give him a wave when they come in for the parade before the class."

Suddenly Maddie heard footsteps running down the corridor, and someone pushed their way through the people at the gate to appear at George's shoulder. "There you are, Miss Maddie!"

It was Toby, with a bundle of clothes under his arm.

"Toby! Is Birdy all right? Where's Theo?"

"They're outside, warming up." He thrust the bundle of clothes at Maddie. "Here, put these on. You can go an' see them for yourself." In his other hand he held out a piece of yellow card that read *Toby Chalk, Groom, Firebird.*

Maddie stared at him in confusion. "Go on," Toby urged. "I'll sit in your seat with your sister and Lord Edwards. You'll need a belt for the breeches an' the shirt will be too big," he added, "but no one will be looking at you for long."

Louisa gave Maddie's shoulders a squeeze. "That's a brilliant idea! Come on, Maddie. Toby is giving you the chance to be Firebird's groom!"

chapter 33

LOUISA RAN TO THE STEWARD in the brown suit and explained that her sister was feeling faint, and was there somewhere private she could sit down for a moment? Looking distinctly alarmed, the man directed them to a tiny office just off the main corridor. Louisa steered Maddie into it. "I'll be waiting outside," she promised.

In a daze, Maddie pulled off her skirt and blouse and dressed herself in Toby's clothes. The breeches slipped straight off her hips but she used a piece of twine she found on the floor to keep them up, and left the shirt untucked to hide the makeshift belt. She had to roll up the sleeves several times, but with luck Toby would be right and everyone would be far too busy watching the horses to worry about a groom dressed like a scarecrow. Wishing she had a neat bob like Lou's or Rosie's, she tipped her head upside down and gathered all her hair on top of her head before stuffing it into the tweed cap.

Louisa grinned when Maddie went back outside. "You look a perfect urchin," she said. "Here, take this." She tucked the yellow card into the pocket of Maddie's breeches. "Toby,

George, and I are going to find our seats now." She gave Maddie a quick hug. "Give Firebird my love!" she added, her eyes sparkling.

Feeling as if her legs were about to give way with nerves, Maddie ran back to the Collecting Ring. She stopped at the gate, waiting for someone to open it for her, before she remembered she was a boy now, and she could do that sort of thing for herself. The latch was stiff, and she was struck by a sudden fear that her disguise would all be for nothing if she couldn't even let herself into the ring.

A steward came over to her. "Having trouble, sonny?" he said, tugging the latch open. "Here you go."

"Thanks," Maddie muttered, ducking her head as she slipped through.

Behind her, the big doors opened, and a black horse trotted out. Loud applause followed it, almost drowning out the announcer. *"And that was clear at five feet seven inches for Ace ridden by Major Archibald Havers!"*

A thin-necked dapple gray cantered into the arena. Maddie guessed that the High Jump was more than halfway through, which didn't leave much time to find Firebird and Theo. She jogged along the edge of the arena, flattening herself against the wall when horses cantered past, so close that they flicked sand into her face. Reaching the entrance, she clung to the frame and peered out. Several horses were being walked around on the stony space of ground. On the far side were rows of temporary stables, the white canvas roofs flapping in the breeze. Maddie wondered which one was Firebird's.

She scanned the horses—bay, gray, black, gray again. There was a sudden flash of amber behind a bay horse, a small, neat shape walking with her neck arched and her tail streaming out behind her. *Birdy!*

"Theo!" she called, then coughed and lowered her voice. "Er, Master Theo?"

He reined Firebird to a halt and grinned down at Maddie. He looked very smart in his khaki uniform, with a wide brown belt over his jacket and gleaming black boots. "There you are, Toby! I think we should take her over a practice fence now, don't you?"

Maddie wanted to throw her arms around Firebird like she did at home, but no groom would do that here. "How is she? Did she get frightened on the journey? What's her stable like?" she asked all in a rush.

Theo smiled. "She's absolutely fine. I think she slept better than we did! Toby put so much straw in her stable we could barely find her this morning. There was no way he was going to risk her knocking a leg."

"Good," said Maddie, running her hand down Firebird's foreleg anyway. It felt cool and smooth, and the mare stamped her hoof restlessly as if she knew there was work to be done.

Theo nodded toward the Collecting Ring. "It sounds like the High Jump is nearly finished. Let's have a go at the practice fence before everyone has the same idea."

"Are you nervous?" Maddie asked as they headed for the entrance.

"A bit," Theo admitted. "I saw the plan of the course this morning, and there's going to be a triple bar instead of a water jump."

Maddie nodded. "That's all right. I know it's harder without the canter poles, but keep your legs on her three strides before the jump and remember that you always feel as if you're going faster than you really are."

"Yes, sir," Theo teased, touching the peak of his cap.

Maddie blushed. "Sorry. I just feel as if I'm going to be jumping this course myself, I've been thinking about it so much."

"I know. And we couldn't do it without you." Theo's face was serious now, but there was no time to say anything else because they had reached the entrance to the Collecting Ring. He shortened Firebird's reins and pushed her into a trot, tucking in behind a bad-tempered-looking bay that flattened its ears and swished its tail at them.

Maddie went to stand with the other grooms, all dressed in breeches, shirtsleeves, and flat caps like her. She squeezed next to the shortest one, a thin-faced lad with black hair who was muttering to himself in Italian. He had his eyes fixed on a beautiful white horse that was cantering showily toward the practice rail in the center of the ring. He let out a satisfied whistle as the horse landed safely on the other side. *"Bellissimo!"*

Maddie hoped the white horse was practicing for the High Jump, because it would be stiff competition if it was in the Gold Cup with Birdy. To her disappointment, she heard the loudspeaker announce that the High Jump had been won by Major Archibald Havers riding Ace. The white horse must be in the Gold Cup after all.

She looked around for the other horse she knew would be hard to beat: Nightwatchman. There were several dark brown thoroughbreds cantering around. As she scanned the arena, one of the other grooms nudged her in the ribs.

"Is that your fellow waving to you over there? Look lively or you'll be out of a job!"

Maddie ran over to where Theo was waiting. "Hurry up," he said, sounding tense. "I need you to put up a practice rail for me. The class will start as soon as they've built the course."

"Yes, of course, sorry," Maddie stammered. She headed carefully into the center of the ring; the last thing she needed was to be knocked off her feet by a passing horse.

She waited by the jump stand until the white horse had cleared the fence again, giving an airy flick of its heels as if it could jump much, much higher if it tried. Then she propped one end of the rail on her shoulder, just as she did in the pad-dock at home, and slid the cup down a few holes. Firebird needed to start off lower than this. The weight of the poles and the feel of the cup in her hand felt so familiar to Maddie that she started to forget where she was. All that mattered was helping Firebird warm up, letting her stretch and spring until she grew her invisible wings.

She stood back to let Theo canter her over the fence, trying not to grin too broadly as the mare soared over. She nodded to Theo like she had seen other grooms do, and raised the pole a few inches. A lad appeared on the other side and shifted the other cup. "Thanks!" Maddie called.

"No problem," he called back. "My chap's just warming up too. You in the Gold Cup?"

Maddie nodded. The lad grinned. "Looks like you're the competition then." He glanced to make sure there were no horses coming, then jogged over to stand next to Maddie. "I've not seen you 'ere before."

She shook her head.

The lad raised a hand to a rider on the far side of the arena, then turned back to Maddie. "That's my fellow over there. You want to watch him," he warned. "'E won the cup last year, an' we're pretty sure 'e can do it again. You've 'eard of Nightwatchman, right?"

Maddie froze. She hadn't seen this lad when she and

· 327 ·

Jonathan visited Mr. Stillwell's yard, but if the trainer was here himself, he could easily recognize her. Staring at her boots, she muttered, "Yes, I've heard of Nightwatchman."

The lad was too busy watching his horse to reply. Maddie listened to the pounding hooves get nearer, then stop abruptly as the horse took off into the air. There was a thud as he landed, and the groom clapped his hands. "Good job!" he called to the rider.

Maddie looked up in time to see Firebird canter up to the rail. The little mare sprang over, her tail whisking into the air behind her. She cleared it generously, and several people turned to look.

"Nice little horse," said a voice behind Maddie.

Her heart plummeted. It was Mr. Stillwell! Theo had halted Firebird at the end of the hall and was looking expectantly at her, waiting for her to raise the pole. She gave her head a tiny shake.

She heard Mr. Stillwell's groom tell him that he didn't know the name of the chestnut horse, but he'd just been talking to the rider's lad.

Before Maddie could flee, a familiar voice demanded, "You there! Is that your mare?"

34

MADDIE TURNED AROUND slowly, shoving her hands into her pockets and hunching so that she looked like a timid groom rather than a girl in a rather feeble disguise. "What's that, sir?"

"That mare," Mr. Stillwell repeated. "She's got a cracking jump. I was wondering what her breeding was."

Maddie shrugged. "Dunno, sir. I've not been working for Major Harman that long. You'd best ask him."

The trainer nodded. "I might just do that." Maddie fled before he could say anything else. She darted over to Theo, who was looking very puzzled.

"What's going on?"

She quickly explained about the trainer.

"Well, he won't recognize me," said Theo. When Maddie raised her eyebrows, he added, "He'd remember Jonathan from his scar, wouldn't he? But don't worry, I'll try to keep out of his way just in case."

The man at the doors lifted his megaphone. "Gentlemen, we are ready to start the parade. All competitors for the Gold Cup, please."

"That's us," said Theo.

"This is the easy bit!" Maddie reminded him. "You won't have to jump anything this time, so it's a good chance for Birdy to get used to the ring."

Giving Firebird one last pat, she squeezed among the other grooms crowded around the double doors. She found a gap at the edge where she could see into the arena. There were twenty horses in the parade, all polished and well-muscled, with gleaming bridles and long legs stamping restlessly on the sand. Firebird was a whole hand smaller than most of them, looking like a child's pony among the thoroughbreds. But her coat shone under the lights, and she arched her neck so that her mane flowed like a golden wave. Maddie thought her heart would burst with pride. *Brave little desert horse,* she thought. *I wish Jonathan could see you now!*

The announcer was reading the names of the horses and riders over the loudspeaker, sounding almost as excited as Maddie felt. The crowd clapped and cheered as each competitor was announced. The loudest cheer came for Captain Gavin Acheson and Nightwatchman. The beautiful white horse was popular too, even though it wasn't ridden by a British competitor.

Maddie held her breath when Firebird's name was read aloud, bracing herself for a confused silence. Would people think the little chestnut mare had been entered as some sort of joke? But as soon as the announcer introduced Major Theodore Harman riding Firebird, a small section of the crowd started clapping so loudly that the rest joined in. Maddie grinned when she saw George and Louisa standing on their feet, with Rosie, Bertram, Lily, Clarissa, and Algernon cheering madly beside them. Toby was there too, waving his cap in the air.

As soon as the riders had filed out of the main arena, the first competitor was ushered in. Maddie went over to Theo and held Firebird's bridle while he checked the girth. Her brother looked deathly pale and his fingers shook as he fiddled with the buckle.

Firebird's coat glistened with a faint sheen of sweat, and Maddie could feel her heart pounding when she laid her hand behind the mare's shoulder, but her breathing was even and regular, and she stood still while other horses milled about them.

"We're twelfth to go," Theo said.

"Oh," said Maddie. She looked around to see what other grooms and riders were doing. Those who were jumping early in the class were cantering in circles and putting their horses over the practice rail, while others walked around the arena on a loose rein. "I think you should keep Birdy moving," she suggested to Theo. "We don't want her to cool down too much."

He nodded and gathered up the reins. "Good idea." As he

rode off, he glanced back. "You'll stay here, won't you?"

"I'm not going anywhere," Maddie promised.

The first horse refused three times at the second fence and its rider came out looking very red in the face. The second had two fences down, and the third must have run straight through the triple bar, judging by the deafening clatter of poles.

Some of the grooms muttered comments about "a tough course," and suggested there might not be any clears at all. Maddie began to feel sick. Then a French rider emerged with just half a fault, having rattled the top rail on the triple bar, and the Italian on the beautiful gray scored the first perfect clear, cantering out of the arena to rather muted applause. Maddie guessed that the crowd were happy to cheer for a good-looking horse as long as it didn't beat all the British competitors.

Four rounds before Firebird's, Maddie went over to the practice fence and beckoned to Theo. He nodded and turned Firebird toward the jump. She took off too close to the fence and sent the rail flying with her front legs. Maddie winced as the pole thudded onto the ground. Theo circled away, shaking his head.

"Try again!" Maddie called, heaving the pole back onto the stands.

This time Theo sat deep in the saddle and kept his legs still, so that Firebird cantered steadily up to the rail and sprang over it with her hocks well underneath her. Maddie started to wrestle with the nearest cup to raise the pole, but Mr. Stillwell's lad came over and tapped her on the shoulder.

"I think the steward's calling for your chap," he said.

Maddie looked around in a panic. "He can't be! There's at least two more riders before us!"

"Looks like one of them pulled out," said the groom. "Your chap had best be quick, or he'll miss his turn."

She ran over to Theo, who was trotting in a small circle. "You have to go in now!" she told him breathlessly. "The rider before you pulled out!"

To her surprise, Theo just nodded. "Fair enough," he said. He smiled down at her. "If we aren't ready now, we'll never be."

Maddie reached up and untangled a knot in Firebird's mane. "Just remember to keep her steady, and sit still for the last three strides before each fence. If you've got her right by then, there's nothing more you can do to help her."

"I'll remember," Theo promised, and Maddie stepped back. "Good luck!" she whispered.

Firebird looked tinier than ever as she trotted away. The previous rider cantered out with the announcer totting up his faults behind him, and the huge doors closed behind Firebird as if she was being swallowed up. Maddie darted for the gap she had found earlier, pushing her way in next to an elderly groom who tutted under his mustache.

"Next we have Major Theodore Harman riding his own mare, Firebird,"

said the announcer. *"Good luck, Major Harman!"*

Theo cantered Firebird in a circle and turned her toward the first fence, one of two uprights along the left-hand wall. Maddie felt so dizzy that she thought her legs would buckle.

With a toss of her head, Firebird leaped over the first fence. Three quick strides, and they were over the second. Maddie heard a strange sighing sound, and realized that the entire crowd was holding their breath and letting it out when Firebird landed safely. They loved the brave-hearted little chestnut horse! It was clear she wasn't the usual sort of show-jumper, with her flowing mane and broad dished face.

The groom beside her grunted approvingly as Theo cleared the second pair of uprights. Now he was cantering down the center of the ring, with just the triple bar to clear. *Faster, faster,* Maddie willed him, waiting for Birdy's hoofbeats to speed up. This jump was lower than the uprights—only a little over five feet—but well over six feet wide. Firebird needed a good run at it to clear the spread.

They reached the fence, and the little mare sprang into the air like a cat. Maddie held her breath. After what felt like several minutes, Firebird landed cleanly on the sand again. It was a clear round!

With the sound of clapping ringing in her ears, Maddie ran over to the double doors. Theo rode out, slapping his hand against Firebird's neck and grinning.

"Well done!" Maddie cried. She patted Firebird's shoulder over and over. "You clever, brilliant girl!"

The mare tossed her head and snorted, scattering foam onto Maddie's shirt.

"I reckon she enjoyed that," said Theo, sounding breathless. "I'll definitely go for three strides between the uprights again in the next round."

Maddie stared up at him. She'd forgotten there would be another round to decide the winner, because the white horse had jumped clear as well.

Theo swung his leg over Firebird's withers and jumped down to the ground. "Walk her around, please," he said. "We need to keep her moving." He nodded to where the Italian groom was leading the gray horse around the edge of the arena with the stirrups run up. Maddie was about to shoot Theo an excited grin when she remembered she was supposed to be an ordinary stable lad. Instead she just nodded and clicked her tongue at Firebird.

The mare trotted a few paces, in high spirits from her jumping, but calmed when Maddie put her hand on her neck and murmured to her. After two circuits of the arena, loud applause announced ahead of the loudspeaker that a third horse had jumped clear. Maddie wasn't surprised when Nightwatchman trotted through the doors.

The first round ended with no more clear rounds, leaving

three horses to jump again. Theo walked over and swung himself back into the saddle—one advantage to Firebird's short legs was that Maddie didn't have to give him a leg-up. He looked too nervous to speak.

"Good luck," said Maddie.

Theo nodded and gathered up the reins to push Birdy into a canter. There was no need for Maddie to adjust the fence—Mr. Stillwell's lad had set it at a height that would stretch the horses' legs without over-facing them and making them too scared for the course. Maddie went to the gap by the door, feeling so sick that for a moment she wished she'd never even heard of the King George V Gold Cup.

The elderly groom was still there, and this time he smiled when he saw Maddie. "That your mare, is it?"

She nodded.

"She's a grand little lepper," he commented, using the old-fashioned word for a show-jumper. "Not English bred, I'd say?"

Maddie shook her head. Suddenly a fanfare sounded from a balcony above her head, and she jumped.

"Ladies and gentlemen, we present the second round of the King George the Fifth Gold Cup!"

The gray horse with the Italian rider was first to go. They cleared the first two uprights easily, then turned for the second pair. Two strides from the fence, the rider hesitated and twitched the reins. The horse's head shot up and its front legs swept the rail from the stands. Two faults!

The Italian rider sat very still and kept the horse collected for the next fence, which he cleared. They flew over the triple bar and reined to a dramatic halt in front of the Royal Box, where the rider swept his hat off his head and bowed low as the crowd applauded.

The gray cantered out as Nightwatchman cantered in, like relay runners passing a baton. The audience cheered so loudly that it was impossible to hear the announcer, but there was no mistaking this horse and rider. Nightwatchman was clearly the favorite to win the Gold Cup for the second time.

Captain Acheson took his horse over the first two fences as if they were nothing more than poles on the ground. They swerved around the end of the arena for the next pair of uprights, Nightwatchman's hooves scattering sand against the wooden boards in front of Maddie. *Flick* and *flick*, and they were safely over. Now they just had to come down the arena again, over the triple bar. Maddie stared at the horse's legs approaching her on the far side of the enormous fence.

Into the air they flew, Nightwatchman's rider thrusting his hands so far forward they were nearly touching the horse's ears. And then came the tiniest tap, like a very small person knocking on a door. The pole trembled in the cups, but rolled back into place and stayed there. Half a fault!

Nightwatchman landed and his rider bent forward to clap

his neck, clearly delighted with the almost-clear. Maddie's head spun. Firebird could win the Gold Cup—but only if she jumped clear. She closed her eyes and bent over her hands, which were resting on the edge of the ring.

"Wake up, lad!" said the groom next to her. "Here's your fellow now."

Maddie lifted her head to see Firebird cantering into the ring. The triple bar looked big enough to be a stable for her. Even Theo looked smaller than the other riders, his slender frame sitting straight and quiet in the saddle.

Maddie couldn't remember how to breathe. One and two, and Birdy was over the first pair of uprights. Was it Maddie's imagination, or was this round going more quickly than the last? *Slow down,* she begged her brother. They thundered past Maddie toward the second pair of uprights, and the little horse crouched down on her forehand before leaping over them. They were too high, surely! But no, she was clear, once, twice. Just the triple bar . . .

Maddie shut her eyes. She listened to the hoofbeats speed up, galloping faster and faster, then silence. The only thing she wanted to hear was the sound of Firebird's hooves landing on the other side. No tap, no thud of a falling pole . . .

But everything was swallowed up in the huge cheer that exploded around her. Maddie opened her eyes. Firebird was cantering around the arena with Theo standing in the stirrups, patting her neck over and over. Every single person in the crowd was on their feet, clapping and waving. Lou was hugging George, and even Toby looked as if he was yelling at the top of his voice.

Firebird had won the King George V Gold Cup!

The old groom gave her a prod. "Go on, sonny."

Maddie stumbled past the other grooms just as the big doors swung open to let Theo canter out. People swarmed toward him, stewards, grooms, other riders, clapping and calling well done. Even Mr. Stillwell was striding over, nodding appreciatively.

Maddie backed toward the gate, suddenly feeling shy. She wanted to tell Firebird how well she had done when they were in the quiet of her stable, just the two of them. This was Theo's moment.

"I knew she could do it," said a voice behind her.

Maddie spun around and stared at the man standing behind the gate. "Jonathan!"

She raced over and gave him a hug. "It's so good to see you! Did you see Birdy? Wasn't she incredible?"

Jonathan nodded. "I'm very proud of both of you—and Theo. She deserved to win."

"How are you?" Maddie went on. "Did you get the job with the diamond company?"

"Yes, I did. It's all right, actually. I'm lodging with some friendly folks, and I've found some horses to ride." He smiled, the edges of his eyes turning up exactly as Maddie remembered. She didn't even notice his scar now—all she saw was the man whom she had loved as her brother. "I owe everything to you and Theo, I know that. More than I deserve, that's for sure."

Maddie shook her head. "You brought us Firebird," she reminded him. "That was the best thing anyone could have done."

She reached out and grasped his hand. "Will you come over and say hello to Theo? I'm sure he'd like to see you, and so would Birdy."

Jonathan shook his head. "No, I'll not stay. I just wanted to see Firebird win, that's all. Tell Theo I was here, won't you?"

Maddie nodded, trying to swallow the lump in her throat. Tears threatened behind her eyes, and she blinked them away fiercely. "Keep in touch, please?" she whispered. "I miss you."

"I miss you too, Mouse. You and Firebird both. You look after her for me, you hear?"

"I will," Maddie promised. She thought of all the years ahead of her, riding Firebird over the estate, jumping with her invisible wings. Sefton Park was her home now, where she and her family belonged. The only thing missing would be her other brother, the first Theo.

She squeezed her eyes tight shut to keep back the tears, and when she opened them, Jonathan was gone.